DEAD WORLDS
UNDEAD STORIES

VOLUME 7

EDITED BY
REBECCA BESSER

OTHER LIVING DEAD PRESS BOOKS

THE TURNING: A STORY OF THE LIVING DEAD
THE DEAD OF SPACE BOOK 1 AND 2
PLAYING GOD: A ZOMBIE NOVEL
PLANET OF THE DEAD
ZOMBIES IN OUR HOMETOWN
NIGHT OF THE WOLF: A WEREWOLF ANTHOLOGY
JUST BEFORE NIGHT: A ZOMBIE ANTHOLOGY
THE BOOK OF HORROR * KNIGHT SYNDROME
THE WAR AGAINST THEM: A ZOMBIE NOVEL
CHILDREN OF THE VOID * DARK DREAMS
BLOOD RAGE & DEAD RAGE (BOOK 1& 2 OF THE RAGE VIRUS SERIES)
DEAD MOURNING: A ZOMBIE HORROR STORY
BOOK OF THE DEAD: A ZOMBIE ANTHOLOGY VOLUME 1-5
LOVE IS DEAD: A ZOMBIE ANTHOLOGY
ETERNAL NIGHT: A VAMPIRE ANTHOLOGY
END OF DAYS: AN APOCALYPTIC ANTHOLOGY VOLUME 1-4
DEAD HOUSE: A ZOMBIE GHOST STORY
THE ZOMBIE IN THE BASEMENT (FOR ALL AGES)
THE LAZARUS CULTURE: A ZOMBIE NOVEL
DEAD WORLDS: UNDEAD STORIES VOLUMES 1-7
FAMILY OF THE DEAD, REVOLUTION OF THE DEAD
RANDY AND WALTER: PORTRAIT OF TWO KILLERS
KINGDOM OF THE DEAD * DEAD HISTORY
THE MONSTER UNDER THE BED * DEAD THINGS
DEAD TALES: SHORT STORIES TO DIE FOR
ROAD KILL: A ZOMBIE TALE * DEADFREEZE * DEADFALL
SOUL EATER * THE DARK * RISE OF THE DEAD
DEAD END: A ZOMBIE NOVEL * VISIONS OF THE DEAD
THE CHRONICLES OF JACK PRIMUS
INSIDE THE PERIMETER: SCAVENGERS OF THE DEAD

THE DEADWATER SERIES

DEADWATER * DEADWATER: Expanded Edition
DEADRAIN * DEADCITY * DEADWAVE * DEAD HARVEST
DEAD UNION * DEAD VALLEY * DEAD TOWN * DEAD GRAVE
DEAD SALVATION * DEAD ARMY (Deadwater series book 10)

COMING SOON

BOOK OF CANNIBALS VOLUME 2 * CHRISTMAS IS DEAD VOLUME 2
EMAILS OF THE DEAD * CHILDREN OF THE DEAD

DEAD WORLDS: UNDEAD STORIES VOLUME 7

Table of Contents

JURY DUTY

ANTHONY GIANGREGORIO

James Wilson stepped off the elevator and into the large foyer with marble walls and floors. He was in the Superior Court house in Boston, Mass.

He had been picked for jury duty, and though he was dreading it, he still boarded a train and came to Boston, doing his civic duty.

The foyer for the second floor was decorated in contemporary modern, with polished stone floors and white, imported marble walls. On each side of the foyer were two banks of elevators, the doors shiny, like stainless steel.

There was a line, fifty people strong and still growing, as jurors stepped off the elevators and lined up one after the other. In their hands, they carried white pieces of paper that had arrived in the mail. As James studied the faces of his fellow jurors, he saw the same grim countenances on each of them. All had lives to get to and jury duty was a nuisance none of them had chosen. Still, more than a hundred of them had arrived.

Getting in line, James couldn't help but people watch, especially the women. In his early thirties, it was in his blood to admire the pretty ladies.

All walks of life were here today, a real melting pot of America. There were Spanish, Asian, Haitian, black, white, brown, young, old and middle-aged. There was nowhere else James could imagine where such a diverse assortment of people were gathered together.

"Some line, huh?" a man asked.

James glanced over his shoulder to see a middle-age man with a balding pate, pale skin, and a beer belly he carried proudly, wearing a white shirt, blue slacks and loafers. James was in a similar outfit, only with a tan shirt and black slacks.

"Yeah, it's always like this when I come here."

"Oh?" the man inquired. "You've been here before?"

"Yeah, a few years ago," James replied.

"You get picked?" the man asked.

"Nah, I sat around for a few hours and then went home."

"That's good," the man said. "I'm Steve by the way." He smiled, offering his hand to shake.

"James. Nice to meet you."

"Likewise," Steve replied as they shook hands.

The line continued to move, albeit slowly, but twenty minutes later, James reached the door to the jury pool room. Stepping through the doorway, he was ushered to a desk where he was signed in and given a number.

As he went to find a chair, he read his number. "113? Is that good or bad?"

Steve moved up next to him and James realized he had made a friend whether he liked it or not.

"Depends if you're superstitious," Steve replied.

Moving past the desk, James studied the room. It was large, with at least a hundred chairs in it. They were blue, and all of them were lined up in rows of twelve. Almost all of them were occupied now, a few bored faces glaring back at him, though most had their noses buried in books or newspapers. A few had laptops perched on their laps as they tried to get some work done, despite being trapped at jury duty for the day.

James picked a seat between a heavy set man—who filled his chair without leaving an inch to spare—on his left, and a young Asian man on his right. One seat over was an older black woman. She had her head down and was snoring softly. James couldn't help but smile at this because she had the look of a cleaning lady, or someone who worked hard for a living. He assumed she worked nights, and instead of going home and getting to bed, she had to come here.

From somewhere up at the front of the room, someone was coughing loudly. In fact, it was so loud that James wondered if the person was coughing up a lung.

"Hey, James, how you doing?" Steve asked from behind him.

James turned in his chair to see Steve's grinning face.

"I got a seat right behind you; lucky, huh?"

James forced a smile. "Yeah, lucky me." He tried to give his most apologetic smile. "Look, Steve, I have a lot of work to do, so..."

Steve looked at him for a full ten seconds before he finally understood.

"Oh, shit, sorry. I won't bother you anymore."

"I hope you understand. I don't want to be rude," James said ruefully. Now he felt guilty at coming off as antisocial.

"No, James, it's okay. I totally understand. I have a book with me. Go 'head and do what you have to do."

"Okay, thanks for understanding," James replied.

Steve patted James arm and then leaned back in his chair. James was relieved; it seemed Steve did understand and Steve seemed nice enough that he didn't want to offend the man; after all, the man did try to befriend him.

James leaned over and opened his briefcase, planning to get some work done before the court officer got started with the introductions.

As he began working, the infernal coughing at the front of the large room continued, sounding like a habitual smoker was getting his payback.

* * *

The next three hours went by in a boring daze for James. After the introduction by the court officer and the prerequisite video about the civic duty of all Americans to serve on a jury, everyone grew comfortable and tried to pass the time.

James concentrated on his work, but with each passing hour, it grew harder and harder to focus. The reason for this was because of the infernal coughing coming from the front of the room.

It was at the point now where the man—James had found it was a man earlier—acted like he had pneumonia. The coughs were deep hacks that wracked the man's body like he was being pummeled by invisible fists. A few times, the court officers—a man and a woman—had asked the man if he needed help.

James thought they should have excused him for being sick, but as most people know, it takes a lot more than a bad cough to get a person excused from jury duty. So the man had taken the glass of water offered to him and was left alone.

By 1 p.m., the man was pretty much alone in his corner of the front of the room. The coughing was so annoying that anyone sitting near him had moved away.

It was twenty past one when the man did more than just cough.

He was having a really bad bout when he suddenly began to gasp, then, like he was slapped from behind, he toppled out of his chair to fall face down on the low-weave carpet, a bit of blood dripping out of the corner of his mouth.

Cries of shock and surprise filled the room as jurors called out for help. A woman in her forties dropped to the man's side, trying to see what she could do. Checking his air passage, she wiped away the blood and began to perform CPR on him, but no matter how hard she tried, he remained immobile.

James was still in the back of the room, and from his vantage point, he couldn't see a thing. Heads and shoulders crowded around the hapless man, all eager to see what was happening.

A court officer—James saw it was the woman—forced her way through the throng of people to see what was happening. The room was in chaos, everyone on their feet, wanting to know what was going on.

"He's dead," the forty-year-old woman said blandly as she stopped performing CPR on the still man. She touched his neck again and shook her head, not finding a pulse.

The room filled with "Oh my God's!" and "No shit's?" as the crowd crammed forward for a better look.

The female court officer knelt down beside the other woman, both looking down at the dead man. The man's eyes were still open, and the woman who had performed CPR on him reached out and closed them with her fingertips. "It's so sad, someone needs to call someone," she said softly.

"We already called, an ambulance is on the way," the court officer said.

The woman who had performed CPR leaned both hands to either side of the dead man as she prepared to push up on her arms and legs so she could stand, when the dead man's eyes snapped open like they were spring-loaded.

Before anyone knew the man was alive again, he turned his head sharply to the right, and with his mouth wide open, he moved his head in and sank his teeth into the woman's right wrist.

Everything seemed to happen in slow motion.

The woman with a dead man eating her wrist, screamed in pain, not understanding what was going on while the female court officer jumped back in shock as blood squirted from the wound and into her face and on her white shirt, staining it red.

She pulled her revolver and aimed it at the man, yelling. "Stop that, get away from the woman now or so help me, I'll fucking shoot!"

The dead man ignored her threat, still feeding.

Deciding she had done a textbook warning, she shot the man twice in the chest. The bullets impacted and shook the man, blowing fist-sized holes out his back, but the man seemed not to care. After recovering from the rounds, he went back to his meal.

Meanwhile, the crowd of onlookers began to yell and scream, as three male onlookers who were watching everything play out, lunged at the dead man and tried to pry his teeth off the beleaguered woman's wrist.

The teeth were in there like a bear trap, and as the arm was yanked away from the bloody mouth, tendons and muscle tore as fragile veins were severed.

The woman fell backward and landed on her butt, all the while waving her arm around, the blood shooting from her wrist wound splashing those around her.

As each droplet landed on another juror, all hell broke loose and the people tried to get away, as if the blood was acid and could somehow kill them.

At the same moment, the dead man was rolling onto his side, seeming to still have more than a little life in him. He growled loudly and shook his head like an animal, while blood dripped from his mouth and off his chin to splatter the carpet with small circles of crimson.

The three men who had tried to help the woman were still holding on to the man, and one of them got a rude shock when he felt a sudden pain in his forearm and he saw the dead man was now eating him!

Another man punched the dead man in the face, the teeth knocking out on impact. With eyes wide with hunger and rage, the dead man turned on the next available target, a small man with a toupee who had been the last to help.

Before the Good Samaritan could so much as utter a warning, the dead man jumped him, both falling to the carpeted floor. The small man hit his head on a chair on his way down and he saw stars for a few seconds, now dazed and confused.

He came back to his senses when the dead man sank his teeth into his throat, tearing out a large chunk of flesh before diving back in to slurp at the flowing blood.

Trapped under the dead man, the supine man kicked his arms and legs as he screamed to the rafters in agony. But no one came to help him, for chaos now ensued in the jury-pool room.

The male court officer, acting fast and wanting to contain the violence, followed protocol and locked down the room, closing all the doors and locking them. For all that officer knew, a biological outbreak was occurring, which wasn't far from the truth.

The small man with his toupee now knocked off his bald head and a torn-out throat, stopped kicking as the last of his blood pumped out of him and spread across the carpet in a growing halo. The original dead man climbed off him, his face now lathered in scarlet, his eyes darting back and forth, as he searched for another target. He found it in the form of a young blonde woman huddling in the far corner, crying tears of terror.

Like a wild animal, the dead man jumped onto a chair, leaped to another one, then seemed to fly across the room with his leap. The young blonde woman managed one scream before she was attacked, then her cries became muffled as the dead man fed on her, his face buried in the crook of her neck.

The now bald Good Samaritan's eyes snapped opened and he rolled to his feet, growling and moaning like he was in pain. His eyes darted back and forth, and as a shrieking woman ran past him, he reached out his hand and grabbed her by the hair. Yanking back, he pulled her to him, then forced her to the floor where he sank his teeth into her cheek. She screamed so loud for a moment her voice topped all others, then her screams turned to sobs as the man feasted on her again and again.

The young blonde woman was dead on the floor, her eyes staring at nothing. But no sooner did she die, then her limbs began to twitch and her pupils began to move again.

Swiveling her head slightly, she found she couldn't move too well thanks to half of the flesh and muscle torn away from her throat. Coming to her knees, she crawled across the floor, slid under a chair, and sank her teeth into a juicy ankle.

The old woman looked down to see a bloody face feasting on her leg and she cried out for help. But there was no one to help her, and she was pulled from her chair where she was climbed on and promptly torn apart, the Good Samaritan joining in the fun, the dead man and woman like a gore-covered tag-team.

They feasted on the old woman like she was a gazelle and they were lions, after taking down their kill in the wild. Red-tinged hands dug deep into wrinkled skin, tearing off the offending clothing to get at the soft flesh and entrails within. The old woman was alive for most of her death, her mouth stuck in an 'O' shape as her eyes popped out of her head like a character in a Tex Avery cartoon.

That ended quickly when another raging, undead killer reached down with two fingers and plucked one, then two eyeballs out of their sockets.

Like they were quail eggs, the killer popped one and then the other eye into his mouth, chewing happily as eye juice squirted between his lips like he had eaten a grape tomato.

When he was finished, he turned and went after another hapless soul.

James and Steve were standing in the far corner of the room, along with another man who was still holding his laptop. All three were staring in wide-eyed horror at the carnage before them.

"We're trapped!" Steve yelled. "The fuckers locked all the doors!"

"It's procedure in a situation like this," the third man said.

Steve looked at the man as if he had sprouted horns. "And what fucking situation is this exactly?"

"Fuck if I know," the man shrugged. "But acts of violence, like a riot, are locked down until it can be contained."

"This isn't a riot," James said as he watched a man get taken down by three blood-soaked people with mortal wounds to their bodies.

As he stared at the gore-fest, his mind tried to take it all in. He watched one blood-covered, animalistic person at a time attack a normal person, taking them down and killing them in the most horrific way imaginable.

Then, after less than a minute after death, the victim woke up and began attacking others, now joining the killers who murdered them.

One of the raging killers broke through the pack and came at the three men. James held his fists up, ready to fight to the last, but the undead killer went right for the third man, as if he was a missile homing in on its target.

The third man yelped in terror and used his laptop as a weapon, swinging it sideways and connecting with the attacker's face.

Teeth and pieces of the inset keyboard went flying in all directions as the dead killer went falling backwards.

The third man had broken the dead man's jaw, and it now hung like a trap door on loose hinges.

But the man wasn't down yet, and with a growl and a roar, he lunged for the third man again. Both went down in a tangle of arms and legs as James jumped back, not wanting to get involved.

But when a young woman with a curvaceous form and a hunger for human meat came at him, James had no choice but to punch her in the face. The woman took a step backward as her head snapped back from the blow.

No sooner did she do this then she righted herself and came at him again.

She never got close though, because Steve used a chair to whack her on the back, right at her shoulders, sending her to the floor with a broken neck.

She twitched and writhed on the floor as her nerve endings shut down, then went limp, her eyes still open and glazing over in death.

The room was slowly shifting from screaming, suffering normal people to walking dead killers with a taste for human flesh.

Steve and James backed into the furthest corner, both standing back to back as close to one hundred jurors slowly stopped feeding on their victims and turned their attentions to the last remaining normals in the room.

James looked around, at the barred windows, the locked doors, and the blood-covered faces dripping gore from chins and mouths, and he realized he was absolutely and totally screwed.

Just before the undead horde came for him, he couldn't help but roll his eyes and say, "Civic duty my ass, I should have said I was a racist on the return flyer."

THE UNDERTAKER

JOHN FOSTER

As always, it began in a graveyard, and as always, it began at night.

A hollow-eyed man edged reluctantly among the granite markers. He was an undertaker of sorts, and he worked by the light of the full moon.

Only two hours earlier, the shrill ring of the phone had echoed through the rooms of his house. When he answered, a familiar voice on the other end said, "There's another one."

At the end of the conversation he had replied, "Of course," and set out alone.

The October wind whistled through the valley and pried at the undertaker's scarf with icy fingers, flipping his lank hair, and sending shivers down his spine.

Pulling his coat about himself, he stepped out of the windy gust into the lee of a decrepit mausoleum. Faces were carved into the stone. Surprisingly lifelike, yet utterly devoid of expression, as if the stone were elastic and the faces were pressing through from inside the mausoleum. The undertaker stepped away, shaking off the image. It was a trick of the eye, nothing more.

God help him. The reality of graveyards was much more terrifying.

Too soon, he found it.

The hole had a blasted look, like a violent wound in the hard ground. Runnels of dirt were flung nearly a dozen feet in every direction, and the pauper's headstone had toppled into the hole, cracking in two. Taking a deep breath, he slid down into the grave in a cascade of dirt and pebbles.

At the bottom he knelt and lifted the heavy stone of the top half of the marker. The name engraved in it was **PETER KING GOREY**, but he barely noted this in his haste to drop it. *He always looked at the dates first.* Several years ago, he had concluded a pursuit with unusual ease. When he had wiped away the matted dirt covering his quarry's decaying flesh, he had nearly fainted in surprise—it was a child.

That was the only one he had ever talked to, though a smashed palate made gibberish out of its mouthing. After he'd *returned* the child, he had wept over the grave, learning from the inscription that the little one had been only six years old.

After that one, he had been sent away for a while to a place where he could rest. Every job since the child, he looked at the dates on the grave marker before he did anything else.

He shifted position in the tight confines of the hole and his shoulders dislodged more dirt, which tumbled inside his collar and made him shiver. He forced his fingers in between the rigid grit and the stone, lifting the bottom half of the marker, but the moonlight was too weak for him to discern the spidery scrawl. Reaching into a side pocket, he withdrew a matchbook and struck a Lucifer alight. Flickering yellow illumination crawled across the pitted stone and revealed the dates to him. 1963-2009.

He shook out the match and let the stone fall. He leaned back in relief and fingers tickled his neck.

"Yeeaagh!" he gurgled a scream and whirled, tripping over the grave stone, bouncing against the walls of the pit. He clawed against the dirt, fingernails peeling back as he held himself upright and finally managed to turn completely.

It was just a root exposed long ago by grave diggers, and now it dangling from the earthen wall of the grave.

He smeared dirt across his brow when he tried to arm away the clammy sweat, then cradled his fingers until the sharp pain in their tips subsided.

Finally, he was calm enough to climb from the hole.

He was ready to work.

His talent, or curse, was most closely akin to dowsing—save that his abilities sought out the dead, a special kind of dead, and led him unerringly to them. He did not need rituals. He did not need a coven. All he needed was the night, and the grave from which the corpse had risen.

He knelt and let his wounded hands find their way down to the clods of dirt hurled up by the undeads' emergence. He crumpled a dry clump in his hand, letting it trickle between his fingers.

Though he was unaware of it, his breathing slowed and his eyes rolled back in his head so that he saw through the whites. But he did not see the graveyard in which he knelt.

He saw where the dead man was at that very moment.

* * *

The place was a charnel house.

An hour of frenetic driving brought him to the small, Cape Cod style dwelling. From the outside all looked well. A single car was parked in the driveway. A Halloween pumpkin, as yet uncarved, sat on the step like a featureless orange gargoyle.

The smell hit him before he passed through the front door.

Inside, crusted brown smears of dried blood streaked the walls. Lamps were smashed. Tables and chairs were overturned.

Somewhere a phone was off the hook and the incessant beep-beep-beep clawed at his self-control.

He focused his vision on a single, bloody hand print on the wall. Never mind that the severed hand that had made it was lying against the baseboard four feet below the print. Never mind that the print wasn't made by leaning, in fact, the hand must have been thrown hard to splat against the cheery yellow wall paper. Never mind that . . .

He let his *feeling* extend out from his body through the walls until it filled the house, but Peter King Gorey wasn't present. Not anymore.

Following the sound, he located the phone and then, using a handkerchief, plucked it from the floor. He dialed 911 and whispered, "Help," into the receiver before hanging up.

Then he fled the house as quickly as possible.

The man inside had been torn completely apart.

* * *

He spent the remainder of the night in a drab room at a nearly deserted roadside motel. He turned on every light, and left them on. From a small television in the corner, the fuzzy static of a TV station off the air enveloped him in white noise.

This was a bad one. . . Oh, this was a very bad one.

A sharp *crack-crack* at the door jolted him to his feet, and for a split second, he thought it was Peter King Gorey coming to find him. Then he realized it was simply an impatient knock.

He rubbed his bloodshot eyes, finger-combed his hair back from his face, and opened the door. The man outside was squat and bundled warmly. A bright orange safety vest proclaimed 'AAA Messengers – 24 Hours'.

The messenger took a half step back, quiet alarm registering on his face. Then he stopped and offered a flat package.

"Are you Mr. Undertaker?"

"That's me."

"This is the—sorry to disturb you so late . . . uh, here."

The undertaker took the package and attempted a reassuring smile, "Thank you."

Emboldened by the smile, the messenger took a half step back toward the door. "Hey, uh, is the name some sort of joke?"

A hellish video loop of open graves played behind the undertaker's eyes. "I wish it was."

Something in his voice frightened the messenger again.

"I need you to sign for it," the squat man muttered nervously.

The undertaker signed for the package and the messenger hurried back to his car—orange vest bobbing across the darkened parking lot. The messenger's truck spit gravel from beneath its tires as it fled the motel.

Closing and carefully latching the door, the undertaker sat on the bed and spread out the files contained within the package—the histories of two dead men. One told of Peter King Gorey. A businessman. Family man. His wife and daughter were both dead from cancer. Gorey himself, dead three months later from a massive aneurysm, blood vessels in the soft tissue at the base of his brain literally exploding from pressure.

He rose from the bed rubbing his temples and checked the door again. Locked. He crossed to the tiny bathroom and checked the opaque window set high in the wall. Locked.

He returned to the bed and picked up the second file. Charles W. Bruce. The man Gorey had slaughtered this very night. A realtor. Divorced. He lived modestly, considering his financial success.

He looked for connections—crossovers of their life paths. The dead don't return for small matters.

He found nothing.

* * *

The next evening the motel manager asked him to leave, so the undertaker conducted his business away from prying eyes in a cluster of trees off a side road.

The moonlight was bright enough to cast strange shadows as skeletal branches clattered in the wind. A crackling blanket of dead leaves hugged the hard ground.

The undertaker knelt and tried to settle himself, but his eyes kept playing tricks, insisting that a shape in the dark was moving. Finally, he lurched up and angled toward the shadowy mass in question. It was an upended stump and the wind was tickling thin filaments of its root structure.

Nothing to be afraid of.

The undertaker sucked in a shuddery breath, held it, and let it out. Then he pulled a paper sack from his coat pocket and emptied the grave dirt it contained into his cupped palm.

The gift inside him reached out.

* * *

Black night. The house was high-peaked and looming, sur-rounded by a wrought iron fence as spidery thin as an ink drawing. It was a gothic sculpture crouched on a bluff, connected to the coastal village below by a winding road.

The undertaker sat in his car and let the cooling engine tick as he stared up at the grim cliché house in front of him—the window shutters banging in the wind, which didn't help.

He pushed open the door and unfolded from the car, then shoved the door closed, wincing at the loud bang it made.

Tick . . . tick . . . tick . . . The engine, his heart, the clock counting down the minutes for Gorey's next victim.

The moon was hidden behind clouds. No street lights lined the road. An ozone smell tickled his nostrils.

He stepped forward, but stopped when he realized that the clacking of a swinging window shutter was matching his footsteps. *Lunacy.* He shoved his hands deep into his coat pockets and stepped forward again.

The gate squealed in oxidized protest as he pulled it open.

He stepped through into the yard and sensed a pressure building around him. The shutter was banging faster now, *clack-clack-clack.* He fought to keep his breathing slow, but it wanted to be quick and shallow—air barely pulling into the tops of his lungs before it rushed out again.

If a house could cast a shadow in the dark, then he stood in it.

The *explosion* nearly sent him diving back through the gate and dumped quarts of adrenaline into his bloodstream. The animal portion of his brain screaming "*Flee, flee!*" even as the more encyclopedic section of his mind calmly noted *thunder.*

With a whoosh, the rain came down. Stinging pellets of water struck his exposed face and hands. He hunched in his coat and laughed, the adrenaline strangling his mirth into a breathy cackle. *A storm.* The cliché was complete. His next laugh came easier and was more genuine.

He hurried to the front step and . . .

The door was open.

The undertaker froze, oblivious to the rain pelting him, his eyes unable to discern anything in the pitch-blackness of the foyer. Then he was turning and running across the squishy, wet ground until he banged against the fence. He wrenched open the gate and slipped, falling into the runoff beside the road and soaking his knees.

He hurled his gaze back and saw the black maw of the open door leering at him, poised to vomit forth an unspeakable horror.

Then he was up and at the trunk of his car, fumbling with his keys, missing the lock on the first try.

The doorway was still dark and empty.

He opened the trunk and the wind fought him, driving the rain sideways against his face and neck.

He searched among the shovels, picks, and bags until he freed a long leather satchel. Tearing the zipper in his haste, he yanked out the gleaming black length of a double-barreled shotgun. He broke the weapon open and thumbed in two heavy deer slugs, then stuffed several more into his deep coat pockets.

Cradling the weapon at port arms, he slowly stalked to the open doorway of the house as if it were a crouching animal ready to spring. He couldn't see more than a foot into the interior darkness.

He took a deep breath and thumbed back both of the hammers, silently warning himself not to trip and blow himself to hell.

In a flapping mass of coat and limbs, he charged through the door and into the foyer. He sensed the inner wall at the last moment and spun, slamming his back into it. His gun, eyes, ears, and *feeling* stabbed at the stygian black, but found nothing.

A simultaneous flash-boom of lightning and thunder strobe-lit the foyer and deafened him. The after image of his surroundings danced in his eyes—two doors and a wide staircase going up.

Pulse pounding in his ears, he tried to reach out and sense the presence he sought, but fear blocked him. Would it be the attic or the cellar? It was *always* the attic or the cellar.

He checked the bottom floor first, edging into rooms, waiting for lightning flares through the windows to flash-paint the picture for him. The place was oddly bereft of furniture, save for the occasional ancient overstuffed chair or carved table. Here and there, new appliances contrasted sharply. A microwave. A television. As if the house were caught in a shift between the ages, between Victorian and modern.

When he realized the house had no cellar, he almost gave a giddy laugh. Almost.

Lightning. Pause. Thunder—the eye of the storm was moving farther away.

Too soon the undertaker found himself at the base of the staircase, curving wide above him. His eyes were adjusted now—their pupils black and engorged to gobble every scrap of available light. But the floor above was dark and impenetrable to his vision.

He couldn't ascend the stairs blind. The first floor of the house had sucked his courage dry.

He retreated to the dining room where a silver candelabra rested atop the elegant table.

Flash . . . boom. Light washed through the windows.

He lit the five candles and felt something within him loosen as the warm yellow glow flickered. The candles quietly hissed and popped, as if burning rendered fat instead of wax.

Holding the candelabra before him like a talisman, the undertaker ascended the staircase.

Again the search, room by room

Nothing lurked in the bathroom.

He set the candelabra on the floor and tugged open a closet door with a startling screech. Dirty linens were the only threat. The undertaker moved on.

No corpses or blood stains marred the well-appointed master bedroom with its enormous four poster bed and oak dressers.

He re-entered the hall, following the candelabra as if its circle of light would dart off and leave him behind. Having the light was almost worse than not having it. His pupils had shrunk down to nothing again. He couldn't see anything beyond the sphere of radiance before him, and he felt the continuous need to whirl about and bring the light to bear behind him. Clammy sweat mingled with the cold rain soaking his clothes. He sniffled repeatedly.

The storm outside grew feeble and the rain trickled away.

The next room was a child's bedroom. It startled him with its contrast to the rest of the dwelling, his wavering candlelight dancing over a ruffled girl's bedspread and a litter of stuffed animals. A rugged Fisher Price record player stood proudly amidst a scattering of hand-me-down 45's. The bed was rumpled.

When he emerged again into the hall, he heard it—a slow, thick dripping.

He followed the sound to the end of the hall. Dark liquid oozed from the cracks around a trap door set in the ceiling. *The attic.*

He set the candelabra on the floor and saw a dangling cord barely within his reach. He experimented with different methods for simultaneously aiming the shotgun and grabbing the cord, but he couldn't do both at once.

Drip . . . drip . . . drip.

He let the long barreled weapon point off target and stretched onto his toes, snatching hurriedly at the cord and yanking sharply, and screamed as a shrieking mass flew down at him.

A weight struck his face and a cascade of warm liquid splashed down across him. His shotgun *BOOMED* massively and plaster exploded from the wall as he was knocked off his feet.

The candles were snuffed out and pitch black darkness smothered the hall.

The undertaker crabbed backwards as he heard a moaning from overhead, "Maaaaa . . . maaa . . . maaa," and a scuttling sound in the hall itself.

He levered himself into a sitting position as his thumb flew over the hammers of the shotgun—only one barrel had fired. He threw the weapon to his shoulder, aimed blind and clutched the trigger.

Two feet of flame belched forth from the weapon as the deer slug flung itself lethally at a spot four feet in the air . . . an *empty* spot.

The undertaker held his breath, trying to sort the split second image from the muzzle flash. The spattering rain of blood from the attic, and beneath it, the huddled form of a child.

He strained to listen, strained to *feel*, but his fear still crushed that delicate sense.

"Maaa . . . maaa . . . maaa . . ." still echoed hauntingly down from the attic. In front of him, in the hallway, he heard soft whimpering.

He dropped the first match from trembling fingers, but managed to light the second.

Stepping forward behind its weak glow, he beheld a small girl, she of the stuffed animals and record collection, in a fetal curl and shaking with terror. She was drenched red-black in blood and her eyes were huge white saucers.

"Child?" he croaked through a strangled throat, dizzy from adrenaline. She made no response.

He found the bloody candelabra and plucked a candle from it, then broke open his shotgun to extract the two spent shells, shuddering at how close he had come to blasting the little girl.

With two new slugs loaded, he closed the shotgun. He then unfolded and ascended the attic ladder, following the feeble glow of his candle.

"Moaaaaaaooooo . . ." moaned the thing in the corner. The wife. Her mouth worked, but language eluded her.

"You're safe now," he whispered, but the woman was oblivious to his presence. Her eyes were fixed on something that had happened hours before.

Horror.

The man of the house had been strung to an overhead beam by his feet, directly over the trap door. The girl must have been huddled beneath her father when the undertaker had pulled the door open.

The dangling man had been savagely eviscerated, completely drained of his organs and fluid. The hatred that had fueled the act was a musky stink still befouling the air.

Downstairs, the undertaker repeated his trick with the handkerchief and phone, dialing 911.

Then he fled to his car.

*   *   *

The payphone was in a highway rest area, deserted in the hours before dawn.

"You need to get someone else to do this," the undertaker croaked into the phone. "This is . . . This is . . . horrible. . ."

The voice on the other end was unflinching, "There is no one else."

"Then send me the file, damn it!" The undertaker slammed the phone into its cradle.

*   *   *

The connection to Peter King Gorey was still not apparent, but the connection between the new dead man, James T. Quiring, and the earlier dead man, Clawson, was now apparent. They had been partners in a small, but highly profitable, real estate company.

There had been a third partner in the firm, bearing the name of Lydecker.

The undertaker shivered as he pulled on his clothes, still wet from their washing in the motel bathroom. He was coughing and sniffling continuously from the onset of an ugly cold.

The dead cannot walk during the light of day, but the sun was no threat for the undertaker.

He might be able to get to Lydecker first.

*   *   *

Sunset.

Waiting.

The home was remote but prosperous, the grounds neat and trimmed with obvious pride. A pile of red and yellow leaves waited on the grass for disposal. Corn stalks were tied around the light post at the end of the driveway and a sheet-turned-ghost hung with macabre Halloween glee from a tree branch. A mailbox set at street side bore an ornate cursive L.

Cold and tired, the undertaker huddled around a warm Styrofoam cup of coffee in the driver's seat of his car.

As soon as the last, red lip of sunlight slipped away from the western horizon, he felt it. The rise of a dead man. The animating force was an unnatural scream in the ether.

It was approaching.

He blinked his eyes suddenly, and realized he had fallen asleep. He cursed and looked at the glow of his watch. He'd been out for more then thirty minutes.

Something rustled in the bushes across the property. Unaware of the lurking horror, lights blazed warmly from inside the house. A happy family.

If only they knew.

A dark shadow lurched onto the front lawn.

The undertaker reached back for his shotgun, unable to take his eyes off the approaching shape.

He slid across the seat, eased open the passenger side door, and stepped out onto the dirt shoulder of the road.

It saw him and halted its clumsy walk. The undertaker fought back a cough, and sniffled as the cold air made his nose run. Primitive fear clawed through his fatigue as he thumbed back both hammers.

He hated this part. He never knew what to say to them.

"Stop." Oh, that was good.

Peter King Gorey stepped further into the glow from the light post and the undertaker gagged. Dirt and leaves clung to Gorey from whatever wild refuge he had hidden in during the day. A sharp stick jutted from his collarbone, piercing flesh, unnoticed. His black burial suit was tattered—what was left of it was stiffly crusted with dried blood from Clawson and Quiring. Decay was sinking its destructive claws into Gorey's gray flesh. His eyes had drained and fallen back into the sockets like the skins of empty grapes.

"You can't be here. You're dead," the undertaker said.

Gorey's mouth moved and escaping air wheezed out as it tried to remember speech, "Noooo."

"Trust me. You should see yourself. You've been dead for a while."

Again the pained syllable, "Nooooo."

From twenty feet away, the undertaker lifted the heavy shotgun to his shoulder.

"Staaand aside," Gorey wheezed.

The walking dead man took a step forward and the undertaker blasted him with the first barrel. Gorey spun like a top as his left shoulder separated, but he remained on his feet.

His arm fell to the lawn as shouts erupted from inside the house.

Gorey's pallid countenance contracted, lips pulling back from his teeth in a feral snarl. His right arm lifted, blood-crusted fingers clenching, and he stepped again toward the undertaker.

BOOM. The second slug blasted him straight through the chest and knocked him off his feet.

From the house: "I called the police!"

"Stay inside!" The undertaker screamed at the man who opened the door of the house, presumably Lydecker.

The undertaker hurriedly broke the shotgun open and tugged out the two smoking shells. Fifteen feet away, Gorey levered himself up in a one-armed push up and climbed to his feet.

"Shit!" A shell slipped from his quivering fingers and the undertaker back-pedaled across the lawn, right hand scrabbling in his coat pocket for more shells.

"Murderer," Gorey moaned and lurched forward in a clumsy charge.

The undertaker dropped to one knee as he forced both shells into the gun and snapped it shut.

Gorey's right arm stretched out as he lunged to within five feet.

BOOM. The first slug blew apart Gorey's hip, so close that the muzzle blast set his clothes afire as he jerked away from the impact.

The second slug hit his right knee, ripping the limb in half and knocking the undead man into a crazy half-flip.

The undertaker stumbled up, and back, several more steps as he reloaded. Unable to stand now, Peter King Gorey pulled himself across the ground by his functional right hand. The undertaker lifted—aimed—fired. The blast blew the right arm off and Gorey's locomotion stopped. Another blast severed the rest of Gorey's right leg at the hip.

Exhausted, the undertaker backed away from the still writhing torso of the dead man.

He opened the trunk of his car and laid the shotgun inside.

When he turned back to Gorey, he held a wide-bladed axe in his hands.

* * *

Headlight beams danced through the misty darkness as the yellow dividing line hurtled past to the left of the car. The undertaker's body sagged with an awesome weight of fatigue.

The pieces still twitched in the large Hefty bag he had placed on the back seat.

The undertaker coughed weakly and winced at the pain. He was very tired.

"Murderer . . ." came a moan from the back seat, from inside the bag.

The undertaker sneezed, eyes bleary. "I'm not a murderer. You were already dead."

"Nooot you, hiiim."

"Lydecker?" The question was thrown over his shoulder to the severed head piled in with the arms, legs, and sundry bits of Peter King Gorey.

"And the others . . . ahhhh . . . my wiiife . . . my daughter. . ."

And as the undertaker maintained a steady fifty-five miles per hour on the highway, Gorey continued on. He spoke of a housing project and ground water contamination. He talked of hazardous chemicals and the cover-up by a hungry young real estate company. He described the sound of a little girl crying in pain as bone cancer ate her away. He spoke of what a man feels when he makes the decision to increase his wife's morphine drip, knowing she will never regain consciousness; never say his name again, or hear him say he loves her so dearly. He sobbed in his rasping, undead way, as he blamed himself for not knowing better, for moving his family into the house that killed them.

The sky was still dark when the undertaker pulled his vehicle to a stop in front of the cemetery. The rusting gate protested shrilly as he leaned back and pulled it open.

He threw the bulging Hefty bag over his shoulder and his knees buckled. *Dead weight.* His thoughts whirled in dark directions as he staggered among the resting places and grave markers until he reached the open grave.

The undertaker's fingers felt thick and clumsy as he untied the plastic fastener, then upended the bag so that the various parts of Gorey tumbled into the hole.

He retrieved his shovel and Bible from the car, then returned to the grave side.

Gorey's head sobbed from within the deep hole and the undertaker hurried with his prayer for the fallen. He asked for mercy for Peter King Gorey. He asked that Gorey be reunited with his wife and daughter, and assured the corpse in the grave that it would indeed be so when the dirt-filled mouth mumbled the question up at him—though in truth the undertaker had no idea how things worked on the other side.

By the time the praying was complete, Gorey had stopped making his sounds.

The undertaker knew that Gorey was still aware as he threw the first shovel full of dirt down onto him. He shuddered as the granules and pebbles bounced off of Gorey's severed limbs. Knowing that Gorey's spirit would depart with the rising of the sun didn't make the ugly task any easier.

As the dirt piled around his head, Gorey muttered a last word that sounded like "Kristin." The undertaker couldn't remember if that was the wife or the daughter.

False dawn was tickling the treetops at the eastern edge of the cemetery when the undertaker tamped down the last of the grave dirt. He leaned on his shovel and let the sweat run down his face, breathing hard from the exertion.

The old man would call him within the day to ensure that the 'returning' was complete. He always did. The undertaker thought he would tell the old man that he needed a rest again, after he completed one, final task.

Gorey's words echoed in his mind. The dead do not lie.

The undertaker pulled out onto the road and began to drive. He had questions he wanted to ask.

So he would drive to Lydecker's house, and he would ask his questions.

And he would bring his shotgun.

THAT DAMN WOMAN IS ALWAYS RIGHT

DANE T. HATCHELL

There were many things in life that bugged Richard. Life seemed to be a train of anonymous things that worked in partnership to aggravate him throughout the day.

Even though he couldn't rightfully blame his parents, having the last name of 'Condon' passed on to him in itself brought ridicule. Most people mispronounced his name at a cold reading; even though it should have been as plain to read as the nose on your face.

A casual glance from a reader at an appointment book would usually generate a "Hello, Mr. *Condom*." Of which Richard would usually just sigh and say, "It's Con-don, with an 'n'."

He was *warmly* called Condom by his classmates, starting in middle school, and the fact that his first name was Richard only encouraged further abuse. By the time he reached high school, his buddies shortened Richard to 'Dick'. His immature friends loved to shout, "Hey, Dick!" at him across the hall between classes. Sometimes the adjective *big* was added in front of his name.

"Remember, it's your turn to pick up Rhonda from practice this afternoon," his wife Marge said. She was the greatest annoyance in his *house of cards* life.

The newspaper crunched under his tightening fingers, "Of course I remember." He liked his quiet time in the morning, and didn't like his ritualistic reading of the paper interrupted. "I'll be there at five thirty."

"Five o'clock, five thirty is Jimmy's Karate class," Marge told him.

Richard was a very intelligent man, and amongst the volumes of information and minutia in his mind, it was the fine details in his personal life he couldn't keep straight.

That damn woman is always right, he thought.

So, he apologized, said okay, and went back to reading the paper.

There was an unusual story on page 16A that gave a vague account of an incident where the clerk at a convenience store sustained injuries from an attack by a diseased man. The situation ended when an on duty policeman, buying a candy bar, shot the ill man in the head. The clerk had to be hospitalized and was under observation.

Now, what kind of disease would cause a man to go crazy? Rabies? he wondered. *Damn illegal immigrants.*

He glanced at his watch and cursed, threw the paper down on the table like it had just insulted him, and told Marge it was time for him to go to work.

He went to give her a kiss on the lips and she did that *turn the cheek thing* at the last minute. Instead of a nice moist kiss, he got a taste of dry, bitter makeup foundation.

Richard made the usual scowl when he pulled away, and Marge said, "Didn't want you to smear my lipstick."

He grunted and thought, *That damn woman is always right.*

So, he told her he loved her and would call her from the office later.

His daily grind included a fifteen minute drive to work, and as he predicted, the usual gang of idiots on the road were in full force. Every morning he risked his life driving–dodging others, trying to avoid their two ton battering rams of destruction.

Richard didn't leave his frustrations to the imagination, and made sure to annoy some inconsiderate drivers in return. The texting woman; the mascara applying teenage girl; the 'Car and Driver' reading young man; he gave them all a honk of his horn and an instructive index finger lashing. A gesture of the middle finger kind was usually given back in response.

He made it to the office parking lot, narrowly avoiding a jay-walker, and had to pass three empty spaces because the vehicles were parked partially in the adjoining spaces.

He didn't dare risk scratching the paint on his new SUV. Sometimes he wished he drove a 1983 Oldsmobile. They had real chrome plated steel bumpers, not the plastic covered crap that was used now. He imagined himself parking so close to those selfish bastards that the drivers would have to enter their vehicle from the passenger's side.

He considered keying the space hogs as he walked through the parking lot, but remembered the security cameras and headed straight to his first stop, the Café Coffee, for two cappuccinos.

Inside the Café, he was once again the third or fourth person in line, and was waiting *again* on an indecisive patron who had to have the entire menu explained to him or the office gofer that was getting coffee for the office of thirty.

Finally, as each grueling second passed, feeling like an hour of torture, he stepped up to be served. The bright red-haired, freckle-faced girl that asked for his order was cute, in a trashy sort of way.

He surmised from her gum chewing and vocabulary that she had spent more time on her back with her feet pressed against a car's head liner than in the local library.

The front door to the coffee shop opened, and Richard heard a gurgling moan bubbling up from behind him.

He spun around and what he saw made his bowels quiver. A woman, five feet tall and two hundred pounds wide, lumbered her way toward him. Her skin looked black from rot and her lips were drawn away so much from her mouth that she maintained a perpetual ghastly smile.

A putrid smell assaulted his nostrils, forcing him to gag as bile rose into his throat. The front door burst open and four police officers slammed into the back of the roly-poly walking corpse, sending her straight into Richard.

He raised his right arm for protection as she crashed into him and felt her teeth clamp down on his forearm. Fortunately, his wool business jacket offered some protection.

The zombie sent him to the floor, on his back, and landed on top of him. His arm felt like a vice was squeezing down on it, and then the air from his lungs was forced out with the added weight of the policemen piling onto the woman's back.

Richard struggled for air, and one by one the policemen rolled off of her and started working her over with night sticks. They were whacking her repeatedly across her back and side; the dull thuds sounded over and over, but brought no cries of pain from the living dead woman.

Richard collected enough air to find his voice. "Get her off me! Get her off!" he screamed.

The police seemed to be oblivious to him, and his plight, until they heard his cries. One of the officers pulled out a taser, yelled for the other three to stand back, and fired.

The two metal darts, carrying the thin metal wires, traveled the short distance into the dead woman's back. Fifty thousand volts traveled through the wires and into her, causing her muscles, including those in her jaw, to contract. The five seconds of electrical discharge was enough for Richard to free his arm from her mouth and roll out from under her.

The policemen immediately fell on her with their knees on her back, pinning her to the floor, overpowering her arms, and finally cuffing her.

Richard pulled off his jacket and rolled up his shirt to examine his arm. His jacket and shirt mostly protected him from her sharp teeth, but there was the tiniest amount of red seeping up through his skin where her teeth had left a U-shaped indentation. The bruising of his arm was worse than the actual bite itself. It was already turning a nasty brown-yellow-green and hurt like hell.

"What's wrong with her?" he asked, almost rhetorically. The police already had the unruly woman standing, and with one on either side, had her arms locked and were pushing her out of the door, avoiding her thrashing head and gnashing teeth the entire time.

"Hey, man, you okay?" the last policeman out was kind enough to ask.

"I. . .appear to be so. Do you need a statement from me?" Richard asked.

The answer was clear as the officer turned and left to join the other three outside the coffee shop. Richard and the freckled, red-haired girl stared at each other for a few seconds, and he noticed her name tag. Her name was Judy.

"Well, Judy, was that a regular customer of yours?" he asked, trying to make light of the terrifying and surreal event.

"You okay, mister?" Judy asked.

"Sure, I'm okay," he said. "I wonder if she's married, she was kind of cute."

Judy took a step backwards as she looked down at the counter. Richard realized she was upset over the event, too, and was in no mood for his sarcastic humor.

He made an animated happy face, and in his best radio DJ voice said, "Judy, why don't you just comp me two cups of your famous cappuccino, and I'll be on my way."

She didn't say anything. She took two to-go cups and filled them with coffee, then topped them off with frothy milk. Her eyes darted back and forth at her task and then at him, making him feel like some sort of intruder.

She put the coffees in a cardboard base and carefully placed them in the bottom of a paper bag, before sliding them toward him.

"My boss is going to want to know what happened here," she said. "Can you leave your name and phone number? You know, for insurance purposes."

"Don't worry. I'm not trying to win the lottery by suing the owner over some deranged vagrant." He pulled his wallet out of his pocket and handed her a card.

"Thank you, Mr. . . *Condom*? I'll make sure my boss gets this. He'll probably want to talk to you."

Richard grabbed the bag off the counter and headed out. He looked back as he opened the door, "That's Con-don, with an 'n'," and left without waiting for an apology.

* * *

The sign on the building read, ***Brinkly Printing Co.***

Richard had spent the better part of his last ten years working for the company. Being a salesman was a predictable job; you just had to learn how to handle the highs and the lows and focus on being patient. Save your money when you're rolling in it, and pull from your savings when times were a little lean.

"Hey, sleeping beauty, you're late," a man in a chair rolled out from the first cubical, blocking his path as he entered the office.

"Andy! I feel so guilty. I should have gotten an extra cup of *fuck off* while I was at the coffee shop," Richard said with a frown.

"The other salesmen have been here for over thirty minutes," Andy informed him.

"It can tell time, too! My, it's amazing what modern science can do with dog shit," Richard said. "Look. Your grandfather may have started this company sixty years ago. But he's gone and your family sold the business before you were old enough to piss standing up. You're not my boss; you're not anybody's boss. Ass kissing Vice President Jenkins is not an official job position, but it's what you excel at. Now move before I move you."

Andy made a half snarl, turned in his chair, and duck-walked back to his desk.

Richard continued to the back where the other salesmen's offices were located without any further harassment. He came to a door with the name **Drew Wilson** etched on a brass sign, knocked twice, and let himself in.

Drew was behind her desk with her reading glasses hanging low on her nose. Her eyes peered up at him over her half-glasses as he closed the door behind him.

Her long blonde hair hung alluringly, hiding her left eye. Her plumb-red lips glistened, and moved to form a little 'O'. Richard could feel things getting a little tight in his pants.

"I'm sorry I'm late, Drew. I had the most unbelievable morning at the coffee shop." He was all gentlemen when he was around her. The smell of her lavender scented perfume filled the air, and had a calming effect on him.

"What, they made you hand grind the beans again?" she teased.

"Well, I . . ."

"Oh stop, silly, don't be bothered," she smiled as she stood to take the coffee from his hand. Drew flipped the hair away from her eye, removed her glasses, and smiled even wider. Her bleached white teeth looked like the finest ivory.

She wore a purple sleeveless top that accentuated her small, perky breasts. Her black pants fit her ass perfectly and made Richard want to grab a hand full of it.

"Thanks for the cappuccino; it's just how I like it. You better get to your office before anyone wonders what you're doing in here at this time of the morning and not at your desk."

"I know, and I can hardly wait for lunch," Richard grinned.

"Me, too," she cooed. "I'll be waiting . . . and ready."

He grabbed his pants over his crotch and adjusted himself. After all, he couldn't leave her office while *pitching a tent.*

*   *   *

It didn't matter how many times he looked at the clock, he could never make it go faster. He was feeling good about his day. He made three sales on cold calls and had two of his clients call him for reorders. Very unusual for this time of year; things were looking up in the world.

His phone rang and Richard answered in a chipper voice, "Brinkly Paper, you've got Richard Condon, how may I assist you today?"

"Richard, you took the SUV." It was Marge, the fastest way to take a smile and turn it into a frown.

"Yes, I took the SUV today. Sooooo . . ."

"So you were supposed to take the coupe. I've got to go to the school at noon and pick up Jimmy, and some of his classmates, and drive them to the museum," she said.

"I thought the museum was tomorrow?"

"No, tomorrow I take the coupe. You'll need to have the SUV to pick up Jimmy and his Karate class, and take them to the tournament."

That damn woman is always right, he thought.

He apologized and said he would bring the SUV right over.

Richard looked at the clock. It was eleven thirty. It was Friday and most everyone in the office would go to Mr. Jalapeno, a local Mexican restaurant, for lunch. It had been a tradition of sorts for years, and no one seemed to tire of it. It was probably the free chips and the two dollar margaritas that did it.

He had to hurry if he was going to be back in time to meet Drew. She would be in the copy room, waiting for him at noon; waiting for him all alone, with the lights down low and her panties on the floor.

He pulled his jacket off the back of his chair and hurriedly walked down the hall to the front.

"Hey, Richard, what's the rush? You're coming to lunch, right?" asked Shane, a fellow salesman.

"Sorry, Shane, not today. I have some family matters to attend to. Have a good time, bye." Richard didn't break stride as he headed out the door.

* * *

Marge had that *look* on her face when he entered his house and exchanged keys with her. He made some excuse that he was working through lunch and had to get back as soon as possible.

"You do remember that you have to pick up Rhonda at five today, right?" she asked.

"Of course I remember," he said through gritted teeth.

"Oh, really? I'll bet you right now that I'll get a call from Rhonda at five thirty saying you're not there. Then you'll show up home at six thirty saying how it completely slipped your mind because of work," she said as if she was scolding a child.

"You're wrong." His face reddened. "I've got to go now."

He got another taste of the bitter foundation off her cheek and drove out of the driveway like a bat out of Hell.

On the drive back to the office, he began to feel queasy. His heart started beating faster and his chest felt hollow. Light perspiration built on his brow, his mouth felt dry, and his tongue thick. He began to feel so bad that he didn't notice any of the other drivers annoying habits on his way back.

At least the parking was easier this time. Several cars had left to take the office members to the restaurant.

Richard composed himself, and walked steadily back to the office.

Andy was still in his cubical. His excuse for avoiding the Friday lunch was that he felt someone should be at the office for that one hour a week when everyone left in case there was a fire.

Cheap ass prick, Richard thought as he passed him by. No matter, the copy room had a lock on the door.

He felt like he was walking in lead boots, each step he took like a major effort. He stopped by the water cooler and had a drink, his hands shaking slightly as he filled the cup. Fatigue was overtaking him, and his head was heating up. He remembered he had some aspirin in his desk drawer and used his last remaining strength to make it there and plop heavily down in his chair.

He put his palms to his cheeks and felt the heat rising off his face. The pictures of his children and wife looked back at him as the world around him began to spin. He laid his head on his desk, then closed his eyes to invite the darkness.

* * *

When Richard reanimated minutes later, he no longer felt the heat from his fever. In fact, there were few feelings he felt at all, with the exception of a ravenous hunger.

Yet an inner longing dominated his current state of being. He rose from his chair and found it a little more difficult to walk than what his body was accustomed to. His feet moved forward in short, choppy steps, and he now walked with a wider gait.

Out of his office and down the hall he was drawn, an unknown compelling force pushing him on, until he stopped at the copy room door. He put his hand on the door knob and twisted it one way, then the other, until it opened.

The light in the hall cut through the darkness of the room, illuminating two bare legs hanging down the front of a copying machine, Drew's body from the waist up hid in shadow. Richard entered the room, and closed the door.

"Mmmmmmuuhhh," Richard went to speak, but that was the only sound to come out.

"Mmmmmm, right back at you, baby. I was getting worried. I was beginning to think you'd forgotten me. Now, come on over here and make up for it," Drew said, her voice like a soft purr.

Richard lumbered in the darkness, and with outstretched arms, grabbed one of her wrists, then the other.

"Oh, I like a man that takes what he wants," she said with excitement.

Richard was drawn to her by her irresistible smell—one of fresh meat. His head plunged forward and his teeth went to work on her neck.

The pain was so sudden and intense that shock set in quickly, only allowing Drew to gasp before falling unconscious. Richard enjoyed her body in a way he had never done before, now feasting on the flesh that he used to kiss and caress. He ate until the feeling to feed ceased, then he felt the need to leave the closed room and wander the world under the open sky.

Andy was at his desk with his IPod buds shoved deep in his ears. With a pencil in each hand, he was banging out, *Moby Dick* by Led Zeppelin on imaginary drums. A half-eaten cheese sandwich and a bag of chips lay abandoned on his desk.

Andy looked outside his cubicle while thrashing his head back and forth, and caught a glimpse of Richard's back as he was leaving the office. The clock read fifteen minutes to one.

Andy jerked out his ear buds and ran after Richard.

"Hey, Dick Condom, you can't leave now. It's time to get back to work. Mr. Jenkins is gonna be upset if I tell him you're taking half the day off."

Richard stopped just before he exited the door, turned, and faced Andy.

"Good God, man. Are you sick?" Andy cringed, and took a step backwards.

Richard's face and clothing were covered in Drew's blood. He reached a bloody hand toward Andy and walked forward. Andy turned to run but ended up tripping on his own feet, his head hitting the stainless steel trim on his cubical door.

Consciousness momentarily left him, and when he came completely awake seconds later, he felt the full weight of Richard on his back, his deadly teeth gnawing through his skull.

Richard dined on Andy's brains until the screams stopped and Andy's body stopped shivering. Richard's stomach, for the moment, was full, and though he felt a certain satisfaction while Andy was squirming beneath him, the dead body no longer held his interest.

Richard left the office building and struggled to comprehend his surroundings. Sirens were blaring with squad cars, ambulances, and fire trucks maneuvering in and around traffic. The moving objects didn't look like food to him, but he could make out bodies inside of them as they passed.

As he lurched by Café Coffee, something familiar about the facade caused him to pause. He turned to the front door and tried to pull it open. It didn't budge. Then instinctively, he pushed on the door handle and entered, while above his head, a small bell chimed his entrance.

"Hello, what can I get . . . Oh my God!" Judy gasped. "Mr. Condom, what happened to you? Do you need me to call you an ambulance?"

Con-don, flashed through Richard's mind. Something about what she called him stoked his anger. He was compelled to say something, but couldn't remember what or why. It didn't matter, his jaws were aching to masticate, his teeth eager to tear flesh from bone.

His advance struck Judy with fear, and she backed up into the wall behind her. "Mr. Condom, you're not well. You need to stay away from me. Get away!" She grabbed a glass coffee decanter from its station and slammed it into Richard's skull as his hands reached her throat. Glass shards and hot coffee went flying through the air and cut a nasty gash in his cheek.

The coffee on his face mixed with the blood that squirted out of Judy's jugular as he set out to satisfy his insatiable urge to bite, chew, and eat. Mindlessly, he ate until all of the good parts of her body were gone.

Richard felt confined in the empty coffee shop, and returned to the outside world, his belly practically set to burst with all the meat it now contained.

The sunlight was being pushed aside by large, black clouds. The sky was turning a dark gray to the west, and the winds were kicking up. Richard was being drawn internally to a destination that his mind could no longer remember.

As the rains fell, he went unnoticed by the line of cars speeding by him. As the blood on his clothing and face were washed away and diluted, he became just another poor soul caught in the rain without an umbrella.

Walking on the sidewalk against the traffic of a one-way road, Richard noticed a woman in a car, stopped at the intersection, texting on her phone. The traffic light was green, and Richard again felt an overwhelming anger.

Slamming his right fist into the driver's side window, his college graduation ring reduced the safety glass to a thousand pieces. The woman's face lit up in surprise as the glass fell into her lap. He didn't hesitate. He grabbed her by her hair and snatched the phone from her hand, then tossed it into the street.

The woman's foot lifted off the brake pedal as Richard tugged to extract her from the car. The vehicle started moving forward, and slowed as Richard's strength now countered via the woman's neck.

The woman's scream was proportional to the tension he exerted. Her screaming came to an abrupt halt as Richard gave one mighty jerk, and her head detached from her body. He was glad when the annoying woman finally grew silent.

The car moved forward again, coming to a stop against a telephone pole across the road.

He continued his walk, one foot forward, then the next, slowly, methodically. He was unaware that he still had the woman's head in his grasp. He was moving toward a destination that was nothing more than a feeling he had inside.

Block after block, street after street, the darkness the rain clouds brought hid him in plain sight. He slowly walked through the puddles, wet grass, and mud, while sheets of rain cascaded over him.

A black SUV in a driveway struck a chord of familiarity. He searched his mind for an answer, but his mind was vacant.

Still, he turned off the road and onto the driveway. Lightning crashed, illuminating his pale, white complexion and the dark rings that surrounded his eyes. His brooding silhouette moved across the garage wall as he staggered up to the back door, and turned the knob.

Marge was at the stove sautéing onions and garlic when she heard the door squeak open behind her, the sound of the pouring rain, then the closing door, to return to the sounds of the room and the sizzling vegetables.

She looked at the clock on the microwave. It read six thirty-two. She shook her head and made an *I told you so* smirk.

"Well, right on time. I told you that you'd forget to pick up Rhonda."

Richard looked around the kitchen. It all felt familiar, and yet so distant. The woman's words echoed, *I told you that you would forget,* over and over in his head.

Then the last sentient thought Richard would ever have flashed in his mind. *That damn woman is always right.*

So, he ate her.

A VACATION IN HELL

DAVID H. DONAGHE

Roxy had been bugging me about going on a vacation, and since our little bit of misadventure down by the Mexican border, I figured we were due.

My name is Mike Monroe and I own Monroe's Paranormal Investigations. My partner—her full name is Roxanne Delaney, but I call her Roxy for short—is a beautiful blonde with big boobs, long flowing hair, sexy legs, and a hot temper. She's the kind of woman that drives a guy nuts, me especially, but on our last case she got hurt and I figured it was time for some R&R. Besides, I put up a good front but I just can't tell her no when she bats those baby blues my way.

I was sitting in my office, reading the newspaper, and I read an advertisement in the classified section advertising a cabin for rent.

The article said, *Secluded mountain cabin situated in the heart of Humboldt National forest; three bedrooms, fireplace with a clear mountain stream out back. Good trout fishing with its own sandy beach; available for weekends, by the week, or by the month.*

The ad gave a phone number and an e-mail address, so I contacted the owner on the internet and set a date, paying him in advance with my credit card. He faxed me a map and e-mailed me some pictures of the cabin. I had just logged off the web when Roxy sashayed into the office.

I leaned back in my chair, taking in her long golden locks, her full breasts with her large round nipples pushing up the cotton of her wife beater T-shirt. She wore those dammed Daisy Duke shorts that drove me wild, and when she turned around and closed the door, I caught a glimpse of the top of the lacy thong she wore underneath them. After closing the door, she turned around, placed her hands on her shapely hips and gave me that look.

"What are you staring at, pervert?" she asked, though she knew exactly what I was looking at.

A mischievous grin crossed my face and I said, "Only you, dar-lin', and don't make any plans for this weekend."

A sour looked crossed her face. "What now? Not another case."

"Nope, it's time we took that vacation you've been bugging me about. I just rented us a cabin up in the Humboldt National forest. It's got a cozy fireplace, a trout stream out back with a sandy beach to lie out on, and a swimming area. You can work on your tan if you want. It'll be just you and me, baby. What do you say?"

"Can we make it a four-day weekend or maybe even a whole week?"

I nodded yes.

She let out a squeal, rushed across the room, smothered me with kisses, and in the process her left breast hit me in my eye.

"Damn girl, be careful with those things. They could poke a guy's eye out," I said and then laughed.

She straddled me and took off her shirt. "Oh shut up and kiss me."

As for me? I just leaned back in my chair with a big shit-eating grin on my face.

I borrowed a friend's Jeep for the trip. We packed our gear and left that Friday afternoon, heading over to the coast, and then took the 101 north. Roxy wore a little pink tank top, and of course, she wasn't wearing a bra. Her nipples pressed up against the material of her shirt and her long sexy legs stretched out with her feet resting on the dashboard. I reached over and laid my hand on her thigh.

"Knock it off, jerk," she said and pushed my hand away, but I couldn't help but notice the hint of a smile trying to break forth.

"You might as well get some rest," I said. "We've still got a long drive ahead of us. I figured we'd spend the night in Frisco."

"I love San Francisco. Maybe we could do some sightseeing while we're there," she smiled.

"Anything for you, babe," I said. She leaned over, revealing a deep valley of cleavage, and kissed me on the cheek. Glancing down the front of her shirt, I got a clear view of her massive breasts and swerved, almost hitting another car.

"Take it easy, big boy. Keep your eyes on the road," she said and then laughed. She leaned back in her seat as I regained control of the Jeep. "I think I'll get some sleep," she yawned.

I watched her lie back, close her eyes, and drift off to sleep. Taking in the gentle rise and fall of her breasts in my peripheral vision, I settled in for the drive.

Nine hours later, we rolled into Frisco and found a Holiday Inn near the bay. Roxy, now wide-awake, took my arm and we headed to the room. The pressure of her left breast brushing up against my arm, caused a stirring sensation to shoot through my loins as we stepped into the hotel room. Standing inside the room, I took in the plush beige carpeting, the oak entertainment center with the wide screen TV, the other oak furnishings, and the California king-sized bed.

"Pretty snazzy," I said.

She turned, pushed me down onto the bed, took off her shirt, climbed on top of me, and smiled. "This is your lucky day, pal."

Making love to Roxy is like trying to ride a lightning bolt or maybe trying to surf on top of a hurricane. When she unleashes her passion, it's all I can do to keep up and hold on. This time was no exception and after she had her way with me, I laid back on the bed, thoroughly drained, and drifted off into a deep, sound sleep.

We spent the day in San Francisco seeing the sights, such as Fisherman's Wharf and the Golden Gate Bridge. I bought tickets and we took the boat trip out to Alcatraz Island where we toured the famous old prison. Of course, Roxy wanted to go shopping and that took up most of the afternoon, so it was late in the evening when we left Frisco and headed north on 101. At Eureka, we found a cheap motel, and after spending the night, we headed east on State Highway 289 early the next morning after a quick breakfast. The road snaked its way through a cathedral-like forest with giant redwood trees towering above us on both sides of the two-lane road.

"God, it's so beautiful here!" Roxy said in awe, admiring the majestic forest, and while she admired the forest, I took in the soft curves of her large breasts along with her tanned, shapely legs. She wore a pair of cut off jeans that bordered on the obscene, but hey, I enjoyed the view.

"I know what you mean, babe. Oh, and am I ever enjoying the scenery," I said and then reached over and touched her thigh.

"Knock it off, Mike," she said, pushing my hand away, just as a large buck deer, along with three does, scampered across the road. The buck stood in the center of the road for a few seconds, shaking its antlers, then crossed. "Wow, you just don't see things like that in the city," she said as she watched the buck disappear into the trees.

"I know what you mean, darlin'," I said, downshifting to avoid hitting the animal. We had just passed a little town called Burnt Tree Flats, when I noticed an old, primer gray Ford pickup truck parked next to the road with a flat tire and an ancient looking Indian kneeling down next to the rear of the vehicle.

"Pull over, Mike, that poor old man looks like he needs help," Roxy said. Heaving a sigh, I pulled the Jeep over, parking behind the pickup truck, and climbed out. I stepped onto the road and looked down at the most skinny, ragged-looking man I had ever seen. What hair he had left on his head was pure white and his skin, tanned from years of working in the outdoors, looked like wrinkled saddle leather.

"Did you have a blow out?" I asked, swaggering up with my hands in my pockets.

"She's got a slow leak," the old man said, giving me a weary glance.

"Where's your spare? I'll help you change the tire."

Roxy stepped up next to me; the old Indian gave her an appraising glance and a hint of a smile crossed his face. "Got no spare," he said.

"Is there someone you can call? Do you have a cell phone?"

The old Indian looked at me as if I was crazy and just shook his head.

"He probably wouldn't get any service anyway. Here, let me check my phone," Roxy said and after a minute, she shook her head and put her phone away. "I saw a gas station back in that little town," she suggested.

Heaving a sigh, I knelt down and said, "Here, let me help you get that tire off. We'll take you back to town and see if we can get it fixed."

The old Indian tried to protest, but I just took the tire iron away and started working on the tire. He didn't have a jack, so I had to use the one from the back of the Jeep, but within half an hour, we had the tire changed and we were heading back the way we came. The old Indian sat in the back seat as quiet as a cigar store Indian and Roxy tried to engage him in idle conversation, but he just answered in one or two word sentences.

When we reached the gas station, I took the tire into the garage, handed it to the attendant and the old Indian looked distressed when the gas station attendant mentioned the cost of the repair.

"That's okay," I said. "I'll pay for it."

The old Indian's eyes lit up, and after the attendant fixed the tire and when we were on our way back to his truck, I tried to get the old man to open up a bit. "Roxy and I are going camping," I said. "We're renting a cabin in the woods near here."

A worried look crossed the old man's face. "The next valley is better. The land here is cursed. It's not a good place for a white man from town."

"What do you mean cursed?" I asked, feeling intrigued.

"Years ago the white soldiers slaughtered the Pinoleville Band of the Pomo tribe. The soldiers killed the men, raped and killed the women, and then slaughtered everyone. Even the little ones. The tribe's medicine man put a curse on the land. This forest is not friendly to white men."

I glanced at Roxy, noticing goose bumps forming on her legs, and I tried to get the old Indian to open up a bit more about the curse, but he clammed up. After I put the tire back on his pickup, he handed me a small leather pouch.

"What's this?" I asked.

"It will keep away evil spirits. When you get to your cabin, hang it on the front door."

"Thank you, I guess," I replied, taking the leather pouch.

"Whatever you do, if you see an Indian graveyard, don't go inside or take anything from the sacred ground. There are places white men shouldn't meddle."

"I hear you loud and clear. I don't need that kind of trouble this weekend," I said.

The old Indian's eyes widened and I figured he was surprised that I took his beliefs seriously.

"What do you think? The moon will be full in a day or two," I said to Roxy when we pulled away after changing the tire, but she just shrugged.

"I don't care. I've got my Saint Christopher medal. Let's just find this place."

We traveled for a few more miles and then came to a dirt road branching off to our right, leading east into the heart of the forest. I checked the directions I had written down and then the map as I scratched my head.

"I don't know, Mike. I don't think this is the right road. The guy's e-mail said easy access. This seems like nothing more than an old logging road."

"It's the right road. I can't get a signal for my GPS on my cell phone, but it looks like the right road according to the map," I said.

"Whatever, I just want to get there and take a shower," she added.

I turned onto the dirt road heading into the forest and rolled down the window on the Jeep. Tree branches slapped the sides of the vehicle, squirrels chattered in the nearby trees, and a cool mountain breeze tickled my face.

"God it's beautiful up here," I said.

The road meandered through the forest, heading east for a few miles and then curved to the north. The sound of someone chopping wood echoed through the trees, and when the road dropped down into a small valley and the forest cleared somewhat, I saw a campground off to our right and an old Indian graveyard to our left.

Noticing what looked like a group of college kids setting up their tents, I glanced over and Roxy gave me an elbow to the ribs when she saw me checking out a young, redheaded woman in a pink halter top.

"Keep your eyes on the road, mister," she said with a laugh.

"Yes, ma'am." The road continued east, crossed a narrow bridge made from rough-hewn logs, and below the bridge, I heard the sound of a mountain stream dancing over the rocks. "This is the right road. See there's the stream," I said, enjoying the view of the clear mountain brook.

"Yeah, right," she replied.

We continued down the road, cresting a small hill before descending into a small grassy valley. Glancing to my left, I noticed a rustic looking cabin surrounded by a small stand of sugar pine trees, and followed the dirt trail leading down to it.

"I don't know, Mike, this cabin doesn't look much like the one in the picture," Roxy said.

"They never do. This has to be the place."

We pulled up to the cabin, I parked the Jeep and Roxy climbed out. She put her arms above her head to stretch, causing her large breasts to jut forward, and of course, she caught me looking.

"You got eyeball problems? Unload the Jeep, I need to pee," she said and stepped up onto the porch.

"The key should be under the door mat," I said.

She glanced around and then said, "There is no mat, but I'll try the door." She opened it and then paused in the doorway. "It's unlocked. I really don't think this is the right place," she said and went into the cabin while I unloaded most of the camping equipment. I was in the process of unloading a long coil of chain with large heavy links and a stout padlock when Roxy stepped back out onto the porch. "The place is a mess," she said as she noticed me unloading the coiled up chain. "Is that really necessary, Mike?"

"It wouldn't be if you would wear your Saint Christopher medal and take your wolf bane. The moon is going to be full in two days. If you would do what you're supposed to and learn to control yourself, this wouldn't be necessary."

"Yeah, right, well, I'm gonna take a shower and then clean this place up," she replied and headed back into the cabin. "There better be hot water in this place."

After unloading all the equipment, I grabbed my fishing rod, headed out back, and strolled downhill to the streambed. The water dancing over the rocks was crystal clear. I was having the time of my life, and three hours later, I headed back up to the cabin carrying three large rainbow trout. When I stepped into the cabin, Roxy was in the kitchen cleaning the counter tops.

"I brought supper," I said, holding up the fish.

She nodded at my catch. "I checked the place out and cleaned up a bit. It'll do, but it isn't like what I pictured it to be, Mike."

"It's perfect, you'll see. Just let me clean these fish and then I'll chop some wood. After we have dinner, I'll light a fire in the fireplace."

After putting the fish in the small icebox in the kitchen, I headed to the front door and grabbed the ax that I had left there. Remembering the medicine bag that the old Indian gave me, I took it from my coat pocket and hung it from a nail sticking out of the front door. Whistling a little tune, I stepped off the front steps and headed off into the woods in search of firewood.

Thirty-five minutes later, I stepped back into the cabin, carrying an armload of firewood, and after lighting a fire in the fireplace, I fried up the trout and we ate dinner.

After dinner, I rolled the sleeping bags out in front of the fireplace and we spent a cozy night together by the fire. Roxy unleashed her passion, we made love in front of the fireplace, and I drifted off into a deathlike slumber, fully spent.

Waking early the next morning, I grabbed my fishing gear and headed down to the stream. The early morning chill caused goose bumps to form on my legs and arms, but the fish were biting and by the time Roxy made her appearance, I had already caught five fish. I glanced up when she came strutting down from the cabin to the little beach by the edge of the stream. I was just in time to see her toss off her shirt, slip off her Daisy Duke shorts, and jump into the water.

I stood transfixed, watching her pop back up from the waist-deep water, noticing her nipples standing erect from the frigid water of the mountain stream. She shook back her long golden locks, causing beads of water to fly in all directions, and her wet body glistened in the morning sunlight

Climbing onto the bank, she spread out her towel and lay down on her stomach, sunbathing in the nude. My fishing pole jerked out of my hand and moved down the bank toward the water as a fish threatened to take it down to the depths of the stream. Roxy laughed when she heard me let out a startled cry and go chasing my fishing pole. Diving into the freezing water, I went after it. Sputtering and blowing, I climbed back up onto the bank, after retrieving my pole, and reeled in a large brown trout.

Carrying the fish over to where Roxy lay, I put it down and sat next to her.

Roxy laughed and said, "Hey, Mr. Fishermen. Do you normally let the fish take off with your pole like that?"

"Not usually, but I was a bit distracted," I said and my face turned red.

"Why don't you take off those wet clothes and put some suntan lotion on my back?"

"That sounds like a plan," I said. After putting lotion on Roxy's back, she put some on mine and we lay out in the sun for a while. We spent the rest of the day soaking up the sun and playing in the water, but I had already caught my limit, so I didn't do any more fishing.

That evening, just after sundown, I was cooking up the fish and Roxy was taking a shower when I heard a commotion coming from out near the road.

Then I head a woman scream.

Charging across the kitchen, I ran into the small living room of the cabin, unzipped my gear bag, and grabbed my Bush Master AR-15. Like my credit card, I never leave home without it.

Roxy came running out of the bathroom in the nude and yelled, "What's wrong?" Pausing for a fraction of a second to ogle her luscious body, I grabbed her Ruger Mini-14 and tossed it to her.

"I don't know yet, but get dressed. It looks like we've got company!" I yelled and ran to the window facing the road.

Roxy retreated into the bathroom, while I pulled back the curtain and looked outside. My eyes widened in shock when I saw the college kids from the campground down the road slide to a stop in front of the cabin and pile out of a blue Bronco and a red pickup truck. A throng of flesh-eating zombies clung to the tops of both of the vehicles and filled the bed of the pickup truck. A herd of the undead fiends came running up the road behind them, but these were like no zombies I had seen before.

Most zombies were slow movers, but these moved like lightning, and the ones on the tops of the vehicles hacked away with tomahawks, trying to tear through the roofs to get at the kids inside. The flesh-eaters wore tattered loincloths, and wielded knives, hatchets, bows and arrows. I saw vague traces of war paint on the rotting flesh of their faces and arms.

"Not this shit again!" Roxy screamed when she stepped up beside me wearing a black tank top and a pair of jeans.

"Yeah, I know, it seems like we can't take a road trip without having to fight off a bunch of flesh-eating zombies. This reminds me of the time when we went to Pennsylvania for your grandmother's funeral, but this is the first time I've seen 'em using weapons. Cover me," I said and flung open the front door of the cabin.

A stocky, dark-haired young man wearing a black windbreaker jumped out of the driver's side of the Bronco, followed by a petite blonde wearing a white halter-top and a pair of shorts. A sandy-haired, scruffy looking guy wearing a Raider's tank top, and a pair of gangster low rider shorts jumped out of the back seat and his girl friend, a buxom girl with long black hair wearing a blue sweater and a pair of hip hugger jeans, scooted out behind him.

"Get your asses in here!" I yelled and then fired a burst from my AR-15 at the flesh-eaters on the top of the Bronco. The young couples ran toward the cabin in terror, while behind them, a fat guy with a baldhead and a busty young girl with long red hair piled out of the pickup truck. The fat guy ran toward the cabin and his girlfriend ran around the front of the truck to follow him, but she tripped on a rock. As she went down, a pack of zombies jumped on top of her and one of the undead fiends pulled out a rusty knife. Lighting quick, he sliced the front of her forehead, brought the blade around, slicing a circle on the top of her head, and pulled off her bloody scalp. He let out a shrill war cry, holding up his bloody trophy, and then plunged the knife into the girl's belly, cutting her from belly button to breastbone.

After slicing open the girl's body cavity, the zombie stuck his maggot-infested hand into her belly, pulled out a long piece of intestine, and devoured it.

I gave the undead son-of-a-bitch a double tap with my AR. The fat guy turned to help his girlfriend, but another gaggle of the undead fiends slammed into him, taking him to the ground. I could barely hear his terrified screams above the war cries of the undead; they pounced on him, chopping him to pieces with tomahawks and knives. I noticed one zombie, after severing an arm, run off to the side, gnawing on the fresh meat.

I fired a burst into the zombie horde. Turning, they rose from the ground and charged the cabin, while the ones following along behind joined the party. One stopped, took an arrow from his quiver, and fired it at the cabin, which hit the doorjamb next to me. The last of the four surviving college kids ran through the door and I slammed it closed.

"Oh God! Oh shit!" the stocky, dark-haired guy said and then took a nylon backpack off his shoulder and tossed it into a corner.

"And then some," I said and moved to the window next to Roxy. The flesh-eating, Indian zombies charged the front of the cabin, but stopped when they saw the medicine bag hanging on the front door. Letting out a howl of frustration, they backed away.

"Do any of you guys know how to use a gun?" I asked, and the dark-haired, stocky guy nodded. "Good. Roxy, go get some more hardware out of my gear bag. We need to guard the back."

Roxy crossed the room, handed the dark-haired guy an AK-47, tossed the sandy-haired young man another Ruger Mini-14, then tossed each of the girls a handgun. I always come prepared, even on vacation.

"Thanks . . . man. I thought we were goners there for a moment," the dark-haired guy said, huffing and puffing.

"Go into the bedroom and get the dresser. Get one of the girls to help you. Use it to barricade the back door," I said to the dark-haired guy. Glancing at the sandy-haired young man, I noticed he had a bloody arm. "What happened to you?" I asked.

"One of those dammed things bit me," he replied.

"Get the first aid kit," I said, nodding at Roxy. "Take care of his arm. We'll have to keep an eye on him."

Roxy crossed the room to the gear bag, retrieved the first aid kit, made the man sit down on the couch, and saw to the wound, while outside, the zombies surrounded the house.

"What'd you guys do? How did you stir up this hornet's nest?" I asked when the girl with the long black hair stepped up next to me.

"We were in the graveyard at sunset. We were looking for souvenirs. Then they just came up out of the ground. It was horrible. I saw maggots running through their flesh and the smell. It was horrible. They came after us and we ran," the girl cried.

"What did you take from the graveyard?" I asked.

"We were just after souvenirs. I found a rusty old knife and a beaded necklace."

"I found some arrowheads," the blonde girl said, stepping up next to her.

"What about you?" I asked, nodding to the stocky guy with the dark hair. I noticed a strange look cross his face for a few fleeting seconds.

"I didn't find anything," the guy said.

"I found a tomahawk," the scruffy-looking, sandy-haired kid said from the couch after Roxy finished bandaging his arm.

"Hand the stuff over. You should never mess with an Indian graveyard," I said.

"It sounds like you've seen this type of thing before," the stocky, dark-haired guy said. He leaned the AK against the wall, then leaned back with his arms crossed in front of his chest.

"You could say that. My name's Mike Monroe. I own Monroe's Paranormal Investigations. That's my partner Roxy Delaney. And who are you people?"

"My name's Johnny and that's my girlfriend Carol," the dark-haired man said as he motioned to the petite blonde.

"I'm Brian, and that's my girl friend, Bonnie. I don't feel so good," he said, nodding at his girlfriend with the big breasts and the long black hair, as he dropped back to the couch.

A clatter came from outside. I peered out the window to see a hail of arrows hit the cabin; then I heard something on the roof.

"I think they're on the roof," I said. "Johnny, you and Bonnie go guard the back, but first I need those items you took from the graveyard."

They handed me their ill-gotten finds while Johnny and Bonnie headed to the back of the cabin. Roxy stepped up beside me, cradling her Mini-14 below her breasts.

"Cover me, babe," I said, flinging open the door. As I stepped outside, I noticed a tall zombie wearing a faded headdress standing in the middle of the undead pack that looked to be their leader. Bits and pieces of decayed flesh hung from his putrid face and I caught the graveyard stench drifting on the wind. He held up a spear, drew it back, and the entire tribe of the undead bastards began to chant in some forgotten tongue.

"Here! You can have this stuff back! We don't want it!" I yelled and tossed the stuff from the graveyard out the door. An arrow hit the side of the cabin next to me, as the zombies charged. Roxy opened up with her Mini-14 and I slammed the door. At the back of the cabin, Johnny opened up with the AK and I heard Bonnie fire off several rounds with one of the handguns.

"They're coming through the roof!" Brian yelled.

Stepping into the center of the room, I looked up and saw a hole appear as several flesh-eaters hacked their way through the roof. I looked up into the undead eyes of the Indian zombies as they glared back at me and the others.

Slapping a fresh clip into my AR, I brought the weapon to my shoulder, emptied the clip into the ceiling, and we all spent the next twenty minutes fighting for our lives.

Finally, the zombie attack broke off, the Indians retreated back into the trees surrounding the cabin to regroup, and I looked up at a full moon rising in the night sky through the hole in the roof.

"Oh, shit," I said while looking at Roxy. "You were supposed to be chained up." Outside, we heard the Indian zombies chanting once more in their ancient language, building themselves up for another attack.

Roxy looked at me with a wild, feral look in her eyes and said, "Not this time, Mike." She took off her Saint Christopher medal, tossed it to me, peeled off her tank top and slid off her jeans. Her body began to change, elongating and shifting, thick hair sprouting to cover her from head to toe as she transformed into a werewolf. Within seconds, dark hair covered her beautiful breasts, her long sensual legs, and pretty face.

"Take it outside!" I yelled, flinging the door open, while the two young couples inside the cabin looked on in horror. Roxy ran out into the night and I slammed the door closed behind her. "Quick! Help me find something to bar this door!" I yelled.

"What the hell was that?" Johnny yelled, his eyes widening in shock, while the rest of the college kids looked on.

"A few months ago, we were working a case down by the Mexican border and Roxy got bit by a werewolf. Now get me something, quick! We can't let her back in here until after daybreak."

Johnny found some two-by-fours down in the cellar, and helped me wedge them up against the door. I looked out the window and watched the battle unfold. When Roxy stormed out of the cabin in her new form, the zombies charged her. I heard them shout their war cry, as Roxy let out a terrifying howl of blood lust. Then the battle commenced. She slammed into the undead multitude, slashing with her claws and biting with her powerful jaws. Decayed limbs flew into the air and I saw her rip the head off one zombie and then disembowel another, literally ripping the undead corpse to shreds.

After a few minutes of the onslaught, the zombies retreated in disarray and Roxy fled into the night.

The night wore on, things quieted down and we managed to get a little rest, but Brian's condition worsened. His skin began to rot, his temperature shot up, and he puked blood. Bonnie made him lie back on the couch, wiped his forehead with a wet cloth, and he drifted off to sleep while I kept watch the front of the cabin. The zombies were still out there, but they had retreated to the road and were milling around in the night. I guess they were afraid Roxy would come back and finish what she started.

Sitting on the floor, I leaned back against the wall, nodding out for a few seconds, but then I heard a loud, feral growl that brought me fully awake. It must have been about two o'clock in the morn-ing when Brian died only to get up off the couch with a bad atti-tude. The undead thing, that was once Brian, lunged at Bonnie and I brought up my AR-15 and gave him a double tap in the center of his forehead. Bonnie screamed and fell to her knees as the corpse slumped to the floor, half his head missing.

"You killed Brian!" she wailed.

"Believe me, sister, he's much better off," I said as I came to my feet.

A little later, Roxy showed up on the front porch. She was back in her human form, and stood in the nude, pounding on the door.

"Mike, it's me. Let me in," she pleaded.

"Sorry, darlin', no can do."

"Please, Michael, it's cold out here and I'm naked."

"You should have thought about that before you lost control of yourself and took off your Saint Christopher medal. Now go out into the woods and play your little wolf girl games. You're not getting back in here until it's daylight," I said.

Roxy let out a ferocious scream and pounded on the door some more. She changed back into a wolf, clawed at the door for a few seconds while letting out several grunts and howls, then disap-peared back into the woods.

The night wore on. The zombies made one more feeble assault on the cabin, but we drove them off with concentrated fire. The sky outside had turned gray, the sun was just threatening to peek over the mountains to the east, and I accidentally knocked over Johnny's nylon backpack that he had left by the door. An ancient looking skull rolled out onto the floor, its eyeless sockets staring up at me.

I looked at Johnny, an embarrassed expression crossed his face before he looked away from me. Bending over, I picked up the skull, and opened the front door. The leader of the zombie tribe, his rotten headdress fluttering in the wind, gave me a hateful look and threatened me with his spear.

"Here, I guess this was what you were after all along," I said and tossed the skull out the door. The zombie leader nodded, picked up the skull and began walking back up the road toward the graveyard with his undead brethren following along behind.

I stepped onto the porch, glanced to my right, and saw Roxy fast asleep, leaning against the cabin. "Get me a blanket," I told Johnny. When he handed me the blanket, I took it over to where Roxy lay, bent down, and covered her up.

She woke up, blinked her baby blues at me, gagged, and said, "Oh, Mike, I think I'm gonna be sick." She crawled to the edge of the porch on her hands and knees and puked her guts out. The blanket fell off, revealing her best assets, but she was too sick to care.

"Got a hold of some bad meat did you?" I asked and covered her back up.

She looked up at me with crusty blood covering her mouth. "You don't know the half of it. Those things tasted like warmed-over shit."

"Tell me about it. Talk about morning breath," I said, fanning the air in front of my face. "Let's get you inside and washed up, then we'll see about cleaning up this mess."

Roxy showered, dressed and after an hour or so, she was feeling much better. I contacted the authorities using the CB radio in Johnny's Bronco and the local authorities patched a call through to General Kincaid, one of my contacts in the military. A contingent of troops showed up, along with people from the Bureau of Indian Affairs. They re-buried the remains of the dead Indian zombies, posted **No Trespassing** signs in front of the graveyard, put up a chain-link fence with razor wire on top, and contacted the closest Indian reservation to watch the place. They also closed down the campground across the road from the graveyard, so something like this would never happen again.

The authorities came up with a cover story to explain the death of Brian Duncan and the other two college students. They made the survivors sign a security oath swearing them to secrecy before letting them go.

On our way out in the Jeep, when we were passing the grave-yard, I noticed tracks on the ground where the remnant of the zombie tribe crawled back into their graves. When we reached the main road, I started to turn left and head toward the highway, but Roxy spoke up.

"Go the other way, Mike."

"Why?" I asked, but I did what she wanted.

"I'll just bet you that the cabin we stayed at was the wrong one."

"Some vacation, huh?" I said while we traveled through the forest.

"Yeah, a vacation in Hell," she replied.

The road snaked its way through the majestic forest, ascended a rocky ridge before dropping down into a beautiful, pristine valley. A mile up the highway on our right, we came to a wide, well-maintained dirt road covered with pine needles leading deep into the forest.

"That's the road," Roxy said. I turned off the highway and headed into the forest. Two miles further, we crossed a wooden bridge spanning the creek and then took a left turn on another well-maintained dirt road. Five minutes later, I looked off to our left and there was the cabin, looking just like it did in the picture.

"So I'm a guy. I make mistakes," I said as I pulled up in front of the cabin. Roxy climbed out of the Jeep, ran up onto the porch, bent down, and checked under the welcome mat; with me, of course, checking out her shapely ass.

"The key's right here. Right where the guy said it would be. Can we stay?" she asked.

"Sure, we've got all the time in the world."

"That's good, I'm gonna go inside and take a nap. I didn't get much sleep last night."

"Me neither, darlin'" I replied with a smile.

Roxy went inside while I grabbed my fishing gear and headed down to the nearby stream. Maybe this time we could have a *real* vacation.

DARKEST HEART'S DESIRE

MARK M. JOHNSON

The rain poured down as if God had loosed the waters of Niagara from the sky, intending to flood the world once again to purify it of humanity's sin. Duncan lifted his countenance up into the falling rain and let it wash his thinning hair back away from his face. No lightning flashed to light his dark, tortured expression. There wasn't any thunder to reflect his fury.

The storm raged with a constant roar from a black endless sky. Though it was a warm night, the cold rain chilled his skin, and he hugged his arms tight against himself and shivered. He lifted his tortured face into the driving rain again, letting it wash away his indecision, cleanse his suffering, and cool the raging fire within his soul. Falling with the dull roar of a waterfall, the tempest eclipsed even the sound of his gasping breath. He was soaked to the bone, his expensive haircut plastered to his head like a bad toupee.

What the fuck am I doing here? Duncan asked himself. He should be out doing the things that ruthless self-made billionaires did at this time of night, in the places that they did them. Yet here he was, standing ankle deep in the muddy grass between two houses in a middle class neighborhood in Fremont, Washington. This, in itself, might not be very unusual.

Surely, there were billionaire peeping Toms in existence that were unsatisfied by the peeping to be had on the internet. Helplessly pitiful perverts, who would risk their freedom and social standing to creep out into the night and spy through people's bedroom windows. Duncan was no peeping-Tom-pervert, however. Nevertheless, here he was, looking through the side window of a stranger's home like some kind of water logged dark-and-stormy-night-freak.

He had followed Mandy, his wife of two gloriously happy years, from the gym she had told him she was going to for a scheduled early evening workout. He had tried to convince her to drop her old gym membership now that they were married and she had an extensively stocked gym in their home. Mandy only smiled and kissed his cheek, explaining how she really went to the gym for social reasons. "All of my friends are there," she protested.

Duncan, of course relented with a silly grin. "Ok," he had said. "Go have your fun." She smiled her sunny smile and pranced out to the Lexus convertible he had given to her as a wedding present and sped away. As she had driven away, Duncan's smile faded and his eyes hardened. He had known, or at least suspected, where she was going, and why. However, he had to see it for himself to accept what his mind was trying to convince him of. He could have hired someone to do this distasteful surveillance but he wanted to keep this in house, it was just too personal. Like his mother, who had raised him on her own after his father left for greener pastures, he preferred to wash his own dirty laundry.

Duncan knew to whom the house belonged. A muscle head named Cory Allen. The full time fire fighter and part time personal trainer at his wife's gym lived alone in this humble abode. From the research he had collected over the past week, he had learned quite a bit about his wife's personal trainer, Cory Allen.

The guy was divorced; caught red cocked with another woman in his own bed. His former wife, Julie, a real looker, had confessed this tearfully to him when he had questioned her. From the many other women he had interviewed, he had discerned that Cory was a sleaze who seduced women, preferably married women. He had resorted to the threat of revealing the affairs to their cuckolded husbands to persuade the women to talk, and talk they had.

The newly awakened part of Duncan's heart that dearly loved his wife, Mandy, could not bear to accept what was happening. It did not want him to step up to the window and peer through the slightly parted curtains. It was afraid of what his eyes would see. He was terrified of the pain he knew was coming. Another part of his heart spoke louder than the weakened, besotted fraction that was trying to coax him back into his car, insisting on his full atten- tion.

This bitter part of his heart, his inner darkness, which had helped him to destroy other people's lives without remorse as he built his empire and his fortune. The dark and ruthless part of his heart that had driven him his entire life demanded he look, now!

It would not take no for an answer, it meant to have its way.

Taking in a deep breath, he lifted one foot up and almost lost a shoe in the process. Getting the foot firmly back into his shoe, he sloshed his way up to the window and peered in. At first, he saw nothing upsetting. The pouring rain washed down the window and partially obscured the softly lit interior of the home. It offered only a view of the kitchen doorway, part of the dining set, and the china cabinet. Shifting his gaze to the left, toward the front of the house and the living room, he gasped. His mouth twisted and fell agape.

Cory, the personal trainer/firefighter, the sleazy seducer of married women, sat on the couch facing the direction of Duncan's window. From what he could see, the man had on not a single article of clothing. *He's wearing nothing but a shit eating grin*, he thought harshly as he stared. He trembled violently, grinding his teeth in barely suppressed fury. Between Cory's knees, Duncan could see Mandy's long, naturally curly red hair cascading down over her soft, pale, lightly freckled shoulders and back. She was completely naked as well, he could see her bare feet tucked under her ass, as her head rose and fell in the slow, steady, repetitive motion of well-performed oral sex.

Duncan could almost feel Mandy's lips working on him, as she had done this for him so many times, and she was so good at it. "Oh," he sobbed softly, placing his hands on the warm glass of the window. "Goddamn it, Mandy!" His beautiful new bride finished abruptly and leaned back from her lover's erection, and Cory grinned down at her appreciatively. He watched her wipe the back of her left hand across her face, which he could not see, as she rose to her feet in front of the wife-stealing bastard.

"Mother-fucking . . ." Duncan growled. He drew back a fist, as if he intended to punch through the window-glass to stop the betrayal from continuing. He could see Cory's erection clearly, as Mandy climbed up over it. It was easily twice the length and girth of his own, and he felt a moment of envy. Even over the dull roar of the rainstorm, he heard her cry out softly as she lowered herself down, penetrating herself with it.

She began to ride Cory slowly, crying out each time she came down on him. Despite his agonizing fury, the sight of his Mandy fucking another man frustratingly aroused him, and disgusted with his reaction, he could stand to watch no more. Turning away from the window, he fell to his knees. His head fell into the waterlogged grass and mud as he openly sobbed, softly calling out his wife's name repeatedly as he dug his fingers into the muddy lawn.

Duncan was indeed a cold-hearted entrepreneur, but he had grown up a fatherless ridiculed nerd. In his early teens, a beautiful girl named Andrea had coaxed him into her backyard on the premise of pleasures he had only dreamed of, but it had only been the set up to a cruel prank. She had kissed him and the young heart pounding in his chest threatened to burst. She touched him tenderly and whispered in his ear, and then her friends hiding in the bushes sprung their trap.

They had leapt out and grabbed him before he could scramble away, and held him. Andrea's boyfriend, Tom, hit him and broke his glasses. Then Tom and his hatefully laughing friends, tore his clothes from his frail body. The small crowd of laughing boys and girls had chased him all the way home as they playfully tried to rip away the only scrap of clothing he had left, his underwear.

The humiliation and heartbreak he had suffered kept him in his room for the last few weeks of summer vacation. During those weeks of horribly tormented sequestration, his broken heart grew dark and vengeful. Over the years that followed, many girls had expressed honest interest in him. He would always suspect that their flirtations were nothing more than another lie, another cruel joke. Because of his scarred distrusting heart, he grew up into a lonely, bitter man.

When he had met Mandy Chaney a few years ago, a twenty-two-year-old intern at one of his many office buildings, he had been almost instantly smitten with her. The incredibly beautiful woman played down her natural beauty with her choice of clothing and conservative mannerisms. Highly intelligent and competently professional, yet shy, friendly, and playful, she seemed to be his perfect match.

With her heart-melting smile and infectiously innocent laugh, Mandy had him head over heels in less than a week. For the first time since he was a child, he felt the loving part of his heart begin to beat with life again. When they married after six months of dating, Duncan, at thirty-five-years-old, had still been a virgin.

As he lay in the muddy grass sobbing, he thought to himself that now he truly understood the term heartbroken. Although he had been hurt as a teenager, he had never given his heart to anyone as he had given it to Mandy. He always thought the term was a figure of speech, but now as he fell over onto his side, the pain he felt in his chest was as real as the muddy ground beneath him. It truly felt like a heart attack. Mandy had awoken the soft, tender, loving part of his heart that had gone unused for most of his life. She had breathed life into that dusty old chamber that he had walled up and left for dead. Now, Mandy had savagely ripped it open and left it broken and bleeding. However, the other part that had been eclipsed by his love for Mandy, his darkest heart, began to rise to power once again, and it screamed at him to get up off his ass and do something. It demanded blood for blood and its pound of flesh.

Duncan struggled up to his feet and slowly staggered across the front lawn of the wife-fucking-bastard's house on his way to his car parked at the curb. He dragged his feet across the wet grass in the driving rain, muttering hateful thoughts as he dug in his pocket for the car keys he had absentmindedly left in the ignition switch of his car. He would fix them good; he would use his underworld connections and power to destroy Cory's life. First, he would take-away Cory's job, then his money, and then his home.

Duncan wouldn't be satisfied until the bastard put a gun in his mouth. Mandy, on the other hand, his mind rebelled from thoughts of hurting her. *You must*, his darkest heart screamed. *She must suffer as you suffer*. He could destroy her, take-away all he had given, use the prenuptial agreement his lawyer had insisted she sign. He could see to it that she never found work again, unless it was selling her ass on the street. Digging in vain for his keys, he crossed the street to his car parked at the opposite curb. His mind was so awash with thoughts of vengeance and pain that he failed to notice the man staggering down the street near his car until he almost stumbled into him. He came within arms reach of the decrepit man before stopping abruptly, as he realized he was about to walk into someone.

He staggered back a step, holding up his hands in apology. "Oh, excuse me, sir," Duncan stammered loudly, to make himself heard over the roar of the rainstorm. "I didn't see you there."

It was well after ten thirty and the night was pitch black. Twin reflections of the rain shimmering street lights shone in the man's wide, staring eyes. *Some whacked out junky looking for a hand out?* he thought. *Or maybe I'm about to get robbed.* His anger resurfaced vigorously. "Look, asshole," he growled menacingly at the dazed looking guy. "I don't have any cash, and if you fuck with me I'll blow your goddamn head off!" He bluffed with the best, pissed off expression he could muster.

Out of the corner of his eye, he noticed several other people shuffling up the street from the west, both on the walk and in the street. *What the fuck is this?* he wondered. The man's head jerked down and his vacant expression focused on Duncan as he reached out mechanically and grasped him by the shoulders. The unexpected contact refocused Duncan's attention on the stranger.

"Hey, what the fuck?" he asked incredulously, and struggled to back away. The man held him in an iron grip. His huge hands dug painfully into Duncan's flesh. "What the fuck's your problem, man?" he growled, and tried to shove the man back.

The man ignored his frustrations and darted forward, twisting his head to the left. Viciously, the man buried his teeth into Duncan's throat just below his ear, chewing into the soft yielding flesh. He screamed as he felt the man's teeth grinding through the tendons in his neck, but the roar of the wind and pounding rain greedily swallowed up the sound.

He slammed his fists onto the lunatic's shoulders and head, and then in an adrenalin-fueled frenzy, he shoved back from the man and a large chunk of his neck came away in the maniac's mouth. The man swallowed the bloody meat, growled hungrily, and began moving toward him again, reaching out like a drunken fairy tale monster. Duncan screamed again and turned to flee.

The pain was unbelievable. He held a hand to his ravaged throat as he stumbled onto the front lawn of Cory Allen's home. The blood sprayed from between his fingers in a steady cadence with his racing heart. Once again, for the second time that night, he fell to his knees in the wet grass, sobbing.

His vision swam in and out of focus as he quickly bled to death on the front lawn of the man who was taking his wife at this very moment. *How ironic,* he thought and fell over onto his side. He lay there, helpless, unable to lift a finger to stop the man who was now only a few steps away. "Mandy," he cried out softly. His eyes rolled up into his head and his body began to tremble in spasms before he slowly relaxed into the fathomless shroud of death.

The man stopped staggering abruptly and stood gazing down at Duncan's body. Grunting in disapproval, he grimaced and snapped his teeth together several times making a repetitive clacking sound like muted gunshots. The eyelids of Duncan's dead body flickered and then opened.

The eyes gazed upwards, unblinking, into the assault of the hard falling rain that washed over them. His sharp hazel eyes were now vacant and devoid of any discernable emotion, the lights were on, but somebody else had moved in. He stared up at the thing standing over him and groaned. The thing grunted again and turned to shuffle away. The Duncan-thing pulled himself clumsily to his feet and moved to follow, then paused, and glanced over his shoulder at the house behind him.

The sliver of light shining through the front curtains of the house seemed to call out to him silently, beckoning him forward. The Duncan-thing felt something stir in the dark hollow pit of his being, a dark inexplicable anger that pulled him toward the sliver of light. He walked with ever-increasing speed as he closed the distance between himself and the light shining through the curtain.

When he had awoken from the void of death, he had felt nothing but a cold empty longing burning in every fiber of his being. Now with every step he took he felt a heat rising in his mind, an unexplainable rage that drove him on faster with every step. He crashed violently through the window, ripping down and enshrouding himself in the curtains as he fell into the living room of the home.

*   *   *

"Oh yeah," Cory groaned in rapturous pleasure as sweet, little Mandy rode him good and slow. She had been an easy mark to turn. Newly married women, especially the ones married to filthy rich dweebs, as she was, were always easy if you knew how to play them. The rich fucks just didn't know how to please their women. He prided himself in his ability to get any woman he wanted, and Mandy was no exception. She had been quite reluctant at first, but in the end she was his, just like all the others.

Mandy looked down at him with lusty, half-lidded eyes. "Tickle it," she hissed breathlessly. "Now!"

Cory trailed the fingers of his right hand slowly down her belly, down to what she called her 'happy spot', and began to rub her softly there. At the same time, his left hand found her right nipple, catching it between his thumb and forefinger, he rolled it between them, gently pinching. She groaned as her steady motion intensified, and began to pant and whimper as she bounced up and down faster still.

He was grunting, struggling with the effort of holding back his climax, waiting for her to catch up, when the living room window exploded inward with a thunderous crash. Someone came through the shattering glass just to Cory's right, ripping down the curtains as he came through the window. The curtains wrapped around the window crasher as he rolled across the couch and onto the floor.

Mandy screamed in shocked surprise as she jumped up off her lover's lap.

"What the fuck?" Cory exclaimed irately, as he too jumped up off the couch to face the curtain-enshrouded figure on the living room floor. The figure under the curtain rolled over once and started climbing to his feet. Cory was sure now that it was a man that had just jumped through his window. He could see the muddy shoes sticking out from under the cover of the torn curtains, and the mud stained dripping pants just above them.

Although he was still completely naked, Cory did not attempt to cover or dress himself. He looked ridiculously comical with his Viagra induced erection sticking out ominously, as he readied himself for what he was sure was going to be a very short fight. Even as the man under the ripped curtains struggled briefly to remove them from over his head, Cory was already certain who it was.

"Duncan!" Mandy cried out as the curtain came away and fell to the floor.

Duncan looked over at the woman and his lips came up in a snarl as he staggered toward her. In the heat of surprise, both Cory and his married lover failed to notice the bloody rain-washed wound on Duncan's neck.

Cory reached out and pulled Mandy behind him. "Look, man," he shouted with his deepest intimidating voice as he puffed up his chest and flexed his ample musculature. "I can let the window go, I know you have to be fucked up about all this, but no way are you laying a hand on Mandy!"

The tone and posture he had used to great effect to avoid fights in the past had no effect on Mandy's husband. He continued shuffling forward, growling aggressively, baring his teeth like a collared attack dog. Mandy sobbed behind Cory, stammering out unintelligible apologies.

"You're gonna get fucked up good, man. Don't do it!" Cory warned as he took up a well practiced, but not to often used, fighting stance. "Just leave now, before you get hurt."

Duncan continued forward, coming within five feet of his intended victims and reached out his clawed waterlogged dripping hands.

"I warned you, asshole," Cory snarled. He darted forward and punched his lover's husband squarely on the nose. He felt bone shatter under his knuckles like cheap porcelain.

He felt Duncan's nose breaking and pulled the punch, satisfied that it would do the job. Cory could have hit much harder, but he didn't really think it would be necessary to drop the rich little geek to his knees. Besides, the last thing he needed was to accidentally kill the stupid fucker and go to jail for a piece of tail.

However, the punch did little more than cause Duncan to falter a step, as his head recoiled back with the impact of Cory's fist. Reaching out with an almost uncanny quickness, Duncan snared Cory's retreating fist. He pulled the bloodstained fist closer and savagely bit into Cory's meaty forearm just below the elbow.

Cory screamed at the sudden, unexpected pain. "You fucking freak!" he cried as he repeatedly slammed his left fist down like a sledgehammer on Duncan's head.

Duncan pulled away with a bloody piece of forearm in his mouth. Seeing the opening, Cory put his right foot up in Duncan's stomach and kicked out as hard as he could. The kick sent Duncan sprawling backwards over the coffee table and back onto the floor.

"Please, oh God," Mandy screamed for them to stop, but Cory, now thoroughly enraged, completely shut her out as he advanced on his shorter and obviously weaker opponent. Blood gushed from the deep bite wound on his arm, but caught up in the red haze of violent intent, he hardly noticed it.

"You fucking bit me! Oh man. You are fucking dead now, motherfucker! You hear me, asshole? I'm gonna fuck you up good now!" Cory screamed in a blind rage as he stepped closer to the skinny little asshole, intending to grab him by the hair and lift him up by it.

Consumed in a euphoric rapture from his first taste of human flesh, the Duncan-thing sat unmoving on the floor chewing the tender bloody morsel. He saw the man approaching and the movement brought him out of his daze. He swallowed the meat in his mouth and moved to stand, but stopped when he saw the large piece of tasty looking flesh bouncing between the man's legs.

As the man grabbed him by the hair, he reached out and effortlessly grabbed hold of the bouncing flesh and pulled it to his mouth.

"Stand up, you fuck, so I can knock you back down aga . . ." Cory started, but his threats stopped abruptly when he felt the cold hand painfully grab him by his forgotten erection, and then. . .

The Duncan-thing's teeth cut through the hard, tender flesh like a hot knife through butter. Again, the euphoric explosion in his mouth stunned him senseless, as he tasted the glorious, bloody human flesh again.

Pain. Agonies worse than he ever thought possible exploded at his groin and shot like lightning bolts into his stomach and down his thighs. Cory shrieked, in a panic he slammed his knee into Duncan's jaw. The remaining strings of flesh between Duncan's teeth and his erection stretched and snapped like wet rubber bands. Cory stumbled backwards as he continued to bawl in disbelieving agony.

"Oh God," Cory screamed. "He fucking bit it off! Oh Jesus," he sobbed as he held what was left of his bleeding cock in his trembling hands. Looking up, Cory saw Duncan's throat working as he swallowed the piece of cock he had bitten off.

He suddenly realized that Duncan was getting to his feet and screamed in terror as Mandy's husband's vacant eyes locked onto him, growling hungrily. The Duncan-thing licked his bloody lips, growled, and twisted his mouth with a grimace showing his blood stained teeth.

His manly braggadocio now thoroughly cowed, Cory turned and staggered down the hall screaming all the way, he spun and fell into his bathroom, slamming the door shut behind him.

The Duncan-thing wanted more. He eagerly followed the man down the hall until he came to the door from behind which he could hear the man crying out. "Oh Jesus, it's gone," the man sobbed. "Oh God, oh God, oh Jesus, I can't stop the bleeding. Oh God."

The man broke down and sobbed incoherently from behind the locked bathroom door. He shrieked again as the Duncan-thing began pounding on it. He couldn't get through. He threw himself against it repeatedly to no real effect, except that the man cried out even louder with every impact. Then, over the commotion of his growling, and slamming himself against the door, and the man screaming from the other side, the Duncan-thing heard something else.

"Duncan, please stop," said a sobbing voice from behind him, back in the room where he had come through the window. "What have you done? Oh my God, Duncan! Oh my God, I'm so sorry."

His head swiveled around and the Duncan-thing's vacant eyes fell upon her, the woman he had first seen when he had pulled the curtain off his head. In his frenzy to taste the man's flesh again, the Duncan-thing had forgotten about the woman. Clutching an afghan blanket over her naked body, she stood trembling against the wall next to the couch in the living room. Her teary eyes were imploring him, begging him, pleading for forgiveness that he was incapable of giving.

"Please, please, Duncan," she cried softly as tears tumbled down her face in a torrent of regret. "That's enough," she beseeched the man she mistakenly assumed was her enraged husband.

For just a moment, he stood motionless, gazing at her as if he remembered something of this crying woman. Somewhere in the black depths of the Duncan-thing's decomposing brain, he felt something stir. A faint sensation of love, pain, and anger touched his mind and then faded as the darkness of his insatiable hunger took hold again.

Turning languidly, he began staggering toward her in his slow relentless pace. The man's flesh had been rapturously sweet beyond all imagining, but the pleasure already ran thin in his belly, the fleeting satisfaction quickly giving way to the hunger.

However, the crying woman calling him by a name that no longer meant anything to him, her flesh was sweeter still.

THE LIBRARY

DAVID FRENCH

Susan Weland was a typical American teenager. Her concerns were hanging with the right crowd and keeping up with the latest styles. That was, until a couple of weeks ago. Now she was sitting nervously against the wall of her bedroom, no longer concerned with anything but living. The air in the house was stale and humid. Sweat clung to her as she moved closer to her window, hoping for a breeze to blow though the boards.

Her mother and father were sitting on the couch and she watched them. Susan saw tears running down her mother's face. They were speaking quietly to one another, but she knew what they were saying.

The family has been in their small, boarded up house, hiding in the darkened rooms for two weeks, and the pressures kept mounting.

The military had come to their neighborhood on the day Marshal Law had been declare, and offered to take the family to a shelter.

"This is our home. We'll wait it out." Father had replied to the sergeant, and then went back to work boarding up the house.

Everyone else in their Virginia neighborhood had left with the sergeant, or tried to get off the peninsula before it was sealed up.

Susan's parents weren't prepared for the crisis. *Who could have been?* It's not every day that the dead rise and attack the living!

The days were long and hot as the family waited in vain for help. Sometimes, they could hear gunfire or screams in the distance, and this kept them on edge. The nights were the worst, the sounds of the dead outside grew louder as the sun went down. The walking dead would slap and pound on the doors, and sometimes they would poke their fingers through the openings in the boards and peer in!

After two weeks without supplies, the food was almost gone. There weren't any signs of help coming, and it was time for hard a decision. Susan's father decided that he would try to get to one of the aide stations. He couldn't use their car, due to the concrete road blocks set up on the highways and on some side streets by the National Guard. Not to mention, many of the streets were blocked by the wrecked cars of those trying to flee the mass murder taking place.

Her father would have to walk the mile or so—he knew that he would be in danger—but those he loved needed him to get supplies. He went when the sun was at its brightest, thinking that the zombies were less likely to attack, since many of them sought the darkness.

He kissed his frightened family goodbye and promised to return.

He never did.

* * *

Thirsty, tired, and grieving for the loss of her husband, Susan's mother panicked. She opened the front door and ran screaming into the dark street. It was late at night and the dead had come from their hiding places, she was quickly surrounded by dozens of assailants. They tore at her bare limbs with their yellowed teeth. Pale, bluish hands ripped at her white flesh with filthy browned nails.

She looked down to see her own blood dripping from her arms. This brought her back to her senses.

The zombies were enjoying their kill, they were playing with the woman like a cat would a mouse.

Her mother's screams woke Susan, who hadn't slept soundly in weeks. She ran out of the house with a baseball bat and swung wildly at her mother's attackers.

What was left of her mother pulled free for a moment and pushed Susan away, she screamed to her daughter, "Get back in the house! Now!" Too weak to go any further, she fell to her knees, where she was once again swarmed.

Susan stepped back in horror at the sight of her mother's bloodied and shredded body! Turning quickly, she ran back into the house and slammed the door as she was followed by several blood soaked ghouls.

Her mother's screams, or maybe the smell of the fresh blood, brought more zombies to the house, and one of them was Barbara.

* * *

In the morning Susan looked through one of the small openings in the boards that covered a window. She saw her mother's bones in the street. There wasn't any flesh left on them.

The sun being up sent some of the shuffling zombies away to darker places—they would return at sundown as usual.

She began to cry, slapping her hand on the board in front of her in an emotional outburst.

Susan had one eye looking out of the opening, when Barbara heard the sounds.

Barbara's face suddenly appeared in front of Susan.

She recognized Barbara. She knew her as the woman that lived on the street behind her. Susan jerked her head back, away from the opening in fear. Barbara's blood soaked face and chest sickened the young girl.

It was too late. Barbara, being faster and a great deal more aware then the other zombies, had already started planning how to remove the obstacle that kept her from her meal.

Susan watched in horror as Barbara smashed her hands through the glass and grabbed the boards that covered the opening. She began to shake them violently back and forth trying to free them from their nails. When she got nowhere with this action, she began slamming her fists into the wood over and over.

Susan's blood ran cold with terror at the sudden violence.

Other zombies began to gather on the lawn, due to this new noise.

Barbara started swaying like a snake from side to side, and baring her teeth in rage. Finally, she charged the boards, throwing everything she had into them. They gave way with a crash! She was stunned as she landed on the floor with an audible thud at Susan's feet. She lay there for a second.

This gave Susan a few seconds of time to make her escape out of the opening that Barbara had just made. She ran across the porch and jumped over the handrail, landing on the over grown grass in her front yard, and started running.

Barbara was out of the house and on her trail in seconds. The other zombies turned and quickly shuffled along, bringing up the rear.

Four weeks ago Jimmy was one of those guys that you meet outside the 7-Eleven, asking for your change. Now he's a zombie. Zombie-Jimmy was standing near a fence not far from the intersection of the road Susan was running toward. He was hidden by a tall shrub–this was not by design, nothing that happened to Jimmy in life or death was thought out.

Susan saw Barbara closing on her as she looked over her shoulder–she was getting winded and made a fatal mistake. She didn't see Jimmy until it was too late. She hit him hard, running as fast as she could. Jimmy's feet left the ground as he flew backward, but he did grab a hold of one of her arms, and held on. He dragged the girl to the ground with him as he fell.

Susan struck at him with her fists as she struggled to stand, other zombies made their way to the fight. Spinning around, frantically crying for help, she saw a man in a second story window watching her fight for her life. She knew him, not by name, but they had exchanged nods at the 7-Eleven where he worked. She screamed for him to do something, but he backed away from the window to hide in his room.

Susan felt the first bite–the pain ran through her like a hot iron as the zombie's sharp teeth sunk in. Blood was everywhere, but she was still on her feet fighting! They tore the flesh from her arms as she kicked at them–she even bit Jimmy on the hand. Twisting her body, she almost broke free from the cold, merciless hands that held her in place, only to see Barbara running straight for her.

Barbara ran with amazing speed, leaping over the other, slower zombies that were tormenting the young girl. She tackled the dying girl, forcing her down to the cold concrete where she died kicking and screaming, but never gave up until the end!

* * *

Vince recognized Jimmy as he placed the cross hairs of his scope on his forehead. He remembered him as a likeable guy—always joking and smiling as he asked for spare change at the 7-Eleven in the neighborhood where Vince and his wife, Barbara, lived. The hot Virginia sun was beating down on Jimmy's emaciated face, but he didn't feel it. He feels nothing at all, thought Vince. Then again maybe that's not true! He had to feel something. Jimmy had joined in on the kill with others like himself. He must feel hunger, or he wouldn't kill and eat, or maybe it was a lust for violence. Whatever it was, it was over powering, so therefore he felt something.

Vince watched Jimmy just standing there with his zombie friends, digesting Susan Weland. He could barely recognize the girl whom he and Barbara knew from the next street over. He could see her head resting against the curb—her eyes stared straight into his scope as he watched Jimmy slowly take in his surroundings.

Susan's once beautiful, black hair was matted with blood, and her mouth gaped wide opened as if still screaming.

Vince could see her dried blood on Jimmy's face and hands, and he knew that Jimmy had helped rip the girl's throat out. He didn't hear the young girl scream for help, but he felt anger building in him, and he wanted to shoot the bastards. That was when he saw Barbara among the others, kneeling down beside the body. His heart skipped a beat as he saw what a monster the kind and loving woman he had married had become.

He wanted to scream *"Why?"* at the top of his lungs, but she was why he had been searching the city. He knew he had to finish her, and give her peace from the demons that have come to possess her!

As Vince waited for Barbara to rise to her feet so he could get a clean shot, his mind raced back several weeks. Back to when he and Barbara were hiding in her father's small, brick ranch home in Newport News.

It was where his nightmares had begun.

* * *

Barbara's father was lying ill in his bed. They thought it was a cold, but it just kept getting worst. The hospitals and the Army's make shift aide stations were overflowing and dangerous. Barbara thought it better to stay away from those places if they could. The electricity had been off for days, and the food had gone bad in the refrigerator. Both the cell phone and the land line phone were not working—not that there was anyone left to call if you needed help.

She looked over her shoulder at Vince, who was standing behind her. "Dad needs help. He's getting worse. I don't care what it is you bring back, just get him some *help*!" Her eyes pleaded with Vince.

He took his old 4-wheel drive Jeep—it still had his West Virginia plates on it—and headed toward the Army's aide station. He was hoping to get some antibiotics and supplies, but he arrived to an empty lot—the National Guard had left.

When he returned to the house, and he opened the front door, all was quiet. He felt a strange sensation as the hairs on the back of his neck stood up. He started walking down the narrow hall to the bedroom where his father-in-law was when he had left. It was too quiet.

As he entered the bedroom, he saw Barbara's father on the opposite side of the bed, his back to the hall where Vince stood. *There was no way he should be able to stand as ill as he is*, Vince thought as he ran over to help him.

"Barbara!" He shouted loudly, as he ran around to the other side of the bed.

"*Oh, shit.*" Were the next words he uttered. He saw blood smeared on the old man's face and hands.

This was the first time he had seen one of the zombies face to face! He had seen them on the news reports, but had dismissed them as bullshit until *now*!

"Barbara," he shouted again, as he did a quick back stroke, trying to dodge the bloody, outstretched hands that were groping for him.

Something red caught his eye as he looked down at the floor. It was a thin blood trail leading to the back door.

He knew he was being followed by her father, so when Vince reached the backdoor, he swung it open, then slammed it shut, locking it before he ran out into the yard. He saw Barbara facing the river, the wind blowing her long, straight blonde hair to one side. He could see a large red stain running around the collar of her blouse. She was standing awkwardly as he approached her from behind, she took no notice of him as he approached.

"Barbara?" he asked in a whisper as he took several slow steps closer. His eyes darted between her and the door behind him.

She made a loud animalistic growl as she turned on him fast, it reminded him of an angry cat trying to warn off an attacker. It worked on Vince as he got a look at what she had become. He knew she was a killer, a ghoul, a zombie, that wanted to kill him! He could also tell right away that she was different from the slower zombies he had seen on the news.

The water! He remembered the yard next door had a small pier, and he thought this may be his only chance. He spun away from her as she leapt toward him. The chase was on! He zigzagged a couple of times when he sensed she was getting too close, and this threw her off just enough to keep himself a few feet ahead of her. As he took the first few steps on the pier, he realized that she had stopped at the water's edge. He turned to see that she was staring at him with the wild eyes of a crazed hunter.

"I promise, I'll come back for the two of you, and give you rest," he said before jumping into the water, and swimming away.

Later that day, still drying from his escape, he joined a mob of people as they ransacked a sporting good store. This was where he had gotten a .308-caliber Remington 700, and a scope. He grabbed a 45 auto and several boxes of rounds for both guns. He took as many supplies as he could, and pushed them into a large backpack. Then he made his way back through the frightened, and out of control, mob.

Vince thought about what he should do next as he looked for a place to hold up for the night. He tried to make himself as small a target as possible. He decided that he would complete the promise to Barbara, and then head home to West Virginia—he had plenty of family there. Plus, he knew places there in the mountains where no one, not even a zombie, could find him.

The next day, he walked back to his father-in-law's house, hoping to find Barbara near by, but he saw no signs of her. Opening the back door with the keys that still hung at his side, he found her father. The old man made a run for him, but Vince put him down with one shot to the head with the 45. He didn't feel as bad about shooting him as he thought would.

With the first promise fulfilled, he got his old Jeep from the driveway and started looking for a safe place to hold up for a while, thinking he might have trouble finding her. He found a small, hidden garage behind an empty house and made it his home until it was time to head to the mountains.

A few days later, while looking for Barbara, he came across an Army aide station. The National Guard trucks were loaded and pulling out as he parked the Jeep out of sight. They left many supplies behind as they left the aide station. He watched as the last truck in the small convoy drove off into the distance.

Vince, being the only one present when they left, got first dibs on everything. He found boxes of MRE's (Meals Ready to Eat) and ate a couple of them as he rummaged, and drank a lot of Gatorade—it was still on ice.

In the distance, toward town, he heard hundreds of rounds being fired, but the firing wasn't organized. He dismissed the firing and went back to his searching. "Ah, baby," he said smiling, as he opened a large box.

In the box, he got his hands on four M4s, fifteen hundred rounds of 5.56 ammo, and two night vision scopes that were left behind in the rush to leave the chaos of the city. He loaded his Jeep with the booty and headed back to the small garage where he was hiding at night. How long had it been? The days seemed like weeks and he was tired.

* * *

He snapped himself out of his day dream of the past, and put the cross hairs of his scope on her face. He hesitated, looking to see if maybe Barbara might still be in there. Her face and hands were covered in Susan's blood! He knew she was gone and this had to be done.

Once he fired the round, he knew he would have to get out of the area fast! The zombies out numbered the living, and while most were slow and clumsy, others could move quite fast when they wanted to. Some showed the ability to use crude weapons, such as rocks or clubs.

Vince had brought his .308 caliber Remington 700 with the Simmons 44 mag scope to bear on the bridge of Barbara's nose. He judged he was about two hundred yards away and the wind was light. He stood in the back of a Ford F-150 to give him some height. He took slow breaths in and out, trying to relax before his shot.

This was a shot he had made before with ease, it was just that he wanted so badly to make this a clean kill, that he felt a bit nervous! He ran through his mind what he had to do to make it a clean shot. He would have to be looking her straight in the face which he was. The bullet would have to be no higher then the eye brows, no further apart then the eyes, and no lower then the chin, in order to cut the brain stem between the skull and the spine.

* * *

Vince felt confident about the pending shot. He had begun to squeeze the trigger when he heard shots erupt from behind him. He turned to see a young man running into the street, firing his weapon.

Vince spoke quietly to himself. "Please don't run this way." He knew if he could just do this, he could start to live again. But the man turned to run toward Vince, he hadn't noticed Vince until he was within yards of him. The young man was in his mid teens, and he looked up to where Vince was standing in the bed of the F-150.

"Man you better follow me if you want to live! There's a shit load of zombies coming!" shouted the youth as he paused for a moment by the side of the pickup.

Vince turned back to see Barbara was gone. He pulled the rifle to his shoulder, and looking though the scope, he swept the street for any sight of her.

Looking back over to where the youth had just come, he saw a swarm of undead crowding into the street behind him. They were a mess, shuffling their feet, and barely swinging their arms. They made gurgling sounds as they struggled to close the distance on the youth, and him, it was more sickening then it was scary.

"Come on, *man,*" said the youth, as he started to move away from the truck. "I have people that are counting on me! So come on or whatever," he said, waving his hands at Vince in disgust at the delay.

Vince jumped down from the truck and followed him for about a block, to a large manhole cover. Removing the cover, he saw it lead into a large concrete pipe. Once in the pipe, they had to lean over as they walked, neither of them said a word from this point on.

After about three hundred yards, the young man stopped and slowly slid another cover aside. They came out behind an old library. There were many trees and a few houses to be seen. The building was off the main road maybe a hundred yards.

A young girl opened the rear door to the building. She was maybe mid teens, plump with black hair. She showed no expression as they passed her.

There was a second girl in the hall. She was tall, thin, and had blonde hair. Vince saw that they were both armed, but he didn't feel threatened.

* * *

"It's been awhile since I've been inside a library," Vince said jokingly, as he was escorted down a narrow brick hall by the two armed girls.

He was taken to a small room that must have been the employees lounge. In the center of the room was a table with six chairs around it. There weren't any windows, so it was kind of dark.

"Please remove your weapons and your backpack, and place them on the table, then step back to the wall."

He still didn't feel threatened by them, even though they were making demands. He looked at the two girls standing in front of him and frowned, but did as he was told. With his back against the wall, he put his right forefinger to his chest and with a patronizing tone he said, "My name's Vincent Brown, you can call me Vince. And your names are?" He waved the back of his hand slowly around the room, inviting these *children* to be a little friendlier.

The girl giving the orders spoke up, as he hoped she would. "I'm Fay, the one that brought you here is Ben, and the girl watching the door is Janet. Look I'm sorry for sounding rough, but we can't take chances. There's more than thirty of us here and we're three of the oldest." Fay watched Vince's reaction closely.

He turned to look at Ben. "Why did you bring me here?"

"You are the first sane person I've seen in a long time, and we need an adult to help us escape to . . ." Ben was cut off by Fay.

"He doesn't need to know everything!"

Ben responded. "He's not working for the government. I found him."

"Look, you've been running black market goods back and forth with the soldiers, and one of them may have set you up," Fay said, nodding slightly toward Vince.

"What is it that you've been trading for?"

Fay walked slowly up to the table. "We need medicine, weapons, and news! We haven't heard anything from the outside since the blackout."

Ben spoke up, cutting off Fay. "He was getting ready to shoot one of them, and you know the government has ordered the troops not to shoot zombies."

Vince asked, "Why can't they be shot? They sure are killing us."

Fay answered, "Ben talks to the soldiers that he trades with, and they tell him the news, or what they think they know."

That's why they are pulling back, Vince thought. *They're not allowed to shoot, so they don't want to take any more casualties.*

"The government thinks they are close to a cure, and they believe that they might be killing ill citizens," Ben said, turning his nose up and rolling his eyes. "The soldiers told me today that the disease is now in every country, and every city, of the world. We just got it first."

"What is it that you have to trade?" Vince questioned Ben as he walked further into the room.

"Well, you see, we have jewelry stores and pawn shops that are sitting vacant." Ben sat down and drank some water. "The soldiers want gold or silver coins mostly."

Fay spoke up. "I wasn't going to tell everything, but since he's gone this far. We have a ship that's going to take us to a safe place, an island or something we're being told. The captain said he's waiting for a break in the naval blockade. We're just waiting for a signal from the ship, and then we're outta here."

Vince looked puzzled. "So what do you need me for?"

Ben answered. "When you go upstairs you'll see that most of us here are children, and are too small to unload the trucks, and then load the ship."

Vince nodded. "You need muscle."

It was still early when Vince and Ben went into the spacious main room of the library. Looking around the large two story building loaded with books and children, he got a sense of hope as he walked around the tables. He saw the children were preparing themselves to live a remote life. They were reading books on farming practices, mechanics, and medicine.

It was a tempered feeling Vince had, mixed with despair knowing that the world of man was forever changed. What would be left even if the disease was halted now?

Not knowing where the disease had come from, or why it was released on mankind alone, he put the thoughts away and decided that he would help them.

In the corner was a man on the floor in pain. He was barely conscious. As Vince and Ben got closer, he saw that both of the man's legs were broken, and from his glazed eyes and profuse sweating, that he was running a fever. Ben opened a small bag he had been carrying, and pulled out two brown bottles.

"I heard we had someone new."

Vince smiled at an older woman who held out her hand to him, and the two shook hands.

"I'm Jane Bell. Everyone calls me Ma Bell."

"Vincent Brown, please call me Vince."

"On the floor is Mr. John Wells. He's the one who saved these children." She shook her head as she looked down at the injured man.

"I was the manager here, and when things got bad out there, I came here. It is a solid building and I felt safe here. Then one day, John there, showed up with two children. They were in trouble, so I opened the door. Now I'm doing what I can to help him."

Ben put the bottles in Ma Bell's hands, and she hugged him.

"He's the man who saved us all. He got most of us at aide stations. As our parents died, he brought us here. His brother is the captain of the ship that's going to take us to safety." Ben smiled a little and turned away.

Vince turned to Ma Bell. "What is it you need most?"

"Water," said Jane.

"I'm going back out. I'll return before dark."

Jane followed him to the hallway doors. "Once the sun goes down the doors are locked, we won't open them until sunrise."

"I'll be all right. I'm starting to get use to the zombies," he said smiling, as he opened the hallway doors.

He got his 45 auto off the table in the small room, but left his Remington. As he strapped on his 45 pistol, he overheard Janet speaking to Fay in the hall. They were standing next to the glass doors he and Ben had come through earlier.

"Our foraging team is late, should we go look for them?" Janet asked Fay with concern in her voice.

Vince walked slowly up to Fay, who was looking out of the glass door for the missing team. He knew she was the leader.

"I'll keep a look out for them while I'm out, and I'll be back before dark. If all goes well, I'll drive my Jeep up to these doors—it'll be loaded with supplies"

Fay didn't trust him, but what could she do? She noticed that his backpack was empty, and he only had his 45 auto as he passed her.

*   *   *

The library forging team was made up of four teens. Their job was to make sure that there was enough food, water, and whatever else was needed daily at the library. Earlier that morning, the four had left the library in poor morale. The risks to find what was needed were growing and it was taking its toll on them. They knew they were going to have to go deeper into the more inhabited areas if they were to find enough supplies to keep everyone fed. This meant that they risked being shot by frightened, or hungry, living people—it wasn't just the zombies they had to keep a look out for.

Linda was the oldest of the party, and at seventeen, she was the leader. She carried a Ruger mini 14 in 223 caliber, with six full mags and an empty backpack. The other three team members were Tom, Mark, and Brian. They were under sixteen, and they each wore a backpack to carry any food or supplies they came across.

The group stayed to their usual path—the one that they had walked every day for over a month. It was safe in that it kept them away from the streets.

They had picked through everything worth a damn along this route, so now they pushed on further.

"It's getting late. We'll have to turn back soon." Linda was looking at the time on her watch. Their progress had been slow, but it was better to be careful.

"Why doesn't it ever rain? I mean, damn, it's been over a month, and it's hot as hell." Mark wiped sweat from his face as he ducked down between some wrecked cars to rest a moment.

Off to one side of the road was a large grassy area, in it they saw many human bones. They looked like white sticks scattered about after a hurricane.

"Quit your bitchin'. Even if we turn back now, we've got a ways to go!" Linda turned to Mark and the other two, who were now hiding amongst the wrecked cars.

"Quiet, I hear gunfire and it's not far away. I'm going to scout it out a bit, so keep quiet!"

* * *

Vince, after leaving the library, made his way back to where he had parked his Jeep earlier that morning.

He felt bad that he missed his chance to put down Barbara, but he did feel better thinking that maybe he might be able to help the children.

In the distance, he heard shots being fired while he drove back to the garage where he had hid his food and guns. He noted that there were a lot more zombies out in the daylight then usual. He felt sometime was up.

As he loaded his Jeep, he kept an eye on their movement, and noticed that they were all headed in the same direction, toward the gunfire.

* * *

Linda didn't like leaving the team behind even for a few minutes, but she felt that the team had gone as far as they could for today. Two or three miles in ninety degree heat, and trying not to be seen by flesh-eating ghouls, can make for a long day.

She traveled in the direction of the gunfire–from the sounds of it, it was just in front of her.

Linda crept low between two buildings, until she saw a large parking lot. It was completely surrounded by shiny new wire fence, maybe ten feet high, she guessed. There were a dozen or so pickup trucks parked to one side of the lot.

Down either side, and across the back of the lot, was a strip mall, and behind that was more fence with small structures. In the middle of the large lot there was another fence in the shape of a circle, this fence was high as well. Outside of the parking lot fence, hundreds of zombies stood, pulling and pushing on the barrier, trying to get inside.

There was a group of men and women around the inner fence– their faces showed their excitement as they pumped their fists in the air. They must be cheering, Linda thought, but she was too far away to see what was happening.

She saw an area where she might get a better view of the action, but she was also concerned about how long she had been away from her team. She decided that she had to get a better look before she left, so she made her way slowly to higher ground, staying out of sight of everyone and *everything.*

* * *

Brian was sitting with his back against a wrecked car; he looked at Mark, who was sitting next to Tom.

"Did you hear something? I thought I heard something over there." Brian pointed with his nose to his right–the other two didn't pay him any mind.

"Man. The others are going to be mad that we ain't bringing anything back," Tom whispered to the other two.

Brian leaned forward, looking under the cars for feet. "I know I heard something!" The others heard it too, this time.

The three of them peered over the hoods of the abandon cars. Loud moaning sounds seemed to be coming from all around them. They were surrounded! Dozens of zombies, on their way to the fenced in parking lot, had stumbled onto them. With a deep moan from one of the zombies, all of the zombies turned toward the three dumbfounded youths.

"Shit, man! *Run*!" One of the boys hollered, as if the other two needed his directions.

They split up as they ran, Tom and Brian headed back in the direction library. Mark ran in the direction Linda had gone. Following him was a score of filthy, foul zombies.

* * *

With his Jeep loaded, Vince took one of the M4s and placed it next to him in the front seat, while holding his 45 on his lap. He drove slowly, making as little noise as he could. The day was getting late when he saw more zombies then he had seen in a month–they were all heading in the same direction as he was.

At the library he was met by Fay and several others–all armed.

"What's going on out there?" Fay asked as she hopped into the Jeep next to Vince. Everyone at the library knew something different was going on with the zombies.

"I don't know, and why are you getting in the Jeep?" He was puzzled for a moment.

"Across the street is a fire station. Drive to the roll up doors." Fay pointed to where she wanted him to go.

"We'll be seen," he said as he started driving toward the fire station.

Some of the zombies began shuffling in their direction as he stopped in front of one of the large roll up doors. It began to rise and he drove in as instructed by Fay. He parked between two, 2 ton flat bed trucks, and tight in one corner of the old fire station, sat an old Toyota pickup truck. Mounted in the back of the Toyota, over looking the cab, was an M60.

The two flat beds were loaded with supplies—mostly can foods and water bottles. There were more children here, along with four or five older boys, all armed as well.

Vince turned to Fay sitting next to him. "If I didn't know better, I'd say you're going to war."

"No, Vince, we're going to survive. The ship sent the signal and we're a go for tonight." Fay looked around the room at all of the faces.

"Four of our people are still missing, and there's less then three hours of daylight." She had no intentions of sending out a search party. She had too few people, and she couldn't afford to lose anyone.

"You have plenty of muscle here. Why did you lie to me?"

Fay looked away, ashamed, and then turned back to face him. "We've been watching you for sometime. We saw you get to the aide station supplies before us, and we knew you got medicine and food supplies. It was reported that you got these weapons and night vision scopes as well. We didn't know how much or how many, but we need them all." Her mouth hung open as she looked up at him not sure how he would react. He knew he had been used, but he still wanted to be of help. He *needed* to be of help to someone.

The world would be different from now on, and if there were to be people in the world, it would have to come from the will of these children and others like them.

"Which way did the team go this morning?"

Fay was surprised at the question.

"All right, let's get this Jeep unloaded," Vince shouted to the youths standing around the flat beds.

As he walked passed the Toyota, he saw the back of it was loaded with ammo of all calibers. They had thousands of rounds for the M4 assault weapons stacked up in water tight boxes.

He turned to Fay and saw her smiling. "Pawn shops and gun stores. It's America," she said with a shrug.

Outside, the children were finishing off the zombies that had followed Vince's return as quietly as they could. He watched as three small boys roped a particularly ugly zombie around the legs and the neck at the same time.

They pulled in opposite directions taking it off its feet. It landed hard on its chest, twisting and jerking, trying to face its attackers, but the boys held tight as a third boy ran over with a hefty pipe and smashed the back of its head in! Black, thick goo spilled onto the cement as the creature stopped struggling and succumbed to the blows. The three boys nodded in satisfaction and moved on to the next zombie.

Something chirped on Fay's hip, she reached down, produced a tiny radio, and walked out of ear shot.

Vince picked up the M4 that he had driven in with, and saw several unhappy faces at his action. They weren't sure if they were going to let him leave. The supplies he had brought were being strapped down on the flat beds for transport to the ships.

"I'm going out for your lost team. I'm coming back with them."

Fay walked back and announced, "The ships are on their way. The blockade has ended!" Her expression was so hopeful; he knew he was doing the right thing. "I have to tell the others to prepare." She looked at Vince, who was standing in front of her holding the M4. "Let him go. If you don't find the others in time, they all know where the rendezvous point is."

The doors opened and he drove off to find the lost team.

* * *

Linda crawled into position and watched the crowd that had gathered around the inner cage. From here she could see plainly that this was a blood sport, a game to the death. She knew she had been gone too long, so she hurriedly started to leave.

She was about to stand up when she saw she had been spotted by two men in the crowd. They could tell she wasn't a zombie, and she knew they were coming for her.

Linda said the hell with being quiet, it was time to run, and that's what she did. She ran back toward where she had left her team. She had no idea that they were now running for their lives.

The sounds of the pickups starting could be heard echoing through the streets. Mark and Linda met in the middle of a four-lane road, just as the first truck began to circle them. The truck's big tires kicked up gravel and the two teens had to cover their faces.

"What happened, and where are the others?" Linda tried to shout over the noisy truck.

"We had to run away from zombies! I don't know where they are!" Mark shouted back in reply.

Linda looked at the dumb ass hanging out of the truck's window, hollering at her. She smirked at him and gave him the finger.

Three more trucks pulled up and stopped–the men that got out were either drunk or high.

Linda gave up her rifle–as the men were armed and she had no chance of winning.

* * *

Vince, after following the map for less then a mile, found the first lost member of the team. The boy was running as he stopped the Jeep next to him.

"Fay sent me to find you and the others. Hop in and we'll go find them."

The boy bent over, leaning on his knees, trying to catch his breath. "The others are back there somewhere. I'm not going back." Tom pointed behind him. "I've run this far, and I'll make it back on my own." He looked back to the way he had just come. The zombies were still chasing him. "They never stop!" He started running again.

Vince shook his head and started driving again. He drove around the walking dead as he raced against the clock to find the three missing children.

* * *

Mark and Linda were tied up, loaded into one of the trucks, and taken back to the compound. The two sat in the back of a tall truck in awe at the sights of cruelty they witnessed. Bodies hung from the trees by their feet or hands–some were disemboweled, their insides hanging to the ground where the crows pecked at them. Hundreds of dead bodies were stacked, one on top of another, some half burnt, but all were mutilated and twisted.

They felt sick as they were taken inside the first of the two fences, where they were separated as they entered the compound.

"Where did you come from, girl?" asked one of the men holding her, as several other men dragged a body out of the center cage.

Linda looked at the bodies and she knew these were survivors. They had been taken from their homes and forced to fight for the amusement of these assholes. There was no way she wanted these people to find out about the library, and the young people in it, so she lied.

"We've been hiding in my dad's house, and we ran out of food."

The large man holding her pulled her hair back to make her look him in the eyes. "That's too damn bad for you, little girl!" He laughed loudly as he pushed her though the crowd of people, and to the front. He threw her against the bloody fence and held her there by her arms.

Linda had a bad feeling she was about to see Mark at any moment, inside the cage.

* * *

Brian saw the Jeep turn in his direction, he was out of breath and his legs were giving out on him. The zombies were gaining on him and he didn't care who this guy was, he knew he was dead if he kept going on his own.

Vince stopped the Jeep and shouted for the kid to get in. One of the zombies was too close as Brian jumped into the front seat.

Vince grabbed the M4 sitting next to him and fired point blank. The round ripped though its skull. Dark red blood splattered over the hood of the Jeep, and the body shrank to the ground. He fired at the second zombie, a female.

Her long stringy hair covered her face, but he could see her milky white eyes staring at him. The bullet split the top of her head open. Her stringy hair was now matted with her brains and blood. The body fell, striking the side of the Jeep next to him.

In the clear for a few seconds, Vince put the Jeep in gear and drove off, steering wide of the dozens of zombies that were still chasing the boy.

"Tom's safe. Where are the others?" Vince's voice broke up a little as the Jeep bounced over the field.

Brian pointed ahead. "Linda went that way. I think Mark went after her."

It wasn't long before Vince saw the crowd of undead at the fence. He pulled over and parked out of sight.

"Stay here. I'm going in for a closer look."

Brian shook his head and tried to smile. *Not again, this is how it all started,* he thought to himself.

Vince followed the same path Linda had traveled earlier. With one look at the compound, he knew it was an abomination. Behind him, he felt a presence. He turned with his rifle at the ready to see it was Brian.

"I couldn't stand to be left behind *again,*" he whispered. "That's Linda. She's one of us." Brian pointed with his finger.

Vince started looking around for something, he didn't have any idea what for, but he knew something would come to him.

"What are you doing?"

"I'm looking for a way in." Vince saw what he needed, he just wasn't sure if it would work.

"Come on, we've got to move quickly!" Vince needed to make every moment count.

As they started to move, Brian saw Mark being pushed into the cage.

"That's Mark in the center, there. What are they doing?"

Vince turned to see the boy in the cage. He knew what they were doing, but he didn't tell Brian.

"Come on, we've got work to do."

It felt like a hammer struck Vince in the chest. He saw Barbara being dragged into the cage with Mark. She was fighting like a banshee with the two men who pulled her along by long poles with straps that were wrapped around her neck. She was pulled into the ring. She and the boy, Mark, were to fight before the crowd, and they were making Linda watch her friend die.

In just minutes, Vince and Brian were back at the Jeep.

"Can you drive, Brian?"

"Yeah, I think I can."

"Get in the Jeep and wait for me. If you're in danger, drive back to the library. If no one's there, then drive to where you're to meet the ships. Okay?" The boy nodded and sat there as Vince handed him the 45 pistol.

Vince left Brian and headed across the street to a shopping center. There where several large delivery trucks in the parking lot at the strip mall across the road from the compound. Maybe, he thought, he could get lucky and find a truck with keys in it.

He went from truck to truck, until he got lucky. A bread truck with the keys in it, sat where the driver had left it, next to a market.

Dozens of zombies walked by as he opened the door of the truck, none of them looked his way. The noise from the compound grew as Mark and Barbara met in the ring!

"Damn, this old bread stinks!" He didn't dare roll down the window; he knew if the truck started, the zombies would be all around it all too quickly.

He turned the key, the engine turned over, making a lot of noise, but didn't start. It wanted to start–the zombies now took notice and began moving toward it. He could feel the truck being struck by the zombies as they tried to beat their way in with their fists or crude tools.

Vince crossed his fingers and turned the key again, and it roared to life!

"Yeah!" he shouted as he put the truck in gear. There was no time to lose if he was to save Linda and Mark.

* * *

Linda watched in horror as Mark backed away from the zombie about to be unleashed on him. She could see that *this* zombie was different.

"What is that?" Linda asked the large man who was guarding her.

"That's an almost unstoppable killing machine!" He smiled in anticipation of the violence to come, as he answered her. "I caught this one, we had one other like her, but it got loose and killed three of us before we put a bullet in its brain."

"Just three of you? What a shame," Linda mocked the big man.

Mark picked up a knife and felt discouraged as he looked at it. Someone else threw him a galvanized trash can lid with two straps mounted on it. He put his left arm though the straps and raised it to cover his chest. He felt doomed. He had little chance of living through this fight, and that knowledge showed in his facial expression.

Linda wanted to cry, but she wouldn't. Not as long as Mark was alive anyway.

"Go for the eyes! Blind the bitch!" Linda shouted as loud as she could to Mark.

He heard her and nodded. Raising the trash-can-lid-shield, he prepared to fight as the two men with the poles released Barbara. She was like a wild animal. She felt no pain and knew no fear! She ran straight at Mark. Drool ran out of the corners of her mouth as she tried to reach over the shield.

Mark thrust the blade of the knife into her arm as she reached out for his throat. No blood came from the wound, but a sticky black string of slime hung onto the blade.

The living crowd, around the small cage, let out a loud roar! The undead crowded outside the large compound began to moan louder in response to the glee inside.

* * *

Vince pushed the pedal down on the bread truck, and it started to move, slowly. Dark smoke poured from the back of the truck, blacking out the faces of the zombies bringing up the rear.

From where he had started, to the compound's fence, was about three hundred yards. The driveway entrances were straight across from one another—it was only a matter of feet to the compound fence.

Smashing through the fence meant plowing through a lot of zombies, and then smashing the fence, and then fighting dozens of armed men and hundreds of zombies.

"Maybe I should have thought this out a little longer," he said to himself as he was wishing he had a truck that was a little faster.

He looked down at the speedometer and shook his head. He was concerned about his lack of speed as he was reaching the road.

When Vince looked up from the speedometer, he saw someone he was hoping to meet again.

"Jimmy, stay right there you son of a bitch!" Hearing the sound of the engine behind him, Zombie-Jimmy turned around. If he was still alive, he would have had enough sense to get out of the way of the speeding truck, or *maybe not*!

The flat grill of the old bread truck smashed into Jimmy's face, crushing it. His skull split in half and bits of gray matter and hair flew onto the windshield, sticking there.

"Take that, you *zombie bastard*!" Vince shouted. He wanted to smile at his revenge over the killing of the young girl, Susan, but he knew he had to focus on the task at hand.

* * *

Watching Mark bleed, Linda felt responsible, having left her team alone. Her hands were still tied together, and she was trying to remain strong for Mark, who had no chance. She could feel the large man's hands growing tighter on her arms as he cheered for more blood!

Everyone was watching the battle in the center ring—their eyes wide and their mouths open in a state of bloodlust! None of them were ready for what was coming. Their guns were behind them, out of reach, and most of them were drunk.

* * *

Vince's knuckles were white with fear as he gripped the steering wheel. The old truck picked up speed as he held the gas pedal to the floor. In front of him, he could see the zombies, they were everywhere along the fence, trying to find a way in.

"Hang on! I'm coming!" he yelled as the truck struck the fence, smashing a few zombies into it. Blood, or what was once blood, splashed in front of the truck as several of the zombies were torn to pieces by the metal.

There was a horrible jolt as the fence, which was hastily built, gave way and was flattened to the ground under the wheels of the bread truck. Vince lost control as it rolled to the one side of the steep driveway, and flipped, landing on the passenger side. This was good, as the underside of the truck was exposed to the confused crowd, giving him cover as he regained his composure.

The zombies following the truck began pouring in through the opening. They smelled blood and their lust for it was about to be satisfied.

Vince grabbed his M4 with a shaky hand and smashed the already cracked windshield out, crawling out into the parking lot. He was surprised at how quiet it was as he made his way to cover, behind the over turned truck. Looking around the front of the crashed truck, he saw Mark on his knees, his left hand at Barbara's throat, and his right hand thrusting his knife into her over and over!

She didn't respond to the stabbing, but merely pulled the exhausted boy closer to her and sank her yellowed teeth into his cheek. Pulling back, she took a large chunk of flesh from the boy's face. Mark dropped both arms and slumped forward. His blood poured from his wound as his head rolled down.

There was nothing Vince could do for the boy. He looked up from Mark and saw the girl with her hands tied in front of her. He knew it was Linda. She was in the middle of a large group of people—some were pointing at him.

Gun fire erupted from the crowd, and he took cover again as bullets flew in his direction.

The zombies had become so excited over the smell of blood that they rushed the opening in the fence. They took murderous fire, but they just pushed on. Some took shots in the head and fell, but most made it through, and headed for the crowd. Death was the order of the day.

Vince watched Linda as she was held in place by the large man. He kept a hand on her, but it was beginning to loosen as fear took over. He watched in horror as his friends fell, overpowered by sheer numbers.

The black asphalt of the parking lot ran red with the blood of dying. There were a hundred, or more, zombies for every one person. They ripped the flesh from bodies of the living and devoured it in front of them.

"Let go of me, you *asshole*!" Linda shouted at the man, and kicked him in the leg.

He pulled her in front of him and frowned down at her. *"Go, you little bitch*!" He replied loudly and pushed her away!

Linda was free—her hands still tied. She ran over to one of the over sized pickups parked in front of the fence.

The large man was firing a shotgun into the steady stream of zombies, with his back to Linda.

With her hands tied, she pulled herself up, onto the running board of the tall truck she and Mark were transported in. She pulled her mini 14 from the seat; the clip was still in and was ready to fire. She jumped down to the ground and walked up behind the large man. He was breathing heavily, his laughter now gone as he fought for his life.

Linda wasn't going to give him a chance to stop her again. She held the rifle out in front of her and fired! The round hit him in the back and drove him to his knees, exiting his right lung. He fell forward onto his hands. He turned his head and looked up at his killer.

Linda glared down at him. She heard her name over the gunfire as Vince made his way toward her. He had to stay far behind the action so as not to be seen by what was left of the living, or he would be shot.

The crowd had the guns, but the zombies had the numbers, and the zombies had all but won the battle.

Linda didn't know the man calling her, but she ran to him as fast as she could.

"Fay sent me to find you, and Brian's waiting for us."

"Who are you?"

"Call me Vince. We'll talk later."

They ran back to the over turned truck—where Vince cut her hands free. They both looked at the cage, and they both felt guilty, for they had both left someone behind.

The zombies were feasting on the crowd. It was everyone for themselves. Some fought to the death; others made it to their trucks and took off through the back entrances, leaving many behind. There was still gunfire around the compound. The smell of death was everywhere. The sun was down, but it wasn't dark yet as Vince and Linda made their way to the cage.

Barbara was chewing on some part of Mark that she had pulled off after he had died. Mark had come back and was standing next to Barbara.

Vince aimed the M4 at her head, he no longer saw her as his wife, but he couldn't look her in the eye. *This is an animal. A killing machine. A monster,* he told himself. He squeezed the trigger slowly and put a bullet in her head, her now lifeless body fell to the ground. He did the same for the boy, and he felt free.

"Let's get the hell out of here," Linda said with enthusiasm.

Several men, out of ammo, were using their rifles as clubs, beating the zombies as they made their way to the opening in the fence.

Both, he and Linda, had plenty of rounds left, but if they fired their weapons it would mean bringing the masses of zombies to them.

Linda was about to speak when her cell phone rang. All communications had been out since the start of the crisis. She froze for a second, in shock at the familiar sound. She never thought she would hear the sound again.

A herd of zombies turned toward the sound.

"You have a cell phone? After a month without service you couldn't get rid of it?" Vince was bewildered.

She had it in her back pocket, and she pulled it out as fast as she could, but it rang again. The zombies were on their way, fast.

"Come on! We'll have to run for it!" Vince reached for Linda's hand as he started to run for the opening.

"Hello?"

Vince glanced at the girl. She held the tiny phone to her ear. He couldn't believe what he was seeing.

"Fay said, the blackout is over, and the blockade is moving out to sea."

Vince raised his M4 with one hand–it was set on single fire so he wouldn't waste ammo.

The first zombie was reaching for him as he stepped on the flattened fence. The 5.56 round jerked the creature's head violently. A spray of black blood flew into the face of an oncoming zombie, blinding it, and making it step harmlessly to the side.

"Fay said we are to come to the library. I think my battery went dead." Linda put the phone back in her pocket, freed her hand from Vince's, and raised her rifle.

"You back with me now?" Vince asked Linda as he dropped another zombie on the other side of the fence.

"Where's Brian?" Linda looked around for him.

"There!" Vince pointed with his nose as Brian drove the Jeep to them.

* * *

The ride back to the library was slower then they liked, but it was dark, and they had to be careful not to wreck the Jeep. As they pulled up in front of the library, they were met by Fay, and several others, at the front doors. Ma Bell was there, sitting on a short brick wall. Vince saw she was bleeding from a wound on her arm.

"Mr. Wells died, and no one saw it happen. She went in to check him and he attacked her. He pulled himself halfway down the stairs, after two of the smaller children, before she shot him." Fay turned away from Vince and handed a small pistol to Ma Bell, who got up and walked off without a word.

The Toyota, with the M60 mounted in the back, was there, as well as two other pickup trucks loaded with books.

Fay greeted Vince with a half smile. "Thank you. You've done a lot for us." She pointed to the old fire station. "There's plenty of fuel in there, more then enough for you to get wherever it is you're going." There was a shot not too far away; they knew it was Ma Bell.

"What? I'm not invited?" Vince teased with a smile. He wouldn't have gone anyway, but he really felt used. He had given them everything he had, and almost died for them!

Fay said nothing. She just stood there looking for words.

"Don't worry about it. I have other business. Good luck." He meant it.

Linda hugged him as they sat in the Jeep. "I was as good as dead if you hadn't shown up. Thank you."

Ben walked up to the Jeep carrying the Remington 700. "Here you might need this." He placed the rifle on the seat next to Vince and nodded. Vince handed Ben the M4 and nodded.

This is what they wanted anyway, he thought.

He pulled the Jeep into the fire station and closed the big, rolling door. He went back to his Jeep and sat alone, thinking it was the only thing they didn't want that he had.

He heard them drive off to their rendezvous with the ships, and he wished them luck again. In the back of his mind, he remembered something his father use to say.

No good deed goes unpunished.

In the morning he would start his long journey home.

UNNATURAL DEATH

DOMENIC GIANGREGORIO

"This is so boring," Eric whined.

"Just shut up and enjoy yourself," Cindy commanded.

"Enjoy what," Eric replied. "There's nothing to do here."

"Then go get something to eat at the snack bar," Cindy said.

"There's a snack bar?" Eric asked in surprise.

"Why wouldn't there be?" Cindy mused.

"It's a museum," Eric said sarcastically.

"Just make sure to come back qui…" Cindy stopped.

Before she could finish her sentence, he was already gone.

"I guess that answers that," she said and turned around.

"And if you look this way, you will see a rare statue of a zombie that was discovered more than three centuries ago in ancient Egypt," the tour guide said with a grin.

"Ooh, aah," the tourists said.

The statue had on a green smock with what looked like a scarf, and ripped brown pants with nothing under them.

Suddenly, the lights went out, and the only thing glowing was the glow-in-the-dark stickers that some of the tourists had on.

"We're all gonna die!" a tourist screamed.

"Oh no," another tourist said in a terrified voice.

"Good thing I wore clean underwear," a bald tourist said. "Oops, too late."

"It's okay, don't panic, there's nothing to worry about, a circuit breaker probably just tripped. We have them on all day, every day," the tour guide said.

"Let me call security," the tour guide said and walked over to a black phone on the wall.

"Security," came the voice on the other end of the line.

"I need you to switch out those light bulbs in the east wing," the tour guide said.

"They're fine. We switched them out yesterday," the security guard replied.

The tour guide turned away from the phone and looked at the crowd.

"Okay, now you can panic," the tour guide said.

"Well, so much for clean underwear," the bald tourist added.

"What did I miss?" Eric said as he jogged up to Cindy.

"We're all gonna die," Cindy said calmly.

"Oh, okay," Eric said, clearly worried.

"By the way, where were you?" Cindy asked.

"Bathroom," Eric replied.

"In the dark?" Cindy said.

"Yeah, I know where it all is, I don't need a light on to pee," Eric said quickly.

"Be quiet, people, the news is on," the tour guide said. The TV in the security room was on and the tour guide was listening to it through the phone.

"The weather will be sunny tomorrow and, wait..." the TV news reporter said.

"What's going on?" the tour guide asked.

"I don't know," the security guard said, but if you could see this weather guy's face, you'd know it's bad."

"It seems that the dead are coming back to life and eating the flesh of the living, if you are just tuning in, this is not a joke. Something has gone horribly, horribly wrong," the reporter said.

A crash came from the back of the museum.

"What was that?" the tour guide asked.

"Cindy, please tell me that was you," Eric pleaded.

"Okay, it was," Cindy replied.

"Really?" Eric asked, surprised.

"No, you moron," Cindy snapped back.

Another crash came from the rear of the museum, but this time it was closer. Minutes later, another came closer still. Then another, and another, until the tourists ran away in panic.

The tour guide put the phone to her ear to call security. "Hello? Hello? Is anyone there? Pick up, dammit, answer me!" the tour guide said, frustrated.

"Anything?" Cindy asked her.

"Nothing. It's like the line is dead," the tour guide said sadly.

A loud crash came from one hallway over.

"Cindy, take this," Eric said.

He handed her a mannequin arm.

"I don't want this," Cindy said.

"You need a weapon, don't you?" Eric said.

"Yeah, but not this. Give me something stronger," Cindy commanded.

"Fine, I'll give you the arm of the statue zombie," Eric said but when he turned to go to it, the statue of the zombie was gone.

"Hey, where's the zombie?" Eric wondered.

"You're asking me?" Cindy said with a smirk.

"I don't know. It's supposed to be there," the tour guide said.

"Well, it's not," Eric said.

A moaning sound was coming toward them from out of the shadows.

"What the hell was that?" Cindy asked.

"I don't know, but run," Eric whispered.

"There's a fire escape at the end of the hall. Maybe there's something we can use there," the tour guide said.

"It's our only chance," Eric agreed.

They snuck behind a couple of displays and made it to the fire escape.

When they looked behind them, there was a body walking toward them very slowly.

"Quick. Open it," Cindy said to the tour guide.

"It's stuck," was the reply.

"Try harder," Cindy hissed. "It's getting closer."

With enough strength it opened. They hurried inside and closed the door. A fire axe was on a wall, in a red box, behind clear glass.

"Finally, a kick ass weapon," Eric said as he smiled.

He broke the glass with his foot. Banging and moaning was coming from the opposite side of the door. Eric opened the fire door and raised the axe.

"Decapitate it!" Cindy screamed.

Eric swung at head height. There was a sound of metal meeting wood, and the head of the zombie went rolling down the hall like a lopsided bowling ball.

The lights unexpectedly turned on.

"April fools," the security guards yelled.

"What?" the tour guide asked, her mouth open in astonishment.

"We got you," the security guard said.

"Dude, it's the middle of July," Eric added.

"So, this was all a prank?" the tour guide asked.

"Yes," the security guard said.

"What about the lights?" the tour guide asked.

"We shut the main power off," one of the security guards admitted.

"And the news?" Cindy asked.

"We honestly have no idea," the security guard answered.

"What about the moaning?" Eric asked.

"Microphone," the security guard said as he held it up. "Connected to the building's speakers."

The lights went off again.

"Will you guys stop it, the joke's over already," the tour guide said, clearly annoyed.

"But we didn't do that," the first security guard said.

Suddenly in the dark, a scream came from the other security guard.

"Bill, are you okay?" the first guard asked.

For a reply, the first security guard was pulled away and into the shadows.

"Now what are they up to?" Cindy wondered.

Suddenly, Bill's severed head slammed against the wall.

"What the hell?" Eric yelled.

Blood was being splattered everywhere, warm and sticky, the scent of copper filling the air.

"What's happening?" the tour guide yelled.

"I have no idea," Cindy yelled back.

The lights began to flicker on and off.

"Well, at least we know it's not them," Eric said relieved.

The tour guide's cell phone rang.

"Hello. Hello?" the tour guide said, but the line was dead.

"Who was it?" Cindy asked.

"Nobody," the tour guide answered.

The tour guide took her phone and threw it down the hall. As it slid to a stop, out from an aisle came a hand that grabbed the phone.

"Hey!" Eric screamed as he chased after the hand.

"What are you doing?" Cindy called, surprised at him for leaving her. "Get back here!"

"I'm chasing something!" Eric yelled quickly. When he was at the end of the aisle, he stopped and looked down. "Huh?" Eric said.

It was a severed arm dragging the cell phone across the floor. Eric raised the axe and swung for the arm, but only managed to break the phone. A couple of fingers were chopped off in the process.

In the security room, the remaining three security guards—who were now zombies—were pressing buttons randomly. One of them turned on, then off again, a light in the aisle Eric was in. A little bit of blood splattered out of the aisle as Eric used the axe on the severed arm.

Eric, feeling proud of himself, never saw the shadow creep up on him from out of the darkness. He only had time for a muffled scream as he was knocked to the floor and his throat was torn out by a zombie. His blood spread across the floor, lost in the darkness.

"Eric," Cindy called. "Are you okay?"

There was no response. Cindy and the tour guide ran for Eric, and when Cindy turned into the aisle, she stopped cold, her hand going to her mouth in horror.

"Oh my God," Cindy gasped.

"Oh no," the tour guide added.

Eric was standing before them, his throat torn out, his clothes bloody. As the two women stared at him, he smiled widely, his teeth stained with his own blood.

With eyes that were dead yet filled with evil, he raised the axe overhead, then brought it down again and again.

Lost in the darkness, the slaughter went unseen, only the soft dripping of blood to break the silence.

THE DOORMAN'S DEFENSE

JULIAN BOOTE

"**L**et me be clear from the outset; my clients *wanted* to be bitten.

"There was no coercion or persuasion of any kind on my part. By the time they came to me, these poor souls had made their choice. As they saw the world, with its breached barricades, its ever-retreating soldiers, the relentless fear, the hopelessness, there was no other option. The fight against the rising tide had taken its toll. Physically, mentally, spiritually, the sum total of their losses incurred during this, the escalation of our proud nation's tragic demise, was simply too much to bear. The only way out for them was through my coal cellar door, to join that deadly flood greedily lapping at the shrinking shores of this decadent island we like to call civilization.

"And this, ladies and gentlemen, is the nub of this case. The Prosecution would have you believe I deserve the death penalty because of a body count of *one hundred and twelve people*. It's an impressive number, no doubt about it. I confess, until it was mentioned to me in the interrogation room by Inspector Morgan, I hadn't realized there had been that many–sloppy administration on my part. Mea culpa. One hundred and twelve people the honorable Prosecutor has argued, so eloquently, I and my colleague Alvin murdered, but not just murdered. Our methods have–by his reasoning–contributed to this state of national crisis. We have by our actions, er, what did he say? Ah, yes, ' . . . worked as agents against the interests of the realm, its people, and the future of humanity as a whole.' Not only am I a mass murderer then, but– for want of a better word–a traitor. Two apparently irrefutable reasons, therefore, why I should dangle from a hangman's noose.

"My response, and the question that you must answer for yourselves beyond all reasonable doubt, is this: *What did I do wrong? Did I, one, actually commit murder?* And two, have I under the

Emergency Powers Act by my actions aided and abetted toward the destruction of the realm?

"Your answer I believe, should comprise of just one word, 'No'. I did nothing wrong. My actions, I'm convinced, had my clients' and society's best interests at heart. They were motivated by survival, yes, business, I won't deny it, there was that, but with *compassion and containment* in mind. *Compassion*, as I offered a sympathetic end as free of pain and suffering as possible. *Containment,* because my clients would have ended up out there on the streets *anyway*, but in a far more lethal state, capable of killing and spreading this . . . contagion still further.

"Let me elaborate on each in turn.

"Firstly, compassion. I was simply fulfilling the wishes of my clients'–*clients* I stress, *not* victims. And those clients to whom I agreed to offer my services were in no fit state to live. They *did not want to go on*. And how did I know this?

"Well, for one, their stories. Harrowing, positively harrowing, tales my clients told me. Some described how their loved ones first succumbed to the bug, only to revive hours later as a hungry predator wearing a human face that they had to leave scratching and pounding on the other side of a locked door. Others told how they lost friends, or family, to the many shambling mobs roaming– contrary to the media's sanitized reports–only too free in this city.

"Now of course, if these people wanted out, they could have gone to just any licensed ASO. But my clients had their reasons for coming to me, and to me alone, because they knew I offered what no ASO could.

"There was Beth, for example. A devout Roman Catholic, who, because the Church decreed suicide is a mortal sin, felt a bite was her only release from this world without eternal punishment in the next.

"Or there was Romeo and Juliet, as I called them. Two teenagers so desperately in love. A textbook tragedy, in which they had me play a part. They showed up at my door one Saturday afternoon, about three weeks after I started my service. Romeo had saved his love from an attack, but had himself been bitten and was already succumbing. Juliet wanted my help, despite Romeo's protests. Her words to him have stayed with me. "Death is only a door," she said. "Just a few hours, and we'll walk hand in hand again." He didn't want to leave her, and she couldn't live without him. So I played my part.

"One particular client's story I'll never forget. He was a police-man—armed response officer. The escalating crisis meant he hadn't seen his family for days. His unit was called to contain a break out. Hordes of the *things* had spilled from a quarantine zone into a residential area nearby. He told me of his mounting dread as the streets he passed became more familiar, until finally his squad arrived and jumped from their van . . . onto the tarmac of the very street where he lived, and among the dead now walking, were the blood-soaked, mutilated residents of houses the escapees had broken into and . . . his own wife and five-year-old daughter were among them. And this man, weeping before me, told me how, in the midst of the slaughter, he wouldn't let anyone else on his team, but him . . . give them peace. So he'd come to me. His reason, ladies and gentlemen? He felt he'd abandoned his family. He'd left them to die unprotected and alone, in terror and agony, and so rightly—his words, '. . . and so rightly', likewise deserved their fate.

"But hearing their stories wasn't the only method I used to as-sess my clients' readiness for Alvin's and my ministrations. You see, I vetted them, too. I was not, as it's claimed by the Prosecution in their closing argument, indiscriminate in my choice of clients. I made every effort to be sure they wanted to go through with the procedure. I would take them in, sit them down, give them a cup of fair trade coffee or tea, organic soup if I had any in, and I'd de-scribe in detail the particulars, so they were fully aware of what it was they were asking me to do.

"Now, I did this as it became clear to me soon after starting this service that of the many who came to my door, some *only said* they wanted out. They were lost and confused, frightened, as are we all, but not so hopeless as to genuinely want out. It quickly became apparent when I described the procedure and introduced them to Alvin in his pen, watched their reaction as his dull eyes locked with theirs . . . they weren't ready, and they accepted that. So I showed them out. Let me be clear. They were free to leave, and many did. I wanted them to be sure, as did I, this was their wish. So up to the point they were bitten, they could back out, and this happened a few times.

"Every trade has its share of window-shoppers, eh? I don't say that meanly though. Truth is, I like to think such abortive visits to me might have been a wake-up call, that from it these people somehow learned to persevere and, somewhere out there, they survive even now.

"Other prospects however were just . . . perverse. I soon learnt to see the telltale signs; the thrill in their breathing, the almost sexual hunger in their eyes. Especially when they saw Alvin strapped in his chair, his mouth braced, the empty client's seat next to him with its restraints, the bite harness and lever. They almost drooled. It was vile. Them, I cursed and threw out.

"Human nature, you see, is a powerful assessment tool. And I had the scruples to use it, ladies and gentlemen. That is why I can stand before you today and say, hand-on-heart, it was only to those who had no hope, and were clearly suicidal, that I was willing to offer my services. That I had my clients formally sanction as demonstrated by Defense Exhibit A—one hundred and twelve signatures on ASA standard release documents that state my clients submitted to Alvin's and my services *with full awareness and agreement*. How then the Prosecution can claim that these acts were committed against my clients' will is beyond me—as it should be beyond you. Do killers seek permission from their targets? Does a killer ask payment in tinned food, fuel, water, no less? Is that the sign of a mass-murderer the Prosecution claimed dragged his victims kicking and screaming to a ghastly end? Pah! In fact, let's review again the Prosecution's claim.

"What of my clients' passing? Did I consider them humanely, treat them decently? The Prosecution claims I gloried in my so-called slaughter and has labored to paint a picture of unspeakable ill-treatment of my clients. Not so. I did not enjoy it; I did not take gleeful pleasure in my work. In fact, I can think of no more sad or depressing an occupation these days, except perhaps collecting the bodies of the turned and killed again, or having to be the poor soul tasked to fill the plague pits or fuel the incinerators with corpses. No, ladies and gentlemen, I did my best to make my clients' passing as comfortable and painless as possible. How do I justify this statement? Let me count the ways:

"One: When Alvin bit . . . what tenderness! Hard as it may be to believe, he showed only sensitivity and compassion in his duty! No mindless tearing at the flesh, no chomping and swallowing from him, or rolling his eyes at the taste of warm, untainted blood, like those untrained cadavers out there, oh no! His was a *light bite only*. Just enough to pierce the skin is all, and mingle his saliva with the blood he released. And that was it. As all you here know, that's all that's required. Why would further mutilation be necessary? I point to the forensic evidence, supplied to this court by the Prosecution themselves, which shows little damage to those it calls my 'victims', except to their right forearms, where I had Alvin perform the procedure. Nowhere else.

"Two: I made sure my clients didn't suffer. While I still had them to administer, my clients, if they wished to stay conscious, had a local anesthetic before the bite and painkillers through the transition, or they were given a general anesthetic if they simply wished to sleep their way to the other side. And after I ran out of drugs, I relied upon alcohol. A crude, but time-honored method of pain relief, and toward the end, much easier to procure.

"Three: Contrary to the Prosecution's claims, I did not set upon my clients with pliers as they lay, fading and helpless in their cell. No, I waited, patiently. In fact, in the first weeks I even stayed and talked with them while they succumbed, so as to ease their passing. Truth to tell, it was during those times I was to my clients what they no longer had in this world; a comforter, confessor, a friend even. Some even had me read from scripture. Is that the mark of a murderer? Even when I could no longer sit with them, when frankly I hadn't the time as the workload was getting rather . . . burdensome, I still waited until they had passed on before I'd begin, ah, de-clawing them, if I can put it that way, as there was enough time for me to complete my task and prepare them before they revived. Forensic evidence again from my clients that Inspector Morgan's team captured, demonstrates there were no signs of struggle present. Therefore my clients were *not still alive* when I performed my task.

"In short, hard as my work was, I did not forget my humanity. I admit by the time of my capture I was inured to the job of . . . making my clients safe for the outside. But tempting as it was, and I confess I was tempted, I remembered there are expectations, standards to be kept that make a man civilized. And I kept them until the day Inspector Morgan smashed through my door.

"So then, I challenge the Prosecution: Where was my inhumanity? What is my crime? Who is this man they have gleefully dubbed 'The Doorman?!' He is not me!

"For has not the realm for some years now allowed euthanasia in the form of assisted suicide? For this was the service I offered. Perhaps the death penalty the Prosecution seeks is because I'm an unlicensed Assisted Suicide Operative. I have admitted my guilt in this. My services weren't legitimate. But I am *not* one of those back street doormen to the other side. If I have made a mistake—and I mean *a mistake only*—it was that I was too eager to get myself set up and did not go through the proper channels. Not that I would have had much of an opportunity by that time! I have a tendency for being overly keen, you see. Marry in haste, repent at leisure . . . my ex-wives would tell you that! But, does this omission deserve the death penalty? I have read this, the Assisted Suicide Act, cover to cover, and I've reviewed judgments in cases relating to it, and see that my mistake is—perhaps ironically—*not* punishable by death.

"Or perhaps the Prosecution wants my neck because the method I choose counters the current policy in this, our heightened state of emergency? How so? My methods are as humane as anyone else's, certainly any other ASOs'. Gas, lethal injection, a controlled zombie bite . . . What is the difference? And the Prosecution's half-baked rebuttal of my assisted suicide argument by claiming we performed our services without qualified staff, well . . . Is not my colleague Alvin eminently qualified to perform these procedures? At least he, unlike the half of our nation now like him, is biting only those who want out. The rest of the dead, outside these doors, are committing murder. Mindless though they may be, they *are murdering*.

"Whichever way you look at it, the Prosecution's argument fails. How can I be convicted under law? For did not the Prime Minister himself on the 14th May—and ever since—say, and I quote, '*You'll be doing them a service putting them out of their misery*'? By his own admission, has he not now deputized each and every one of us as an Assisted Suicide Operative, in all but name? The government cannot have it both ways, continuing to keep on its statute books an Assisted Suicide Act demanding licensed ASOs only, whilst at the same time encouraging its remaining embattled citizens to 'remove the head or destroy the brain' for the dead's own good! Do we not see a contradiction here?

"So, to my second motivator: Containment.

"The Prosecution accuses me of contributing, ah . . . 'with malice aforethought to the state of national crisis,' and that I have 'bred yet more monsters'. The Prosecution's argument being that the clients, both I and Alvin, turned could then go off and bite others who did not want to die. It's in this they say I am traitorously aiding the destruction of the realm. But their arguments are not true. I say again—*not true*.

"As I've already explained, had I not been there to offer a sanitary and humane way out, my clients would have taken drastic action anyway, stripping themselves naked and climbing a fence of the nearest quarantine zone and into excruciating horror. I ask you, what kind of an end is that for someone suffering. For pity's sake alone, how could I have allowed that? But perhaps more importantly, how could I allow such an irresponsible and *uncontrollable* action to occur, knowing the inevitable outcome? Be under no illusions, ladies and gentlemen, had they not come through me, I guarantee you, all those people would have ended up far, far deadlier than they are now.

"How can I justify this statement? Again, let me count the ways.

"One: My own evidence, in the form of the chronology of the evolution of my service these past months, as well as the discoveries made by Inspector Morgan and his team, have shown that all my earlier clients were fitted with muzzles to prevent them from biting the living. Crude they were, admittedly, but effective. Inspector Morgan's own testimony stated that of all the dead identified as my clients, all those I had muzzled before release had retained them, and they were still secure at the time of capture.

"Two: You have been shown the buckets of human nails and teeth from my cellar, Prosecution Exhibits C and D, claimed by them to be trophies of my 'kills'. Not so. I hold them up as proof of my motivation to preserve society. When I no longer had the time or resources to produce the muzzles, what other resort had I but to pull their teeth? Next, you have all seen reports of living victims shredded by the dead's clawing hands. Was it sensible to try and put gloves on my clients? Hardly! For one, how could I get that many, and how could I guarantee they wouldn't wear out, tear, or be pulled off? So in all cases, their nails had to go.

"Three: My method of release. Now a man who cared nothing for his client or society, the kind of man the Prosecution has painted me, would have simply thrown the revived corpse out into the street the first chance he got. And in this current state of panic, I could easily have done so. But did I? What does the evidence say? The photographs from Inspector Morgan's team have shown you how, by using speakers playing ambient noise and whispers to attract them, I coaxed my revived clients from their cell, through my cellar's coal chute hatch, along the chicken wire passage in my garden, and through a series of one-way gates through the bushes and into the Hampstead Heath Quarantine Zone. An established, and, until only three weeks ago, secure holding area, ladies and gentlemen. Yes, I admit each release was done under cover of darkness, not because I was trying to hide my guilt, but to help keep concealed the source of the new additions from the already quarantined population. I'd have done no one any favors would I, allowing a horde of curious dead to crawl back to my house, and on into Highgate!

"Taken into account, therefore, these actions you can see demonstrate, I was thinking *humanely* of others. I did not want inadvertent infection of innocents as a consequence of my own service, and the Prosecution has offered no evidence any such infections resulted from the actions of my turned clients. Proof then that my precautions worked.

"Still, let me be fair and ask the question: Was I only making the problem worse, simply adding to the numbers that need a bullet bouncing round the brain pan? Perhaps. But it was controlled—a neutered addition if you will. And did my adding to the hordes already confined to the Heath contribute to its fall? Let's be realistic. Hundreds were being pitched from lorries into the Heath every day, thousands toward the end. When my service was running at its peak, I must have added to the population . . . at most, five in one night. Hardly the straw that broke the camel's back!

"For I did not cause this crisis, did I? The virus—if a virus it is—I didn't release. The responsibility in failing to quarantine and eliminate the ravening hordes we now face was not mine. The fifty percent of the country now dark, with its one-time citizens lumbering, mindless, through devastated streets, engines of corrupt flesh powered by a voracious instinct. I had no power to halt that, did I? And I would have, too, had I been capable. I'm no monster, after all. In fact those responsible for these failures, the politicians and the generals, so safely ensconced in their bunkers, their ships, and fortified islands, cowering on Holyhead, the Isles of Man and Wight, Lundy, Lindisfarne, Jersey, the Western Isles . . . it is they who should stand here in my stead. These are their crimes, and they are surely greater than any I've committed.

"For look at me—who am I? I'm simply a businessman—always have been—watching the shift in trends, keeping my entrepreneurial finger in the air to gauge the way the wind is blowing. You know from my previous ventures, already presented to this court, that I'm a survivor, that's my nature. And today, in what has all too quickly become a survivalist paradise, I am merely following my instincts. I saw the market changing, the consumers—no pun intended—literally were. But did I go the route of those others, those *animals* like the Feeders? Was I psychotic or sadistic like them? Gleefully throwing the living to the dead, and for sport of all things? Please! Where is the profit in that? The court has already been presented with the evidence of the stores I'd accumulated from clients. Demonstration enough, my thinking was merely the honest marriage of service for a return. Compassion for coin, you could say.

"To summarize then, these past four months have been as much an ordeal for me as any of you. My only crime, if you can call it that, was wishing to come through this, to gather supplies enough to survive, to make it to a dawning day when rotting flesh could walk no more, and I could step outside my house without fear. My mistake was in letting my own self-interest get the better of me, and failing to see the authorities might have it in them to control this waking nightmare. One such man is Detective Inspector Morgan. I wish to digress briefly and express my deepest respect for the Inspector. His efforts to track me down, and his continued devotion to duty despite only having available to him an overtaxed and severely depleted police force, amidst a workload of appalling scale, marks him as an officer of the highest caliber, and if this crisis reaches a favorable end, he should be rightly rewarded.

"Finally, I appreciate that during this period of Martial Law I have been allowed an especially rare opportunity to state my case, and for this I thank this hastily convened court for its valuable time. My only request is that, if found guilty, the court would find it in its heart to show mercy . . . and send me the way of the clients I have served, along with my devoted colleague Alvin. If he has not already been . . . disposed of. We were business partners, and though admittedly unusual, our working relationship shared a profound understanding of the need for, and benefits of, our service. It seems only right I should join him.

"The way things are going outside, I believe this appears to be our ultimate fate anyway.

"The defense rests."

THE STRANGE CASE OF
THE JAVORSKI BROTHERS
AND THE FLYING CORPSE

SEAN T. PAGE

Once upon a time, there were two Polish brothers, working in London, called Piotr and Nicolai Javorkski. Back in their beautiful home town of Krakow, they were the two best-known roofers in the area, using all of their skills and experience to repair the town's many medieval and delicate tile roofs.

In 2008, the brothers decided to try their luck in London. They had heard that the demand for professional builders in the UK was phenomenal, and that they could earn there in one week, what it would take them a month to earn in Poland.

So, the two brothers set out to make their fortune. Carrying only a small suitcase and their trusty tools, they left their ancient home and arrived at the bustling London Heathrow Airport on a rainy spring day in April.

At first things went well. Piotr quickly picked up work on the new Kings Cross Station development, whilst Nicolai did some casual building contracts for a housing association.

The summer passed quickly and the two brothers started to enjoy their new life.

However, even though the wages were much higher in London, so were the costs. Their rent was more than quadruple what they had been paying back home, and combined with their travel costs and food bills, the brothers were barely better off than they had been before.

But, it wasn't just about the money. The two brothers missed working with the delicate, antique tiles and slates of Krakow. They knew that the city council there was just about to start working on the roof of the famous fifteenth century Cloth Hall, the best-preserved medieval roof in all of Poland. If they didn't get back by the end of the year, their fierce rivals, the Zajac brothers would undoubtedly handle the whole project and become the roofing equivalent of Olympic gold medalists in the city. Neither Piotr nor Nicolai were particularly religious, and the world of tiles is not generally known to be a superstitious one, but in their minds, the Zajac brothers were the closest thing to deadly rivals as one could have in roofing.

Before Piotr and Nicolai left Krakow, they pledged proudly that they would return as 'millionaires' and marry their childhood sweethearts—both of whom worked in hatpin stalls within the cavernous Cloth Hall Market. But, London proved more expensive than they had planned, and Nicolai's love of the fast life meant that whilst they enjoyed their months in the UK, they scarcely had the millions they were hoping for.

As they sat on deckchairs in their dreary North London bedsit, they figured out they had around £5000 between them. They would need at least £20,000 to buy the Meresky roof and tile superstore on Grodzka Street, which had been their objective since old papa Meresky had pledged it to them for what was a well-below market rate when they were young teenagers. If they could get this superstore and the roofing contract on the Cloth Hall, they would reign supreme, at least in the tiling universe.

The plan had been simple. Come to London, make a fortune, return to Krakow, buy the superstore, get the Cloth Hall contract, and marry Maria and Anya. The problem now was that they didn't have the money and if they didn't return soon, the envious Zajac brothers would probably snap up the store as well as the Cloth Hall contract.

Piotr and Nicolai agreed. They could not stay in London any longer. But, if they returned with barely what they had left with, despite the amazing time they'd had, they would be the laughing stock in the close-knit world of Polish roof tiling.

It was into this seemingly impossible conundrum that their house mate, Marissa Sawicki burst, her eyes red with tears. The young Polish student was clearly upset, as she didn't bother knocking on the bedsit door.

A distressed Marissa fell straight into the arms of the more approachable Nicolai, and it took several minutes before either of the brothers could confirm exactly what had happened.

"Something terrible must have happened," said Nicolai to Piotr. Of the two brothers, he had always been the shrewder observer of human nature, particularly around the fairer sex.

"It's Uncle Viktor," she dribbled through her sniffs. "He's died, gone in that crappy old folk's home, and him with those medals. I can't believe it."

Marissa's Uncle Viktor had arrived in Britain in 1940 as a talented Polish air force commander. As a young man, he fought with distinction in the successful Polish spitfire squadron of the RAF. In his latter years, he stalked a different prey, much as he used to hunt the Luftwaffe across the skies of Kent and London, and his 'kills' included many of the most sought after octogenarians in West London.

Still, time waits for no man, and even this exceptional man finally met his maker one cold November morning. And, surprisingly, for a man who had gone on to have a successful career as a scrap metal merchant, he left little but his old, royal blue, faded RAF box at the home.

Inside the box, Marissa discovered a will. It was a document which would change Piotr, Nicolai, and Marissa's lives forever—and lead to some startling new guidelines for the living dead and air travel.

Uncle Viktor had money, but all of it was tied up in Poland. As she explored his papers, she discovered that he owned the freeholds to most of the town, including the roof and tiling superstore.

But, even with the documents, a quirk in Polish law stipulated all of the money would go to the government in Warsaw, as Uncle Viktor had lived abroad for so long. The only possible loophole was if he was actually buried in the old country. Then, things would be different. As his only living heiress, the beautiful Marissa, would become Krakow's richest woman overnight.

The three young Poles sat discussing this situation well into the early hours. As things stood, Uncle Viktor's body had been taken to a local, council funeral home and was due for a cheap 'save a grave' job in the next few days. They had to get to the body first, and then get it back to Poland.

As you've probably guessed, a simple, but somewhat macabre plan was hatched. The brothers would use their remaining cash to buy three air tickets to Krakow. They would get Uncle Viktor's body out of the chapel of rest, dress him up, and get him through customs and onto the plane. Once at Krakow Airport, they would be met by Marissa's childhood sweetheart Mikeal, who happened to be the senior Polish customs official at the airport.

It was the only alternative, as the young student Marissa could scarcely afford the £10,000 that would be required to have the body transported to Poland.

The living may balk at the price of air travel these days, but they will find the dead fair even worse. If one includes the specialist transportation and chilled storage, the legal charges and other bureaucracy, moving a body, even between countries in Europe, is not a cheap affair.

The prize? Marissa gets her inheritance as her uncle will be buried in Poland, the Javorkski brothers get their store and a bag of cash for their trouble, and Uncle Viktor avoids a cheap, council funeral in London and is laid to rest in his ancient family vault. Everyone wins.

A plan with no flaws.

First, they needed to liberate Uncle Viktor from the funeral home.

A dark frosty night in North Hendon, found Piotr and Nicolai on the roof of the Edgware Road Municipal Chapel of Rest. They skillfully loosened the roof tiles and created a hole large enough for them to drop down. Neither brother volunteered to go first.

Eventually, they made it into the upper floor of the chapel, which appeared to be some kind of sterile white mortuary preparation room.

They moved downstairs, guided only by their small, but bright pen torches. Nikolai carried his hammer and torch in cross hand FBI style.

"Look at me," he whispered to his brother. "I'm like Mulder from the FBI." Nicolai started to add dramatic 24-style background music to his jerky, secret agent-style moves until Piotr finally shut him up.

After several minutes of fumbling in the half-light, the two brothers finally came to the funeral parlor itself. With its perpetual dim light and stained glass windows—the whole effect was creepy enough, but add to that the fact there were no fewer than ten closed caskets in the room, then things moved toward spooky.

How could they find Uncle Viktor? Would they need to search every coffin?

"Yoo-hoo, uncle," called Nicolai quietly. There was no reply, only the delicate tap of the trees on the window, and the ever-present hum of the electric substation next door.

"I've found him," cried Piotr. "Look here, see the blue flying hat on top? This must be him."

Upon opening the casket, they were sure. Resplendent in his RAF crest blazer, laid Uncle Viktor.

"He looks pretty good actually," said Nicolai, surprised as he jabbed a finger into Uncle Viktor's sallow waxy cheek.

"Let's get moving, get him in the bag, and for gods' sake, be careful," said Piotr, keen to get out of the temporary resting home for the dead.

They transferred the body into a heavy duty, grey plastic bag they had bought with them. The corpse was surprisingly flexible, and seemed to be unaffected by any rigor mortis.

"See how supple he is," teased Nicolai as he bent Uncle's leg forward and back, in a Charleston style dance move.

"Stop that, you fool," raged Piotr. "Have some respect for the dead." He nervously eyed the other caskets.

As they finished zipping up the bag and were preparing to leave, both brothers turned. There was a distinct knocking noise over the constant hum of the substation. But, this was from inside the chapel. They stared at each other as if to say, "Let's get out of here."

The body was far heavier than expected, but they made it to the stairs. The sound was much louder now. It was coming from inside the caskets . . .

With the skill of men that work on roofs for a living, they moved as quickly as they could up the stairs with the body of Uncle

Viktor. There were several loud crashes from behind them as coffins fell from their stands.

Piotr looked back and started as he saw a figure moving toward them in the red-light of the funeral home.

Both brothers froze in fear as a highly made-up, old mauve-haired lady started to stumble up the stairs, with jerky, rigid movements. Somehow the dead had come back to life and one thing was sure, they weren't back to discuss the latest tiling trends.

"My God, it's Joan Collins," shouted Nicolai. "Let's get out of here."

Piotr recovered his senses and quickly grabbed a couple of chairs, throwing them down to block the stairs. The look-alike Joan-Collins struggled to get past the overturned furniture and emitted a deep groan as she reached out for them, revealing to them both her wicked looking polished white, but razor-sharp dentures.

Other risen corpses started to join her. No other celebrity look-alikes, but all with plenty of moans. They had to slow them down or they would never get out on the roof again in time, not with the body of Uncle Viktor in tow.

Nicolai came bursting back out of the mortuary room, where he had found some kind of medical cleaver, which must have been used in the preparation of the cadavers. Before his elder brother could intervene, he flung it tomahawk-like at the zombie version of Joan Collins.

It struck her squarely in the chest with enough force to knock her, and the other ghouls, back down the stairs, but it wouldn't stop them for long.

The brothers quickly made their way up to the roof and pulled the body through, and out, into the cold night air. As he was last up, Piotr kicked away the piled chairs they had used to climb up.

The whole dramatic scene had happened so fast, they scarcely had time to take it all in. Still, by tomorrow, they would be back in Krakow, so they stuck to the plan.

Shell-shocked by their night-time activities at the Municipal Chapel of Rest, Piotr and Nicolai did not sleep that night. Their brief battle with the dead seemed almost like a dream, as they sipped their very strong coffee, and waited for the mini cab to the airport. Marissa had spent the night at their flat, working on Uncle Viktor, preparing him for his final journey home.

Uncle Viktor was still looking reasonably good for a corpse. Sure, he lacked the healthy glow of a holiday ad, but then the cloudy and damp English climates could do that to any living person. With the addition of some particularly large sunglasses and a jaunty yellow beret, Uncle Viktor was turned into a mysterious Elizabeth Taylor-esque type character, all wheelchair bound and mysterious, with the faint hint of a movie star about him.

On the subject of faint hints, it was also noticed that Uncle Viktor smelt reasonably good. None of them knew how long it would be before he really started to pong. For the moment, a generous measure of Lynx deodorant gave him the attractive and passionate raw smell of living man that they were after.

The brothers mentioned nothing of the trouble they had back at the funeral home. Whatever it was, it wasn't their problem. By this time tomorrow, they would be back in Krakow, Uncle Viktor would be at his funeral, and they would have one hand on the roofing and tiling superstore on Grodzka Street.

Piotr took charge of the old wheelchair they had bought from the second hand shop on Finchley High Street. The body was to be held in a realistic seating position by two belts, which extended around the back of the chair, holding him upright. Nicolai tried to tie an additional belt around his forehead to keep his head from constantly drooping, but the effect was like something out of Silence of the Lambs, so the idea was abandoned.

"Better to say he's sleeping," offered Piotr helpfully. "We can pretend he's taken some medication or something."

The mini cab arrived fifteen minutes late, as usual when one is rushing to the airport. The journey was uneventful and Piotr took the opportunity to test the drug story with the driver. It went down like a dream, no questions asked. The corpse of Uncle Viktor was simply an elderly relative peacefully sleeping. With their knowledge of events at the funeral home, both brothers prayed it would remain so.

At the airport, Piotr took a break to freshen up in the toilets—he had been awake for almost twenty-four hours straight. He left Nicolai in charge of the wheelchair, and headed off.

Things were going well, and with no sign of Uncle Viktor rising from the dead as the other corpses had done, the impatient Nicolai found himself distracted by a brightly-colored new Swatch shop. He eyed some of the bargains on sale from a distance. You can almost imagine the devil and angel on each of his shoulders, whispering their sagely advice.

Nicolai respectfully wheeled Uncle Viktor into a discreet corner by some plastic shrubs and carefully placed a Daily Mail on his lap. The overall effect was of a geriatric passenger who had drifted off whilst reading the latest news. He headed off on a quest for a new Swatch watch.

Piotr panicked on his return, and after a few minutes of frantic searching, noticed Nicolai in the Swatch shop, leaning manfully over the shop counter, chatting up some young Asian beauty.

"Where's Viktor?" he interrupted in Polish.

"He's fine, don't panic. He's just over there. No one will go near him . . ." shrugged Nicolai, seemingly oblivious to the fact that they were trying to smuggle a week old corpse on a plane in one of the most security conscious airports in the world.

Nicolai stopped mid-sentence as he noticed a young lady in a virulent green sweater with a clipboard, crouching down and looking intently at Uncle Viktor, nodding her head, as if in deep conversation.

Both brothers dashed over, sprinting the first half, then slowing for the finish so as not to arouse too much suspicion on arrival.

The pretty blonde with the clip board was just standing up, obviously having finished whatever survey she was completing.

"Excuse me, gentlemen," she said. "Would you mind if I asked you a few questions about Heathrow washroom facilities?"

"What?" asked Piotr as he grabbed the wheelchair and gave the body a once over.

"Are you from the same party?" she queried. "Oh, I'm sorry—need to be from a different party. Anyway, your friend here has answered the questions, so thanks for now. Do have a safe trip."

Before they had a chance to question her, she had flown like a bee to her next victim. "Excuse me, madam, would you mind if I—"

"Why the hell did you leave him? You could've wrecked everything," warned Piotr, to his younger brother.

"Stop panicking. He's okay," answered Nicolai.

Both brothers stopped arguing as they heard a sound coming from the body.

Piotr leaned down and listened. He could hear a faint murmuring noise coming from Uncle Viktor. His lips did not move. It was a sound coming from deep inside his stomach.

"Must be wind or gas escaping," offered Nicolai helpfully. "I read somewhere that the body keeps active for days after death."

"Is that what happened at the chapel of rest, you idiot?" asked Piotr as he stared intently at the corpse. "What if the same thing that happened there, happens to him? You remember the look in Joan Collins' eyes? She was wild!"

Both brothers considered the problem at hand.

For the next few minutes, Uncle Viktor was as silent as the grave. Soon even the worrisome Piotr dismissed it as escaping gas.

"But, we can't take the risk," confirmed Piotr. "We have to make sure that he stays silent on the trip—whatever happens."

Nicolai thought for a moment, something he rarely did. "Suppose we superglue his mouth shut? That way, if he does get lively during the trip, there won't be any moans, and no risk that he is going to get fresh with our fellow passengers," he offered.

"That's the worst idea I've heard since I came to this country, brother. Gluing his mouth shut! This is a decorated World War II veteran, not some jerry-built council project," answered his brother. "On the other hand, we're out of options. I saw a travel store in the other terminal. Go over there and get some superglue. We'll glue it shut for now, then we can open it up again later."

Desperate times call for desperate measures, and if super gluing the mouth of the corpse shut was the only way to complete the plan, then so be it.

The glue plan worked perfectly. There was one troublesome moment when Nicolai had almost connected his hand permanently to the corpse's teeth, but in the end it was an objective achieved. If Uncle Viktor did start to moan, it would be a deep one from inside. His mouth was glued firmly shut.

Having checked in online, Piotr only had to push the body through passport control. In a fine spot of luck, Nicolai noticed the Polish name on the Immigration Official's name tag. Slipping into

Polish, he soon managed to distract proceedings enough for his brother to wheel Uncle Viktor past, his passport resting, and open, on his lap.

The two brothers removed the huge Victoria Beckham sunglasses from the corpse and prayed that no one would need to wake him up to confirm eye color or something similar.

As if to help, the late Uncle Viktor seemed to emit a moaning sound on cue as his passport was inspected—another stroke of luck.

The party moved through security and into the waiting area. The next twenty minutes or so, waiting to board the plane, were uneventful. With all the hustle and bustle of tourists, businessmen, and families, no one noticed the elderly gentlemen sleeping peacefully in his wheelchair.

There were a couple of hairy moments when a young Czech boy managed to get a lolly stuck to Uncle Viktor's sleeve, but apart from extracting a low moan from the body, no damage was done. As long as the brothers kept an eye on the body—they were home free.

Playing the ace card of a disabled war veteran ensured that Piotr and Nicolai not only got on the plane first, but that they also secured the extra leg room seats. As they strapped Uncle Viktor in, Piotr grabbed an airline blanket and draped it over the body. Not completely mind you, he didn't want him to look like, well, a corpse.

The rest of the passengers started to file in, occasionally casting admiring glances over at the sleeping war hero.

Getting through passport control, getting on the plane and sitting down, had been the major obstacles. Now all they needed to do was keep Uncle Viktor quiet for the three-hour flight, then hand him over in Krakow to Marissa's contact. He worked in security so passports wouldn't be a problem at that end.

Both brothers began to relax. Between wondering how they had gotten into this situation, and almost overpowering urges to sleep, Piotr and Nicolai still managed to stay awake. Piotr checked out the in-flight movie. It was horror season on the Polish Airlines, and he didn't fancy watching Romero's new version of the Dawn of the

Dead whilst sitting next to a corpse, which had already shown a tendency to groan.

Piotr leaned back in his seat, listening to some crooner on the smooth jazz channel instead, and was asleep within minutes.

Uncle Viktor's corpse hadn't moved for the last hour, and desperate for a drink in the dry atmosphere of the cabin, Nicolai pressed the overhead button. He waited, but no stewardess arrived. Through a gap in the aisle curtains, Nicolai could see the lavish in-flight party that is Polish Air first class—the rich business people, international jet setters, and the attentive and glamorous stewardesses. Before his brain had fully engaged, he was up and through the curtains. Five minutes later, he was deep in conversation with a first-class passenger, regaling them with witty stories of his life on roof tops around Poland, and in London.

Piotr stirred fitfully in his sleep. No one sleeps well on an aircraft, and even in his extended leg room seats, he shifted from position to position in an attempt to get comfortable. His dreams were active and full of mixed metaphors about poor tiling, English jail, and the perils of traveling with a corpse. He finally woke up, feeling less refreshed than before he fell asleep. He was also dry as bone. He leaned across to take Nicolai's bottle of water.

It took a few seconds before the sleepy elder brother realized that the two seats next him were empty. Sure Nicolai may have gone to the toilets, but where the hell was the corpse.

Piotr looked over his headrest. No screaming anywhere. A good sign. Two stewardesses were pushing the silver buffet trolley toward him from the front. Uncle Viktor could not have got out that way. He must have gone back.

Many of the passengers were either sleeping or watching the in-flight movie, so no one really noticed when Piotr darted out of his seat and made his way toward the rear of the aircraft.

There were two toilets, so he darted in to check the first. It was clear. After a minute or so of knocking, a disabled Russian lady exited the second bathroom, muttering some profanity which probably related to Piotr's unseemly door rattling and attempted entry. Illogically, Piotr poked his head into the vacant cubicle to check on it and quickly wished he hadn't. The pungent eggy smell almost brought tears to his eyes as he backed out of the cubicle.

His Russian foe gave him a sly chuckle as she slowly maneuvered her bulky frame back to her seat.

The wandering corpse was not in either of the bathrooms, so Piotr desperately followed the aisle to the back of the aircraft. There he found a food preparation area used by the serving staff, but what he found was hardly something for the kitchen.

The old man was leaning over what looked to be one of the stewards. At first, Piotr thought he had stumbled on something his infamous Uncle Silas was known for back home.

On closer inspection, he discovered to his horror that the dead Uncle Viktor was feeding on the entrails he had torn out of the now unconscious steward. Piotr looked away, struggling not to vomit.

He pulled the old man away from his ghoulish feast only to get a full view of the 'plate' he had been working on. Uncle Viktor must have overcome this much smaller man and then bitten into his neck. Blood was everywhere, so the steward must have passed out quickly. Then, the dead Viktor tucked into his own freshly prepared in-flight snack.

Two things flashed through Piotr's mind. Firstly, Uncle Viktor was truly one of the living dead, and secondly, that he had to get this mess cleared up or everything was blown. No roof and tile superstore. No marriages to Maria and Anya. Lengthy prison sentences for him and Nicolai, and, undoubtedly, curtains for the cannibalistic Uncle Viktor.

The smartly dressed ghoul stood calmly next to Piotr as the latter planned their escape. It was as if feeding on live flesh had satisfied him for the moment. But, he was still covered in the blood—how the hell could Piotr get him back to his seat, and what was he to do with the grisly remains of the steward?

To heighten the pressure, he could hear the stewardess approaching with the silver serving trolley. Luckily they stopped at the huge Russian woman's seat as she ordered a prune juice and another portion of curry.

Thinking quickly, Piotr pulled the steward's body toward the large chute where the trolleys normally go during take off and landing. A hatch at the back seemed to lead down, possible to a waste area. Perfect, he thought.

But as he yanked the stick-like legs, he despaired when they both came of in his hands. Noticing this, Uncle Viktor knelt down and began to feed again. The show of still warm, bloody human flesh must have been too much for his ghoulish tastes.

Pushing Uncle Viktor away again, Piotr gathered up the various body parts and jammed them down the chute. That should do the trick, at least until they land. He wiped some of the blood from the floor and the hatch area, and replaced a trolley to cover any remaining mess.

However, on turning, he saw his next major problem. Uncle Viktor had blood all down his front, and around his mouth.

The stewardess was less than two seats away now. He had to think fast.

As they entered the food preparation area, they found Piotr carefully wiping red sauce away from his aged uncle's face and front.

"Sorry," he explained in his best broken English. "Ketchup," he said holding up a Heinz squeeze bottle. By cunningly blending some in with

the blood, Piotr had quickly created a decent looking tomato-blood sauce and the perfect excuse for being back there.

"Don't you worry, my love," said one of the stewardesses understandingly, "it's nice to see a young man who cares for the elderly."

Piotr smiled, pretending not to have a firm grasp of English as he led Uncle Viktor back to his seat.

"That's nice isn't it, not something you see every day, eh Maureen," offered the stewardess to her partner in a thick, broomie accent. "I wish we had more of that here, eh love? Be a better place, I can tell you."

"'Least he enjoyed his liver," offered the second stewardess. "Poor old boy still had some of it on his lip. I'll take 'em a tissue on the way through."

"Didn't think we had liver on this flight, Maureen," said the first stewardess, but her voice was drowned out by an announcement from the Captain. They would shortly be beginning their decent into Krakow.

Piotr returned, leading the lumbering Uncle Viktor to his seat.

"Want some peanuts?" offered Nicolai, hardly noticing that the corpse was now, not only up and about, but also seemed to have been out for a wander.

"I swear this to you, brother," raged Piotr, albeit quietly. The threats came as he secured Uncle Viktor into his seat. The corpse seemed to have calmed down after its feed. So long as no one panicked about the missing steward, they should make it through the landing.

Piotr glanced up nervously to see if the other stewardesses were looking around for their missing colleague. Everything seemed calm for the moment.

Nicolai applied another application of superglue to the zombie's mouth to put a stop to any more feasting, and the brothers kept one arm each on Uncle Viktor as they came into land.

The plane touched down in Krakow, a few minutes ahead of schedule.

The disabled veteran routine worked like a dream again on exiting the plane, and they were soon heading across the tarmac toward the new airport terminal.

On reaching the automatic doors, they were pulled aside by a tall blonde, bespectacled security guard. It was Marissa's ex Mikeal.

"Ready to take him from here?" asked Piotr as he pushed the wheelchair toward the young man.

"Are you sure he's dead?" he replied as he caught the sound of a faint moan from Uncle Viktor.

"Well, whatever he is, he's yours," said Nicolai. "Don't let him get his mouth open," he suggested as he tossed Mikeal the remaining superglue.

The two brothers moved off into the terminal with one thought in their minds—to get away from the corpse. The smell was definitely beginning to get worse, with a subtle tinge of decomposition now blending effortlessly with the copious amounts of Lynx Marissa had applied back in London.

As Piotr offered his passport to an attendant who sat bored in his control booth, he heard some sort of commotion going on by the plane outside.

Members of the baggage team were scattering as a small half-figure in a bloody white shirt dragged itself along after them. One valiant handler picked up a shrink-wrapped case and smashed it over the legless creature's head. Piotr had an idea, but then he'd had enough of walking corpses for one twenty-four-hour period.

Piotr and Nicolai quickly left the airport and caught the bus into central Krakow. In just over a week, they would meet up again with Marissa.

And, just like in any fairy tale, everyone really did live happily ever after. Piotr and Nicolai Javorkski finally got their hands on the roofing superstore, and married Maria and Anya from the hatpin stalls.

Marissa became one of the richest young women in Krakow, and was rumored to be influential in ensuring the Javorkski brothers won the lucrative roofing contract to renovate the Cloth Hall.

As for Uncle Viktor, well, they couldn't glue his mouth shut forever, and he was soon up and about again. To keep everyone safe, they entombed him in the substantial family crypt under the cathedral where, with a choice of hundreds of corpses in various states of decomposition and disrepair, he would be kept satisfied for many years to come.

UNLIKELY HERO

RICH RESTUCCI

It's a whole new world. Since the Rottens came, I've been able to go anywhere and do anything I want. I just need to be careful. Always careful. I do miss my family though.

Dad was always my favorite. He would give me treats all the time, and he could make me feel loved even when I was scared or really tired. I would curl up with him when he sat reading in his chair, and he always made room for me, stroking the back of my neck while he read.

Now he's gone. They're all gone.

Eleven days earlier.

My family had, for some reason, just put big boards on the windows and nailed the doors closed. They moved a bunch of furniture around, and everybody looked scared. I couldn't for the life of me figure out why they were wrecking the house. It was business as usual for me, though, and I just tried to stay out of the way.

They were talking in hushed voices, almost whispers, and my curiosity got the better of me. I walked over to them to see what was going on. My dad reached down and picked me up. He stroked my head a little, and told me everything was going to be fine. He put me down and I latched onto his leg.

He said, "Not now, buddy," and gently pushed me away with his foot. I strolled over to the television. It was on and there was some man talking, not the action I really liked to watch. The man on the TV looked scared, but that was nothing new. All the stuff on the TV had somebody looking scared when my dad was watching it.

I got bored with the TV and decided to take a nap. I wasn't really tired, but there wasn't anything else to do, and Dad didn't want to play. I climbed up on the couch and sacked out.

I woke to the sounds of pounding. It sounded like there was a bunch of people thumping the sides of the house with their hands. This was highly irregular; people usually banged on the front door. The smacks on the sides of the house grew louder.

"How did they find us?" my mom asked.

"Quiet!" Dad hissed back. "They might go away if they don't hear anything," he whispered.

Of course, I didn't know what any of that meant, but the tone implied something bad was happening. The pounding continued, and then there was a crash from the kitchen; splintering wood and breaking glass.

"Get upstairs, Laura, and lock yourself in the bedroom!" Dad yelled harshly.

"I'm not leavi..." Mom started to reply, but Dad cut her off.

"Go!" he yelled and pointed up. "If it's only a few I can take care of it." Dad had a hammer in his hand, and he hefted it a couple of times, checking the weight, I think.

Mom ran toward the stairs, and as an afterthought, tried to scoop me up. I was having none of it, and squirmed out of her arms. I hid behind the couch, and she tried to get me.

"What are you doing?" Dad demanded. "Just go!"

Mom bolted up the stairs, slamming the door behind her.

That was the last time I saw her.

Dad said something under his breath, and I peeked around the corner of the couch. He didn't see me. He looked into the kitchen and said, "Shit." Then he backed up, and I could see a shadow in the kitchen move slowly toward him. Then another shadow. Then another.

I heard a weird moaning from the kitchen, too. Dad stood there and let the shadows come to him. I could hear glass from the broken door crunching under the feet of the shadows. Then a woman came into view. She was dirty, and her clothes and hair were a mess. I couldn't tell what it was at the time, but there was something...off...about her.

She stumbled toward my dad, arms outstretched, and Dad stepped forward and smacked her on the top of her head with the hammer! The woman dropped to her hands and knees, blood oozing from around the wound in her scalp. She started to get up, and Dad brought the hammer down on the back of her head. The disheveled woman stopped moving, but two more people came lurching out of the kitchen by then.

Dad smacked one of the people on the head and the hammer stuck in the man's skull. Dad tried pulling it out, but the second man grabbed Dad by the shirt and pulled him close. The man with the hammer in his head started leaning to one side, and stumbled into my dad and the second man while they were grappling. They all went down in a heap, and my dad started screaming. The second man had bitten Dad on the arm! More people were coming into the living room through the kitchen, and they started kneeling down and biting Dad. My struggling father looked at me then with startled eyes and with his last breath he said, "Run!"

That was all I needed. With eyes wide, I sprang up from behind the couch and hightailed it into there. There were two more people in the kitchen, and I skidded to a stop on the linoleum. These people were equally as filthy, and they reached for me, but I was faster.

I bolted around their outstretched arms and through the smashed kitchen door, narrowly missing yet another trespasser. Another few seconds and I was out in the cool night.

I realized I had never been outside the house by myself before. I had tried valiantly to get out on various occasions, but Dad would always stop me. He said it wasn't safe with the street so close. A fleeting moment of panic was almost my undoing. I stopped dead in my tracks while looking up into the star-filled sky. Footsteps behind me gave away another of the weird people, and I regained my composure and fled.

I ran into the neighbor's backyard and heard screaming from my house. I looked back, and could see shadows fighting in an upstairs window. A splash of thick liquid covered the inky panes from the inside, and I could imagine what it was. It was my mom. One final scream, and then the only thing I could hear was the moaning and shrill cries of the intruders.

To say I was terrified was an understatement. I had just seen my family get killed, I was outside by myself, and there were people attacking other people. Fear and confusion were the emotions of the moment. I decided that I wanted to be far away from here, so I just ran. I ran and ran.

Ten minutes later, I found that I was hopelessly lost. There were staggering forms in every direction, and I had no idea where to go. I was small, and well hidden in the hedges of someone's house, but I was filled with despair. What could I do? Where could I go? Who would take me in? I realized I was hungry, too. The incessant moaning was also frightening. From the cover of the hedges, I saw a man run past under the glow of a street light. He ran into the arms of two of the stumbling people, and they immediately attacked and tore into him. It was horrible. The running man started screaming, and other stumblers came out of the shadows.

They ate him alive. I could see the bad men fighting over pieces of the man who had been running. After his screaming stopped, the stumblers continued to feed for awhile. Suddenly, the runner pushed the others away, and they left the runner alone. The runner stood up, but he was different. In the cone of brightness from the street light, I could see that the man had been savaged. His throat was torn, and his stomach area was open.

The man was missing an arm. I could see his insides spilling out, and it looked like some of his innards were missing. He started lurching in my direction, and I hunkered back into the hedges. The new stumbler was coming right for me when an ear-piercing scream sounded from down the street. As one, all the stumblers turned and headed for the scream at a slow, but steady, pace.

My sigh of relief was cut short. I almost had a heart attack when I heard, "Hey," whispered from behind me. I turned and there was a man signaling me to come to him. I could only see his head and hand, as he was in a basement window. He motioned to me with his hand using a *come here* gesture. I was hesitant. Maybe this man was as bad as the others? The screaming down the street had stopped, and I grew very scared. "Come on," the man in the window said. The moans were coming back, so I decided to make a break for the window. I ran for it. The man pulled me inside, closed the window, and held me close.

"Hey," the man said. "You shouldn't be out there all alone."

I just looked at him.

"What's your name?" he asked, but I didn't answer. "It's okay, my name's Paul," he continued. "I've been down here for hours, hiding."

I must have looked frightened, because he put me down. He continued to talk in hushed whispers, but I wasn't really listening, I was exhausted. We sat there for another hour or two; the sun was just starting to stream through the broken basement window.

He started to say something when there was a crash from above. Paul looked scared now.

"They're in the house," he said. He looked around and picked up some type of tool. It looked like a monkey wrench, but I didn't know for sure. He walked to the basement stairs, and looked up. There were many shuffling footsteps upstairs. Another splintering crash, and a thump on the floor. Dust and grit filtered down on top of us.

"That door will never hold," Paul said. "We need to get out of here." Pounding started on the door at the top of the stairs. Paul ran to another basement door and opened it. There was a short flight of concrete stairs up to another set of red metal doors. Paul picked me up, climbed the stairs, and pulled back a sliding bolt on the red doors. It made a metal on metal noise that sounded like a car crash in our attempted silence.

He pushed the bulkhead doors open and stuck his head out to look. There were at least fifteen of them in the backyard. Paul hurriedly shut the metal door and shot the bolt home. Pounding started immediately on the bulkhead doors. We were trapped.

Paul ran back to the side casement window he had used to let me in. He opened it and looked out.

Nothing.

"Okay, little buddy, time to make our escape," he said.

He opened the window and helped me through. I scanned the side yard and still saw nothing. There was another crash inside the house and Paul started to climb through the window.

"They're coming!" he said. "Oh, no, I can't fit!" he added desperately. There was no way he was getting through that little window. He pulled himself back into the house and I could see through the window that the others were coming down the stairs.

Defending himself, Paul whacked the first one in the side of the head with his wrench and the attacker went down like a stone. There were many others behind the first one, but they could only come at him one at a time. Paul smacked a second one and it went down as well. There were too many though. I could see he was in trouble.

There was a screeching sound in front of the house. A car had stopped, and four people got out.

"Dad!" shouted one of them. I heard gunshots! These people had guns! They fired at the stumbling people, and one of the newcomers screamed, "In the head! Only shoot them in the head!" Not knowing what to do, I crept back to the hedges as the people ran into Paul's house. There was more shooting, and about two minutes later, Paul came out with his rescuers.

"Wait," Paul cried, "there's a..."

"Dad, we gotta go!" one of the newcomers interrupted, a young man in his early twenties.

"No, I let him out, he's on the..." Paul began.

"Dad, now!" the same young man yelled.

"Rick! They're coming!" a woman called out from the car.

The newcomers shoved Paul in the car and it screeched away. I was very happy for Paul. He had been nice to me. I was a little sad for me, though. In the space of one night I had lost everyone I had ever known. I was alone again.

I knew I couldn't stay where I was, so I dashed across the street and into the trees lining another yard.

I must have made it unseen, because nothing followed me. I climbed a tall birch tree and hunkered down. I was so tired, and though I was uncomfortable and scared, I soon drifted off to sleep. I would have a better understanding of my surroundings tomorrow.

Yesterday.

I woke up stiff. It was a long night, and I didn't get much sleep. I have been sleeping under bushes and behind trees for a few days now. There was another smell in the air, too. It smelled a little like the garbage can at my house, but thicker, and sweeter.

It was them.

The air was heavy with the stink of them.

One thing of note: It was obvious that the people that still walked around had started to rot. There were crowds of lurching pedestrians, and they all had the color of rancid cream. They had started to smell, too. I could tell when they were around because of the smell. The stink gave them away before the moans did.

In the daylight, I could see that they had terrible wounds, and they were filthy and covered in gore. I kept low, and moved quietly, and they never knew I was there. I was a picture of stealth. Not bad for someone as young as myself.

I caught a rat and ate it alive yesterday. It was disgusting, but I was starving. I remember the cracking sounds it made as I consumed it. It was awful. The blood was hot and sticky, but it made me less hungry. After I had cleaned the rat's blood off of me, I decided to explore some more. I moved into the city slowly, with eyes and ears on full alert.

The Rottens, because that's what they were, rotten, were out in force. It was relatively easy to stay hidden, they weren't that intelligent, but they did seem to have a pack mentality. When one of them would see something interesting, it would moan loudly, or screech, or hiss, or something, and others near it would come stumbling to investigate. They were like ants. You never saw just one ant. Where there's one, there's usually more. They were staggering around, some trailing pieces of themselves in a bloody swath.

I learned that if I darted out into the street and let one see me, it would undoubtedly attract the attention of others. They would come for me en masse, and I would sprint back into the trees, circle around, and come out on the other side of them, with none the wiser to my position.

This tactic worked out well unless there were too many, then I had to abort the mission and hide in the trees. It was during such an event that I almost met my downfall. I had circled around, and I couldn't see the street from my vantage point behind the burned-out hulk of a car.

I decided the risk was worth it, as there was a crashing in the brush behind me, and the cries of the Rottens were close. The smell they exuded was also permeating the air. I dashed from behind the car, and there were about ten of them right in front of me. They immediately started howling and moaning and came at me with outstretched arms. There was nothing for it, so I ran right past them, across the street and into the city. There was a crowd of about thirty of them tracking me before I was able to turn a corner and lose them. I slowed down a little, and caught my breath for a second, only to see more Rottens come around another corner. I ran between two buildings, and emerged in front of a small bridge.

At one time the bridge spanned a forty-foot wide river running through the town. The bridge was damaged though, and only half of it was there. The other half had fallen into the swift flowing river when a large truck had flipped over and exploded.

Now, half of what was left had burned anyway. There was no way across the river here. I turned back and noticed Rottens coming from three directions. I backed up toward the water and looked into it. It was murky, with no indication as to its depth. It was either the Rottens or the water. There were few of them across the river, as compared with this side, which had an ever increasing number, all eyes intent on me as their lunch. A simple jump, a little wetness, and I could swim to the other side in relative safety.

No way.

Few things terrified and disgusted me more than the Rottens, but one of them was getting wet. I hadn't yet resigned myself to a painful death at the hands—and teeth—of these disgusting creatures though, so I made a mad dash to the right. I sprinted as fast as my legs would carry me.

There were about fifteen or twenty of them between me and freedom, and I wasn't to be stopped. I sprinted straight at them, and because they were spaced out some, I was able to get through without being touched. I outdistanced the crowd that was stalking me, but there were more in twos and threes in all directions. A large building loomed in front of me, and I ran up to it. A broken basement window allowed me access to the building's interior. I squeezed through the window, and into complete darkness.

After an hour in the dark, my eyes became accustomed to my surroundings.

I found I was in a cage.

Truthfully, I was the only thing not in a cage, I quickly found out. I was in a corridor with floor to ceiling cages containing the oddest assortment of things. The things inside the cages looked like personal stuff. I deduced it was a storage area.

There was a broken door at the top of the stairs, so I quietly climbed them, carefully sticking my head out of the door at the top.

Nothing.

I listened for anything and heard distant moaning. The wind had blown some leaves through the open front door of the building. I could see some Rottens milling about out front, and I could smell them, too.

I walked softly past a few doors, one was open, but no one was home. I went inside, and it was just like the house my family had lived in before the Rottens came. There was nothing to eat here, so I took a quick look around and left. There were more doors on this floor.

All closed.

I wondered if this building was a dwelling for many people, and if each door was its own house. A set of metal stairs led to a second floor, so up I went. More doors, two open, three closed. I could smell the Rottens, but couldn't see or hear them now. I peered around the corner of the first open door. No one. After a quick exploratory jaunt through the place, I discovered a large bag of food spilled open near a bowl on the floor.

The picture on the bag had a dog on it. Dog food. Figures. I ate some, and it wasn't really that bad. There was what could only have been a dried blood smear near the food, but no one was around. After eating and drinking some water out of the toilet, I decided to further explore this new territory. I went toward the far end of the corridor when I heard a thump.

I froze.

There was a body near the end of the hall on the second floor. It had been partially eaten, and its head was virtually destroyed. It had a gun in its gnarled hand. There was also a Rotten, but it was stuck on the other side of a skinny door with a glass window. This was undoubtedly the sound I had heard before, as the creature was thumping around in what must have been a very small room.

The Rotten didn't see me, so I doubled back and continued up the stairs. More metal stairs led upwards, and I wanted to fully explore, so I followed them.

I followed the stairs up as high as they would go, two more levels, and there was a closed door at the end of the stairs. I went back down to the third level, and all the doors were closed except one. The door was splintered, and there were dark stains and smears all over it. I cautiously peeked into the room and was rewarded with more stains, and another body. This one was little more than scattered bones and clothes, but it was fresh. A skinless, jawless face peered up at me. Nothing but eyes and some hair. It was terrible. Even more so when I moved and the eyes followed me. It was alive! Just a head, and a bit of spinal column, but alive. I stepped closer to investigate, but stayed out of its reach. The thing couldn't do anything, it had no appendages.

It couldn't even bite me, it had no lower jaw. I was about to snicker to myself when I heard movement in one of the rooms behind me. A Rotten came stumbling out of an open door and looked right at me. It moaned and two more came out of the room behind it. They had been so quiet! I ran.

They followed, moaning and howling like they do. I took the stairs to the bottom floor, intent on escaping out the front door. There was a pack of them at the door, though. One had fallen over and tripped its brethren, slowing them all down. We saw each other at the same time, and they started their caterwauling.

It was either head to the basement or back up the stairs. I could hear the ones above descending the stairs, so I took off for the basement. I was down there for a few seconds, looking for a hiding place, when they reached the stairs. I had no choice but to try and escape.

I climbed some boxes near the broken window and climbed through. There were no Rottens in sight, so I stopped to catch my breath. One of them reached through the window and almost had me. I jumped out of its reach just in time. It lacerated itself on the broken glass of the window repeatedly as it tried to get through, but it couldn't fit.

I ran again.

Today.

I slunk around a wrecked car, and hid behind the rear tire, I peeked out from underneath. The street was clear. I quickly walked toward a small building. There was food in the window, but the door was closed.

It was then I heard an approaching vehicle. It was a van of some kind. The driver hadn't seen me, so I hid behind a trash barrel and watched them. It stopped across the street and a side door opened. Three figures climbed out, all with various hand weapons. One had an axe, and the other two had baseball bats. I remembered how Dad loved baseball...

"Two minutes!" one said curtly.

The three people ran to the door of the small building. They carried sacks of some kind. The man with the axe smashed the glass door and the three of them went inside. A little girl climbed out of the van with another man.

This man had a big gun. The girl sat on the edge of the van in the open door. The man scanned the area, but didn't see me. He also didn't see the Rotten that was staggering toward the van on the other side. I could hear the people in the building moving around and they were very loud.

The man stepped away from the van, and the girl called out to him, "Don't go so far away, Daddy!"

"You're right, honey, what was I thinking?" the man said. He slapped himself in the forehead with his palm and pretended to get dizzy from the slap.

"You still got it, Daddy!" the girl laughed.

Neither of them could see or hear the Rotten as it approached. It was almost on top of them. It lurched to the van and started to come around the side where the little girl was sitting.

The man had turned his back on the van to survey the area; he was chuckling to himself. The Rotten would be between the van and me in two seconds, and on the girl in five.

I let out a warning.

The man turned at my warning and saw the Rotten closing. He pointed his weapon, fired, and blew it right out of its shoes. The shot was incredibly loud on the quiet street.

"Get in the van, honey!" the man yelled.

The Rotten started to get up, and the man calmly walked over to it and shot it in the head. The man looked around to see who had alerted him, and I stepped into view.

He looked at me in surprise for a second, then beckoned for me to come to him. I started to come when the people from the building came running. They had full sacks, and one had a big bottle of water on his shoulder, with his arm over the bottle, and the baseball bat pointing back over his head.

"What happened?" the man with the axe demanded. "You all right?"

"Yeah, one of the infected snuck up on us. I took care of it."

"Nice," said one of the men. They all jumped in the van, and the man with the gun looked at me again.

"You comin'?" he asked

That was all I needed. I ran and jumped in the van. The others looked surprised, and I went right to the little girl. She looked a little older than me.

"Oh!" she said happily.

"Where'd she come from?" the driver asked.

"Dunno, but she saved me and Samantha," the man with the gun replied.

"Daddy, can she stay?" Samantha asked.

"She saved our butts, kiddo, and we're not leaving anyone to be eaten," was the reply.

"What kind is she?" Samantha asked.

"Calico, I think," her father replied as the van pulled onto the street and drove away, leaving the town behind.

MAN FESTIVAL

ALAN SPENCER

The minivan struck the curb, the collision nearly stripping off the front fender and popping the passenger side tire, but Jerry Noonan didn't care as he pursued their prized victim through yet another city block. The chase was in honor of the special day dubbed 'Man Festival', a grown-up boys' day out. No rules applied to this holiday, except to keep paving the way for further destruction and mayhem in the name of a good time, even if they were in their late sixties, and never mind that they were among the ranks of the living dead.

Gaining on their prize, he stuck his head out the open window, hollering at the man fleeing from the vehicle, "Hey man, how do you kill a zombie?"

The fleeing person half-turned his head and shot them a vexed expression while mouthing the words, "*No, no, please, no more of this,*" and then doubled his pace, weaving into a side street, trying to throw them off-course. The man was propelling himself onward with the fear of being eaten by zombies, but Jerry and his best friend, Tommy Neilson, had better plans for their victim.

"He's run about two miles so far," Tommy calculated, strategically planning their next move. He put on a visor, blocking the sun from his eyes. His entire face was beginning to revert from a mushroom gray to a blue-black bruise hue; the internal rot was advancing in the eighty-degree heat. They'd both have to hit the cryogenic chambers on their way to lunch to repair themselves. "Let's finish him now. The loaf's going to keel over any second from a heart attack."

Whooping and jeering like a wild man, Jerry hurled the words out the window as they drove up beside the desperate man, "What was it everybody used to say about zombies, how they could kill them? Do you recall, Tommy?"

He shrugged his shoulders, playing dumb. "Only this guy would know, but he's not spilling his guts."

The victim lashed out, knowing nobody on the sidewalks—all of them being the living dead—would help him. "I've never done anything to you. I only want to see my wife and kids again. I have no intention of hurting any of you people. You keep us around so you can play games with us, so go to fucking Hell! Eat shit and die! I'm not your slave, so fuck you!"

Then the man stopped running. He stood defiantly in place.

Jerry braked, beginning the stand-off on the side of the street.

Tommy fired the question this time. "How do you kill a zombie? Seriously, answer the question. What do you have to do?"

The man put his hands behind his back and tightened his mouth.

He wasn't going to speak a syllable.

"Fine," Tommy sighed, turning to his friend. "Then we'll have to answer that question for him."

The *THOOM* spewed out of the tip of Jerry's sawed-off 12-gauge, and they both shouted in unison, "YOU HAVE TO SHOOT THEM IN THE HEAD! YEAAAAAAAAH!"

Dressed in a green vest and matching reflective pants, the city worker limped toward the van and the headless body sprawled out on the street. He was an old friend of Jerry's, dating back from high school, a man name Pete 'Petey' Norris. He was limping due to the new titanium kneecap they'd transplanted in his left leg. He was looking good despite the way half his face was dripping fluids, resembling the yolk of a half-cooked egg sunny side up.

"You got yourself a real dead one, huh guys? I envy you two. You turned into zombies at the right time. You retired rich, and now you're living the good life." Petey sighed, opening up his trash bag and piecing together the remains of their victim's skull that were spread out in varying consistencies on the baking street. He snuck tastes of gray matter, also licking and sucking the blood off brittle triangles of skull fragments. "*Mmmmm*, now that's good meat." He peered up at them as another glob of clear ooze slipped out of his left eye. "You sure you're donating this body to the shelter? You don't want it for yourselves?"

"Absolutely. Those people could use a decent meal," Jerry insisted, re-loading his 12-gauge and sliding it back under the seat. They had better things to do during Man Festival than enjoy one headless body. He also thought of the zombies who didn't have limbs or could only function with antifreeze circulating through their bodies like a form of permanent dialysis; this was the treatment of the dead who either couldn't afford health care or were too damaged to live full and unfettered lives. "Hey, Petey, you'll retire in a year or two, and this will be you, hunting and eating your ass off every day."

"Yeah, I'll just wait in the meantime, you lucky son-of-a-bitch."

Tommy stepped out of the van, walking toward Petey. "Are you about to do what I think you're doing? I've seen the city workers do it so many times." Cupping his hands together, he begged, "Can I help, pretty please, Petey?"

Their friend limped to his work truck, giving in, and upon returning to the body, the man lugged one axe in each hand.

"Already got you covered, my man," he replied boisterously, handing Tommy the other axe. "Let's cut this guy into pieces and put him in a bag. I've got another call downtown, so let's get this done, chop-chop."

* * *

After Tommy got his hands bloody, Jerry drove them to the clinic made up of all-glass windows called The Cryogenic Preservation Associates. Entering the front room, a young receptionist, who'd applied massive amounts of make-up to look lifelike, though her eyes were still sinking in the back of her head, a tad too deep to pull off the trick, welcomed them. "You're both in room 202. Enjoy your treatment this afternoon."

"Thanks, Heather," Jerry said, appreciating the attention. He gave her a roll of four twenty dollar bills as a tip. "Hope you're getting through school okay."

She perked at the sight of the green. "Oh yes, I'm two semesters away from completing the insemination course. I'm working with real live people now. We've got them in rooms, male and female adults. We're engineering a spray that we shoot into the air ducts, so when they breathe it in, you see, it makes them super horny, then they mate, and then we have more children. Oh, and my boyfriend, he's working on speeding up the aging process so we can keep our meat supplies up."

"Wonderful," he clapped, honestly cheering her on. "This is the future of America, and it's looking pretty damn good."

She batted her eyes, touching her fingers to her cheeks (in doing so, mimicking the process of blushing), "You're embarrassing me. What are you guys doing today, anyway? You both seem extra peppy."

Jerry turned to face her one more time before entering the hallway that led to their chamber. "It's Man Festival!"

* * *

The room resembled a sauna with a wooden bench to sit on, but instead of lava rocks, there were two large air ducts at opposing sides of them. Once the device beyond the walls kicked on, it droned like a broken motor, and white particles were spit out and attached to their skin, resembling the foam from a fire extinguisher. The particles kept absorbing into the rotten flesh, making it stronger, solid, and seeping in deeply, it rejuvenated their organs, artificially preserving them.

"So what's next on today's roster? " Tommy asked, reaching into the mini-freezer on the floor, and sorting through the random items ranging from fleshy femur bones, a head of a woman whose lips were purposefully set in a smile with staples, a pile of hands severed at the wrist, and a bag with six inches of long intestine. The hungry man chose a hand, biting into the middle finger first; his ritual. "I know one thing. I'm starving."

Tommy offered him the hand whose middle finger was literally bone, and Jerry took a hearty bite from the stump, licking the blood that sopped free like gel. "This is damn good shit. Not that bush league junk I get in the mail from China. It comes in bulk, but it tastes like shit. Filler quality at best. This is Grade A hand." He then considered his friend's question. "Let's hit the buffet after this."

Tommy reclaimed the hand and literally flensed the flesh from the rest of the appendage. When the blowers stopped, he voiced his opinion, "Then let's get out of here. I'm glad I can't feel pain anymore. I bet it's cold as Alaska in this damn box."

* * *

The Anatomical Buffet was an establishment where any piece of the human anatomy could be fried, baked, char broiled, flambé, stir-fried, or turned into a dessert. This wondrous eatery was located at the Open Field Mall. They were nearing the buffet itself in the middle of the department stores and boutiques, when the iron-barred cage caught their attention. It was stocked with real life humans in handcuffs being held captive in the Precious Moments Photography and More display window. They would've bypassed it if it weren't for Jerry's ex-wife being one of the captives. Tommy even recognized her, the blonde woman who stayed skinny no matter what she ate, though looking at her now, she was thinner in the face, worn down from years of being stalked by the living dead.

His friend whistled, saying, "Well, Jesus be damned, look who it is. It's your ex."

Linda was hunkering down in the corner, slumped between a set of bars, when she came alive after eying Jerry for a few minutes, and seeing through the seaweed texture of his flesh, she finally remembered him. "Jerry, oh Jerry, thank God it's you! I can't believe this. It's really you." Her determination to win her freedom gave her the strength to beg him. "Liberate me, Jerry. I'll do anything, just save me from these horrible people. You might be a zombie, but I know you're not like them. You're a good, descent person as you always were. You'll buy my freedom, won't you?"

He scoffed at the notion and outwardly burst out laughing at her empty compliments. Zombies could pay a hefty sum of money to keep humans as slaves in their homes, but he had no interest in keeping her around. He'd divorced her for a reason, and today, as would be the rest of his days as a retired zombie, he was at liberty to do as he wanted, and freeing Linda didn't fall under that to-do list.

Jerry whispered to his buddy, "You want to do a photo spread? Skip the buffet and eat my ex-wife?"

* * *

The two were inside of Precious Moments Photography and More, and Linda was shackled by the wrists and ankles in rusty chains, also stripped of clothing. A green screen was stretched out behind her and a pudgy zombie in an angora sweater, blue jeans, a green beret, and a curly mustache began talking up the options with Jerry while Tommy stood in the background, admiring the naked female flesh in chains.

The photographer—named Jean-Luke—lead him to his computer monitor, the worker flipping through different scenes that would be their backdrop in the picture.

"Okay, Jerry, this is what I've got." The scenes changed according to his explanations. "You're in the Carpathian Mountains, and we can dress you up like a vampire . . ."

"Nope."

"You're a rugged man," the photographer announced with flamboyant zest, selling the scenario, "draped in your rubber apron, welding your cleaver, about to butcher the meat and shove it through the grinder, and you're really hungry, because you've got a man-sized craving for . . ."

"Sounds good, but keep going."

Tommy chimed in, "Yeah, what else you got? I'm buying, so he's going all out."

He was touched by his friend's offer. "Are you sure, man? That's easily eight hundred bucks."

"Nah, it's on me. We've been bosom buddies since they ripped us from the teat." He threw his arms up, "This is Man Festival, remember?"

Jean-Luke was affected by the man's banter. "It's Man Festival, well why didn't you two blokes tell me?"

He walked to a side door marked 'employees only' and let out five women dressed down in lacy nightwear, French bodices, and S&M gear; their flesh was pale and tinged with green-black patches, and blood congealed under the surface in blue hues. They were the kind of women you'd see on runways after they'd ravaged the super models walking them, sloppy with their gore and un-apologetic at their slovenliness. Women who liked meat and weren't afraid of getting their hands and bodies bloody in the process, and Jerry was into it.

"Yeah, bring these lovely ladies into the picture!"

Jean-Luke snapped his fingers, indicating it was show time. "It's time to earn your meat, ladies. These chicks are voracious, gentlemen, so watch out." He motioned his two patrons in close for a huddle. "I can tell you guys are no nonsense, so I'll cancel the bullshit pitch. You don't want to tear into your damsel's throat with the Eiffel Tower in the background. You want dirty women, blood and guts, all of that shit. You want a raunchy set. And don't be ashamed; I love capturing these moments. Fuck artsy."

Jean-Luke eyed Tommy, the money man. "It's up to you, Daddy Warbucks, but you can get the full-out female cannibal eating experience, and you get to keep the entire photo shoot on your hard drive." He nudged Tommy in the ribs. "And you can join in, if your buddy lets you."

"Hell yeah, Tommy's in. I'm in, too," Jerry whooped, stepping up to the undead females, embracing each one with a side hug. "Man Festival is in session!"

Linda peed herself, visibly trembling after computing what was about to happen. Jean-Luke closed the front of the store, pulling down a set of dark drapes, and as the women crowded Linda, the photographer announced in jubilation, "It looks like we're going to have to lay the tarps down for this one."

* * *

After forty minutes of flash photography and group consump-tion, Linda was two hands hanging on shackles, the rest of her was nothing more than a soupy bone pile of liquid fat and unwanted gristle, which Jean-Luke expediently wrapped up in the tarp and carted off to the trash. After the women were excused to shower off, Jean-Luke printed two T-shirts featuring Linda being eviscer-ated by six pairs of hands, Jerry and Tommy front and center with the females taking their lead.

"You think I could get this in sweater form and send it out as Christmas presents next year?" Tommy asked him as they walked out of the store with jealous eyes looking on at them and their T-shirts. "Or should I do a calendar spread?"

He gave the answer quick. "You should definitely do a calendar spread. You can make everyone jealous all year." He thought back to what Linda said to him, about wanting to be liberated. "She always thought she could make me do anything. Get me to give up custody of my son and pay her a shit load in child support as a thank you. She might've succeeded in taking my money, but in the end, I ended up taking her flesh."

* * *

Still hungry, they visited the Anatomical Buffet, and as Jerry eyed the sneeze-guarded displays of dead torsos open to free picking, garnished with baby carrots and mustard greens, he couldn't avoid the train of thought Linda had provoked.

It wasn't about her, but his other wife, Angie, who had perished during the zombie outbreak. She'd been ravaged to the point she couldn't come back as one of them; simply a head on a spine, as he recalled. The dead had smashed into their house without warning, and that was all he could remember, until he woke up craving flesh and not caring who it came from.

His son had also been slaughtered during the outbreak, as were his sister and parents. Tommy was his childhood best friend, and the only friend who'd survived up to this point as a zombie. Tommy was all he had left in life.

As Tommy loaded up his plate with a fleshy, fat tit and a pile of eyes swimming in fruit cocktail sauce, he noticed Jerry hadn't put anything on his plate yet.

"Hey, what's wrong, man? This is Man Festival, not 'That Time of the Month Festival'. What's ruining your fun, pal?" His face turned sallow. Though constantly battling rigor mortis, it was more of an overall tightening of his face, a uniform emotion. "It's Angie, isn't it?"

He nodded, that yes, indeed, she was on his mind again. "I can't help it. Seeing Linda reminded me of how it used to be."

Sitting down with only a tibia bone surrounded in barbequed flesh, he joined Tommy at one of the many tables to dine.

Shoving a spoonful of the eyes into his mouth and squashing them individually with his back molars before gulping them down, Tommy posed the scenario, "Would you prefer that you'd died, too? If you were gone instead of Angie, don't you think you'd want her to live on and be happy? Enjoy the fruits of life. Shit, we'll all be dust eventually. It's only a matter of time before our flesh doesn't hold up, and then we're eating tidbits at the soup kitchen, and then we're a meaningless pile of bones. Enjoy this, Jerry, that's what I'm saying. Live your life before you're not even *dead* anymore."

He shoved his fork into a shred of meat trapped between two creases of white bone and forced it out like crab meat, sampling it with menial vigor. "Maybe you're right, but I miss her. I wish she was alive and around like we are."

"I miss my wife, too. But there isn't a damn thing we can do about it. We're lucky we're around to keep each other busy. And we're really fucking lucky nobody..." With a pause and a meaningful look at each other, they said together," SHOT US IN THE HEAD!"

Tommy eyed his friend for another minute, and viewing no turn around, played his final card. "After we eat, I'm buying you a hooker."

* * *

Sinking into the plush red velvet bedding, Brandy relaxed beside Jerry, nuzzling him from behind, the coupling of two undead corpses in a post-coital spoon. He'd undergone a penile injection nicknamed 'The Pink Juice', and his flaccid dead worm of a dick rose to the occasion, giving Brandy a steady paycheck and a way to earn her meat.

"*Get it up, get it done,*" he muttered so low even Brandy didn't hear him as they lay in subdued quiet; it was their mantra before entering the suites at the upscale brothel called 'The Gentleman's Club', a business of legalized prostitution. At the finishing moment, he didn't ejaculate, but it was the memory of it, the action,

150

the smells, the closeness of flesh, that mimicked the sexual experience—though Brandy was quite ripe, the smells ranging from the tang of chemical preservative to raw meat wilting in the sun.

The action between the sheets always cheered him up, and he mentally thanked his friend just as the timer dinged. The half-hour was up.

Brandy released herself from him, exiting the suite. Finished with the moment, he put his clothes back on and left the suite as well.

He met up with Tommy in the lobby, an area with pink carpeted walls that featured racks of pornographic movies and novelty items ranging from dildos in all colors of the rainbow, balls and gags, engineered KY jelly to cause dead flesh to undergo a burning sensation, leather zipper suits, and various other items he didn't care to invest his attention in. He was old school. He didn't require buzzers and whistles to enjoy fucking.

He followed his friend out of the lobby and back to their van. The sun had set, and it was night. The highs of the day were beginning to mellow, and the march to their vehicle was a somber one.

Man Festival was nearing its end.

Instead of getting into the driver's seat, Tommy stepped to the back cargo area and opened it. "You thought that was it, huh, buddy? There's only one activity more enjoyable than sex."

Jerry's melancholy lifted now, he was beaming with joy, staring at the two Browning rifles tucked under a white blanket.

He knew where Tommy was taking him, and they both jumped into the van, ready to go human hunting at the range.

*　*　*

The hunting range was called The Red Zone, a ten-mile wide property of dense woods, abandoned houses, creeks, lakes, caverns, and open fields where humans acted as wildlife game, hiding and fighting for their lives as the undead embarked on a turkey shoot.

"I'll pay for this," Jerry insisted, writing out the check to the cashier wearing an orange and black camouflage vest. He was an older man chewing on a phalange in the corner of his mouth as if it were a toothpick. "Here you go, paid in full. One night's hunt for two guys on the prowl."

"You bring your own guns?" the cashier inquired, turning around to point at the walls displaying thirty different rifles. "If you want stopping power, or if you want to blow them to smithereens, you have all the options in front of you, gentlemen."

They unstrapped their Browning rifles, showing them off proudly.

"I see," the cashier said, smiling at them in approval. "Then on you go. Walk down that straightaway, make a right, and enter the facility. Once you pass the barbed fences, you're on your own. Enjoy the shooting, gentlemen!" He snuck in one last sales pitch, "And if you want a mounted display, come back when you're done with the desired appendage."

* * *

Stalking the darkness, they scouted the horizon with their night vision goggles, waiting for a smudge of red against black—that profile of heat. Jerry took the lead, anxious to blast another human.

If you're going to kill them, you gotta shoot them in the head, he kept thinking, building himself up.

It wasn't but a half hour into the expedition, stalking the edge of a creek, when they caught a human shape hunkered between two large boulders.

"*Shhh*, look to the left," Jerry whispered, pointing ahead. "There it is. Fresh meat at your nine o'clock."

"Who's got dibs?" Tommy challenged, ready to aim his gun, but Jerry beat him to it, moving on, preferring the close range action over the sniper kill. "Oh, I see. It's a competition, huh? We'll see who gets off the first shot, you son-of-a-bitch."

Jerry knew he had to move fast, slipping through a thick set of brambles and stamping through the cold creek water, almost taking a tumble when the rocky floor suddenly changed to mud.

Righting himself, he crept onto land again. The human hadn't moved, oblivious to their approach.

On his knees now, he crawled forward, having no idea where Tommy snuck off to, and keeping his momentum strong, he used a tree to bring himself back up to his feet. Ten yards from the human, he decided to take aim. He licked his trigger finger, though there was no saliva on his tongue, when suddenly there was the sharp sound of something metallic.

Firing a shot into the sky, he tumbled backwards, striking the ground, landing on his back. Jostled to the core, the sensation of every bone shifting in his flesh cage kept him motionless. In the background, he heard Tommy calling out to him, saying his name frantically. "Christ, you stepped in one of the traps! Jerry! Jerry, don't move! It's going to be okay, Jerry. Oh God, Jerry!"

And Jerry kept shouting, "Don't let him get away! Don't let the bastard get away!"

Through the thick, the winds carried the moans of the dead from near and afar. The single crack of the double-barreled shotgun echoed off every tree in Greenland Woods and slowly dissipated. The bullet hit its mark, shattering half the skull of the zombie who leaned against the tree in a sitting position.

Before being half decapitated by the blast, the zombie's eyes were glued to nothing, eying the distance without preference of purpose, so deep in thought.

"The bear trap got him," one of the hunters said, not the shooter. "He didn't gnaw his leg off like some of the other putrid bastards."

"This puss head's too stupid for that," another commented, spitting out the nub of his cigarette, the speaker also not the shooter. "He didn't even see us coming. What the fuck was that maggot buffet thinking? He was in the dead zone."

The third hunter, the actual shooter, approached the corpse. Staring down at his old friend, he mournfully spoke under his breath, "This was supposed to be a boy's night out; this wasn't supposed to happen. I-I couldn't save you, no matter what I tried." He paused, giving himself a chance to hold back his bitter tears. "Rest in peace, my friend. I'm so sorry."

Another series of shots, and another hunter cheered, "Bull's-eye!"

"Another stiff for the pile!"

"The area's clear."

Tommy apologized at the foot of Jerry's corpse one more time before moving on with his rifle in tow, as he kept helping the local militia rid the town of the recent outbreak of the living dead.

And knowing that one day, when they didn't need him any more, he too would share Jerry's fate. He was just glad he could give him the best day of his undead life before he was executed.

ADMIT ONE, UNDEAD

REBECCA BESSER

Troy Jones, Grace Hanson, Alex Keeler, and Nick O'Hara were sitting in a small, family cemetery in the woods behind the Hanson's farm. The full moon was slowly rising on the horizon, the landscape growing darker and darker with each passing minute. It was the perfect time and place for what the group had planned. What better place and time to try and raise the dead?

Of course, everyone except Alex thought it was a joke. Waiting to get started, they sat drinking the beer Nick had taken out of his old man's fridge, and smoking the weed Grace had provided.

"You know what we should do after we're done with this sh . . ." Troy stopped in mid-sentence when Alex's elbow made contact with his stomach. "Hey, what was that for?"

"You were about to say shit, weren't you?" she asked with her hands on her hips. "I can't believe you're being such a dick."

"Sorry, babe," Troy said, trying to placate his girlfriend. "You know I don't believe in all this supernatural, voodoo stuff."

"It's not voodoo," Alex said, huffing and crossing her arms.

Troy leaned over and kissed her cheek. "I'm really sorry."

Grace held a joint out to Alex. "Here, this will make you feel better, and get you in the mind set for the ritual."

Nick laughed and almost spit beer on them all, but covered his mouth at the last moment.

"Anyway, as I was saying," Troy said. "I think after we get done with the 'ritual', we should go to the carnival in Dresden."

Grace grimaced with disgust. "We aren't babies anymore. Why would we want to go to some stupid carnival?"

"Yeah," Nick threw in for good measure as he finished off his third beer.

"Because, we'll be all messed up," Troy said, grabbing a bottle for himself before Nick drank it all. "Everything will be awesome!"

Grace took the joint back from Alex and took a long drag.

"Sounds fine to me," Alex said with a giggle. "I love cotton candy. Haven't had any of that for a long time."

Nick nodded eagerly. "You think they'll have nachos? I could go for a big bowl of nachos right now. All covered with cheese."

Troy laughed, and took his turn with the weed. "They'll have all kinds of food. We can eat 'til we puke and then go on some rides or something."

Nick stood up and made his way over to the edge of the woods, weaving back and forth the entire time. Unzipping his pants, he moaned as he relieved his bladder.

Grace giggled. "If we are going to go to the carnival, I guess we'd better get this thing started. I've got the munchies bad!"

Alex laughed, dug through her bag, and retrieved a bottle of what she said was a 'potion' that would bring the dead back to life. She also pulled out the book with the incantation, which was supposed to give the potion its 'power'.

Troy rolled his eyes and winked at Grace. She covered her mouth with her hand to suppress a giggle.

They had been to various cemeteries, and done the same ritual many times before. It never worked. But, for some reason, Alex was obsessed with the occult and raising people from the dead. She said she wouldn't give up until she had done it. So being the supportive friends that they were, they went along with it. Besides, they always had a great time partying out in the middle of nowhere.

"You guys ready?" Alex asked as Nick sat back down. "Everyone join hands . . ."

The ritual had begun. They said what they were told to say, chanted when they were supposed to chant, and lit the candles Alex had set up in front of each one of them, around their chosen grave. After all that was done, Alex poured the 'potion' on the grave, starting at the head, straight down the center, to the feet.

They waited, watching. Nothing happened, as usual.

"Okay," Alex said with a sigh. "I guess it didn't work...again. We did everything right. I don't know what went wrong."

Troy leaned over and gave Alex a one-armed hug, kissing the top of her head when she let it fall on his shoulder.

"It's okay, babe," he said gently. "We'll try again another time. I'll buy you the biggest bag of cotton candy we can find. Will that make you feel better?"

Alex giggled, rose up on her knees, wrapped her arms around Troy's neck, and kissed him.

"I guess that was a yes," Troy said with a grin, as she pulled away.

"Let's get going," Grace said, standing and brushing dirt and dry leaves from her butt. "I'm starved! I hope they have hotdogs. A hotdog with all the fixin's sounds really good."

Nick stood and grinned. "I've got a hotdog for you, if you want to eat one."

Grace rolled her eyes and shoved Nick playfully. "That's not what I meant and you know it. Quit trying to pimp yourself off on me."

They were all standing now, and turned to walk back to Troy's car that was parked behind a corn field where no one could see it.

"Hold on a sec," Nick said, turning back. "I gotta leak the lizard again."

Troy, Alex, and Grace shook their heads and kept walking.

"We'll meet you at the car," Troy yelled back over his shoulder.

Nick waved an acknowledgment as he unzipped and peed on the grave they had just been sitting around. He started singing and watched the lightning bugs flitting around him.

When he looked down again, he saw that one of the candles had fallen over and there was something white sticking out of the ground beside it. Zipping up, he knelt down to see what it was, thinking they might have dropped something.

Just looking at it, he couldn't figure out what it was, so he touched it. It was hard and kind of smooth. Tugging gently, he extracted it from the hard packed dirt.

It was a human finger bone!

With a yelp, he dropped it and stood up, wiping his hands on his jeans. His eyes scanned back and forth over the grave to see if there was anything else weird. As he watched, the earth shifted. He turned to yell to the others as the hand the finger had come from shot up out of the ground and grabbed his ankle.

Nick screamed.

Kicking and trying to dislodge his leg from the vise-like grip, he was shocked to see a head and a torso break through the ground. Bugs and dirt clung to the skull. The eyes were nothing more than hollow voids, staring out at nothing.

Nick was too paralyzed with fear to even scream. He just stood there in shock, watching the body pull itself out of the grave.

Holy shit, he thought, *it worked!*

As he came back to his senses, Nick tried again to kick free, but the grip was too strong.

The person they had brought back to life gave Nick's leg a sudden jerk and a twist, throwing him to the ground.

"Maaaaaa," it moaned, as it sank its teeth into the exposed skin of his ankle.

Nick cried out with pain, groping at the ground around him, trying to get away or at least find something to beat the thing off him with.

He screamed again as he felt his flesh tearing, and looked back to see the zombie happily munching on what it had torn off. He started to cry, instantly sobered by what was happening to him.

He tried more frantically to get away, his hand landing on a rock. He grabbed it, turned on the ghoul, and slammed the rock down on its head. It took five hard *whacks* before the creature stopped moving. Its bug-filled skull now lay shattered around it on the ground. Insects swarmed and ran in every direction, trying to figure out where their home had gone.

Nick dragged himself away, out of the zombie's grip, and fell back onto the ground, panting and sobbing. After a moment, he sat up and looked at his ankle. It wasn't as bad as he expected. Only a small piece of skin was missing.

He glanced over at the skull, wiping tears from his eyes with the back of his hand. The ghoul was missing quite a few teeth, and that was probably why he hadn't sustained a more serious injury.

Hurriedly, Nick stood and ran toward the path where the others had disappeared on their way to the car. He hobbled awkwardly because of the wound, but he wanted to get away from the cursed place as fast as he could.

* * *

Troy, Alex, and Grace were sitting in the car, waiting for Nick. They had the radio blaring and were rocking out to their favorite band, while smoking another joint. The passing of time didn't register to them.

They all jumped when Nick tore open the rear passenger door and started ranting.

"We did it!" Nick yelled to be heard over the music. "We brought that bastard back from the dead, and he bit me! It was a zombie! The damn thing bit my leg! Look!"

He pulled up his pant leg and showed them all the two inch by one inch bloody wound where a patch of skin was missing.

Alex frowned, turning down the radio. "Are you making fun of me? Because I don't like it. Is this some kind of a sick joke?"

"No, no," Nick said, shaking. "I'm telling the truth! Come look, the body's still there."

Grace said nothing, just watched as Alex bowed her head and stared at her hands.

Troy noticed Alex's dejected posture as well. "Get in the car, Nick, before I decide to get out and kick your ass."

"I'm serious, you guys," Nick pleaded. "Listen to me! There was a zombie, a real zombie, and it bit me!"

Troy slammed his fist down on the back of the front seat. "This is your last chance. Shut your hole and get in the car, or I'm leaving you here."

Nick swallowed hard, glanced over his shoulder, and decided the safest idea would be to get in the car. He didn't like that they didn't believe him, but he could convince them, over time, he supposed.

Nodding silently, Nick slid into the back seat with Grace, looked down at the floor board, and shut the door securely behind him.

Alex was sniffling in the front seat, Troy was trying to calm her down, throwing dirty looks at Nick every now and again. Finally, Troy got her to stop crying and they departed for the carnival.

Grace leaned over to Nick and snarled. "Nice one, jackass. You shouldn't make fun of Alex and tease her like that, you know she's sensitive. Why do you have to be such a dick?"

Nick didn't answer. He just looked out the window. Maybe they were right, maybe nothing did happen. It could have been his imagination. He was drunk and high after all.

The rocking of the car made Nick tired. He knew they had an hour drive to where the carnival was, and since no one was talking to him, he decided he might as well get some rest. His ankle was burning and he was feeling very lethargic. It didn't take him long to fall asleep.

* * *

When they arrived at the carnival, Grace shook Nick, waking him. He opened his eyes with a moan.

"We're here," she said and got out of the car.

Nick caught another dirty look from Troy as he got out also. Apparently, Alex had already made her exit, because she was standing in front of the car. Troy walked over and hugged her, rubbing her back in a comforting manner.

Nick felt bad for upsetting Alex, but if she would just listen, she would realize she had succeeded and would be happy. He didn't know how to convince her. Besides, Troy was very protective. Nick knew he wouldn't be allowed within five feet of her for the rest of the night.

As Nick stood beside the car, he became dizzy and disoriented. The world spun around him in a blur of lights and colors. Sounds faded in and out, and a couple of times his vision went black and he couldn't see at all. Of all his senses, taste and smell were the strongest. He could smell all the people, all the food, all the exhaust fumes from the running machinery. He could taste a cheese burger like he had just taken a bite.

"You coming?" Grace asked.

"Huh?" Nick licked his lips and shook his head. On top of everything else, he felt like he had a fever.

"Are you coming? To the carnival? Or are you going to stay out here by yourself all night?"

"I'm coming," Nick said and followed his friends as they wove through the mass of parked cars and made their way to the ticket counter.

It was hard for Nick to keep up. His leg hurt like hell. He had to keep stopping and rubbing his calf and thigh. The bite on his ankle was hurting worse, but he didn't want to say anything, afraid he would piss everyone off more.

Nick dug out his wallet, and grabbed Grace's wrist as she slid her hand into her pocket. "I got this."

She looked up at him and opened her mouth like she was going to refuse, but stopped. She frowned.

"You don't look good, Nick. Are you sure you don't want to go lay down in the car for a while?"

Nick shook his head, grinning. "No, I feel great. Honest."

Grace was still frowning as he bought their tickets. She took the blue ticket that said **ADMIT ONE**, and shoved it into her pocket to keep it safe.

"You sure you're okay?" Grace asked again, laying her hand on his arm with concern.

"Yeah," Nick said. "Let's go get that hotdog you wanted."

Grace giggled. "Okay."

Troy and Alex were already in line at the French fry stand.

Nick walked up to Troy and handed him a five dollar bill. "Grab me some nachos, and some fries for Grace. Do you guys want anything from the sandwich stand?"

Troy looked at Nick for a moment, his eyes hard, letting Nick know he wasn't forgiven yet. "Sure. Get me a hotdog with everything and Alex a cheeseburger with just ketchup. Think you can handle that?"

Nick decided to ignore Troy's sarcasm. "Got it. See you guys in a sec!"

Grace smiled as Nick joined her in line. He marveled at how pretty she was. It still caught him by surprise how much they had all changed over the last few years. It seemed only yesterday they had been freshman, and in a couple more months they would be graduating from high school. He had never thought any of them would be attracted to each other, having been friends for so long.

But when Troy and Alex started dating, he couldn't help thinking maybe he and Grace might get something started as well.

Nick smiled back. They talked and joked as the line slowly moved forward.

Finally, it was their turn to order. The smell of raw meat drove Nick crazy for a moment. He had a sudden urge to jump over the counter and stuff as many raw burgers in his mouth as he could. Closing his eyes and taking a few quick, deep breaths, he regained control of himself.

Nick quickly rattled off what they needed and then looked around for Troy, to see if he needed to buy drinks, too.

He found him and they made eye contact. Nick cupped his hand and tilted it up like he was drinking, then nodded yes, and shook his head no. Troy nodded yes. Nick gave him a thumbs up and ordered drinks before paying.

Laden down with sandwiches and drinks, Nick and Grace joined Troy and Alex at the small table they had found. It was sticky from ice cream drippings that had dried and left a pink and white goo, but after covering the mess with a couple of napkins, it was nearly perfect for the teens.

Alex wouldn't look at Nick, but he was glad to see she was smiling and laughing. He still hadn't figured out how he was going to convince her that he hadn't been making fun of her, but were telling the truth.

Soon, Nick forgot all about the misunderstanding as he felt Grace's leg press against his under the table. At one point during their meal, she gave him a hug and kissed his cheek in jest. He couldn't help but blush, which made everyone laugh.

After they finished eating, they decided to go on some rides. Taking their tickets to the ride booth, they got their wrist bands, and then made their way to the Ferris wheel, waited in line, and took their ride. Troy and Alex went in one seat, and Nick and Grace went in the next.

They moved slowly as the empty seats were filled. At one point, they stopped at the top for a long time. Nick looked behind them, ready to wave at Troy and Alex, but they were too busy making out to notice him.

Nick glanced sideways at Grace, wondering what it would be like to kiss her. He put his arm across the seat behind her, and was about to ask her if she liked him, when they started moving again. Grace squealed with delight and sat forward, and then back quickly, making their seat swing. They laughed and enjoyed the rest of the ride.

When it was over, Nick started to feel nauseous. He had never had problems with motion sickness before, in fact, he was the one that usually rode the wildest rides with no problem whatsoever, no matter how much he had eaten. But right now, he felt very sick.

Troy looked at Nick. "Are you all right, man? You look like you're gonna hurl."

Nick was about to say he was fine, but instead ran to the nearest trash can and threw up everything he'd just eaten.

When he was done, Nick looked up to see Grace standing beside him.

"You okay?" she asked gently, rubbing his back.

"I think I'll live," he moaned. "I don't know what's gotten into me. I don't ever get sick."

But something was nagging at the back of his mind—the zombie, the bite. He had seen plenty of movies about the undead and he knew how it all worked, but he thought you had to die before you turned into a zombie. He wasn't even close to dying as far as he knew.

He started to feel sick again, and stuck his head back over the trash can just in time. It was too dark where they were for him to realize he was now puking blood.

"I'll go get you something to drink," Grace said and rushed off.

Nick nodded and turned, letting his back slide against the metal barrel that served as waste disposal. He sat on the ground, leaning against it with his eyes closed, waiting for Grace to come back with a drink.

"I got you Sprite," Grace said, kneeling down beside him.

He weakly lifted his hand and took the cup. "Thanks."

"Do you want to go back to the car?" she asked. "I'll go with you. I don't think you should be alone right now, as sick as you are."

Nick nodded.

"Okay, I'll go tell Troy and Alex. I saw them standing in line for another ride."

Nick watched Grace's butt as she scampered off, thinking it would be nice to be alone with her. He just wished he didn't feel so bad. Pushing himself up from the ground, he wiped his mouth on the wet napkin that was wrapped around his drink, and threw it in the trash. Stumbling along, he started toward the car.

Grace caught up with him when he was halfway there. "Why didn't you wait for me? I would have helped you."

She ducked under one of his arms and wrapped her arm around his waist.

He turned his head and smelled her hair.

This was definitely a good idea, he thought.

Before long they were at the car. Grace helped him into the back seat, and went around the car and got in beside him.

He laid his head on her shoulder and moaned.

"Is that better?" she asked as she stroked his hair.

"Yes," he sighed.

He was almost asleep when his stomach began to gurgle again. Hurriedly, he sat up, opened the door, and threw up more blood. The dome light gave off enough of a glow for him to see that his vomit was red, but he was too weak, and his brain was too tired, to process what was happening.

Closing the door, he lay down, using Grace's leg as a pillow. Soon he fell asleep. Not long after, so did she.

In her sleep, Grace didn't notice when Nick stopped breathing and died. She didn't notice when he opened his eyes again, or that they were now vacant and cloudy. But she did notice when he started grabbing at her.

"Hey, what're you doing?" Grace mumbled as Nick's rough handling woke her up.

"Maaaaaa!" Nick moaned, as he took a hold of her shoulders, violently pinning her to the seat.

"Get off me, Nick!" Grace yelled, beating on his chest. "You're hurting me!"

He didn't respond to her, just held her down and lowered his head toward hers. She thought he was trying to kiss her.

"No, damn it," Grace said. "You're such a creep."

She brought her knee up and slammed it into his crotch, but it had no effect on him. Panicking, she threw open the car door and screamed. It was cut short as Nick clamped his teeth on her throat and tore out her windpipe.

Blood sprayed everywhere as he tossed his head back and forth, tearing off a chunk of flesh to enjoy. After chewing and swallowing, he bit off another, and another, devouring her until her blood went cold.

No longer satisfied with his kill, Nick staggered out of the open car door and followed his nose. He smelled blood—sweet, hot, living blood. People were close by, and a lot of them.

His body was slow, not wanting to work like it used to. Inwardly, he was frustrated at how long it was taking him to get to the food he sensed was near.

Finally, he arrived at the ticket stand. The man behind the counter was alone, reading a book. He set it down without looking up.

"How many?"

"Maaaa . . ." Nick responded, before reaching out and grabbing the man by the neck, dragging him across the counter.

The man screamed and pawed at Nick's face.

Nick grabbed the man's wrist and bit off his fingers, one by one. Blood shot out with each crunch of bone and rip of flesh.

The man flailed and screamed, pleading for mercy, calling for help. No one heard him. The noise of the people and the carnival attractions covered his torture.

After sucking all the blood he could out of the man's hand, Nick went for the main course. He threw the man to the ground and knelt over him.

He tore open his stomach and devoured whatever he could reach, thrusting his face into the man's chest cavity, eating like a wild animal that had been starving for weeks. The man convulsed as his body died, his eyes stared off into the distance, where people played and laughed while he was consumed.

When Nick was finished, he got up and moved further into the carnival.

People screamed as they noticed him. His clothes were soaked with blood. It still dripped from his teeth and chin. A small piece of intestine still clung to his bottom lip.

Nick growled and clawed at people as he went through them. In places where they were bunched into crowds, he went through biting as many people as he could. It was like a snack buffet to him. A young girl here, an old man there, then a teen—there were just so many to choose from and enjoy.

He had a bite of them all.

* * *

Troy and Alex had just gotten off of another ride, *The Tunnel of Terror,* and were trying to decide what to go on next, when Troy noticed the screaming.

"What the hell is going on?" Troy yelled, standing on his tip toes, trying to see why people were freaking out.

"Maybe they have someone dressed up as something scary," Alex said. "Let's go see."

She grabbed Troy's hand and dragged him into the fleeing, screaming crowd of people–stopping dead in her tracks when she spotted Nick biting everyone.

"Oh," she breathed. "He was telling the truth."

"Holy shit!" Troy yelled, staring in amazement as one of his best friends tackled an old woman to the ground, biting and ripping at her flesh. Blood shot out onto the people that were still trying to get away. Behind Nick was a swathing path of bodies, lying, bleeding, dying.

They stood mesmerized, watching Nick feed on his kill. But when the bodies left in Nick's wake began to get up and look for food of their own, they finally got moving.

"Quick," Troy said, tugging on Alex's hand. "We have to get out of here or they'll get us, too! Damn, there's at least twenty of them."

As Troy turned, he ran straight into the ticket man's soggy, wide-open chest. Blood squished between them and entrails fell on Troy's shoe.

The man stared down at Troy, and lifted his arm to grab him, but Troy was too fast.

Darting around the zombie ticket seller, Troy and Alex escaped. He didn't follow them, because people were still running in his direction—from Nick and the other zombies that were amassing behind him. He grabbed a screaming teen girl and soon ended her horror in a bath of blood. Grinning, he lapped up the blood like a thirsty dog.

Troy and Alex left the carnival for the field surrounding it, figuring they would be safer there. They circled around to the parking lot, which was just another part of the field where the festivities had been set up.

Alex barreled around the car to the passenger's side, slamming the rear door that had been left open, as she got into the front beside Troy.

He started the engine and stomped on the gas pedal so hard, they slammed into the cars parked across the dirt road behind them.

"Careful!" she cried out. "We don't want to get stuck here!"

"I know, I know," he growled, pulling forward and then backing up again, cranking the wheel at a sharper angle. Shifting into drive, they were off, flying down the dirt road at a reckless speed.

A clicking sound rose from the back seat. Troy and Alex looked at each other with fear in their eyes.

Cautiously, Alex peeked into the back seat, ducking down again with a squeal.

"What is it?" Troy asked anxiously. "What's back there?"

Alex swallowed hard. "Grace. But, well, she's not Grace anymore."

"What do you mean?"

"She's one of them," Alex said with tears in her eyes.

"Shit," Troy said, swerving to a stop alongside the road. "We've got to get her out of here."

Getting out, he walked around to the passenger side of the car, yanked open the back door, and instantly turned away to vomit.

The back seat of his car was covered in blood and guts, and Grace, if you could still call her that, was nothing more than a mangled mess of limbs.

Her arms hung by strained tendons. Her legs had been completely ripped off, and her head hung at an odd angle, held on by nothing more than an inch thick piece of skin.

She looked as if she had been hacked and stretched by a berserk psychopath.

But what really freaked Troy out, was her face. It was eaten away to the point of not being a face any more. Stringy bits of red muscle hung down, making her look like a shaggy-faced, red dog.

She was opening and closing her mouth rapidly, which was the source of the clicking noise.

"What should I do with her?" Troy asked, wiping his mouth with the back of his hand, gagging again as he looked into the car.

"I don't know," Alex said, peeking over the seat again. "I guess just drag her out and leave her. I mean, it's not like she's Grace anymore."

He nodded and tentatively took hold of one severed leg, tossing it into the ditch that ran alongside the dirt road, with a shudder of revulsion.

He quickly did the same with the other. When he went to pull her out by her arm, it tore the rest of the way off and sent him sprawling to the ground. The limb landed on his chest, the hand convulsing and gripping his shirt.

Troy screamed, grabbed the arm, and threw it over his head into the ditch with the legs. Lying back, he closed his eyes and took a deep breath.

"You okay?" Alex asked with concern.

Troy lifted his head. "Yeah, I think so."

Standing, Troy took hold of Grace's other arm, twisting it and pulling steadily, cringing at the squishing, tearing, snapping noise it made. It broke loose with a loud *pop*, jarring Troy, but he didn't fall.

"That's gross," Alex said, and gagged.

Troy gave her a *no shit!* look and tossed the arm over his shoulder. It landed in the ditch with the other limbs.

He stood there, looking down at the creature that used to be one of his best friends, blown away by what she had become.

"Why did we do this?" he whispered. "Why did we have to bring someone back from the dead? Two of our friends are now zombies! It's so wrong."

Tears slid down Alex's cheeks. She felt responsible for all the bad things that were happening. Nothing anyone did could stop it now.

"I'm sorry," Alex whimpered.

Troy shrugged, not looking at his girlfriend. Without showing anymore emotion or revulsion, he gripped what used to be Grace's waist and dragged her out of the car. Her head thumped off the seat, onto the floor, and then out onto the ground.

The zombie kept snapping her teeth together, hoping to get a bite of one of them.

Troy ignored the sound, and left her body with her limbs. But as he turned to walk back to the car, he got a little too close to her mouth. She barely pinched his skin with her teeth, and made him jump away.

He ran to the car, not thinking he was really bitten. He didn't look at his ankle, and he didn't see the single drop of blood leaking out of his broken skin.

*   *   *

Troy took Alex to a cabin in the woods, owned by his parents and only used for vacation.

"We should be safe here for a little while," he said, getting the key from a key box that looked like a rock. "I know there is a good bit of water and food stored in the pantry. My parents always keep it fully stocked."

"Sounds good," Alex said quietly. She knew Troy was upset, and she still blamed herself. If she hadn't pushed everyone to try and raise the dead, none of this would have happened.

"I'm going to go take a shower," Troy said. "The bedroom is that way, if you want to go lay down. I'll be there in a few minutes."

Alex nodded and went through the doorway he'd indicated and just stood looking at the bed. She was frightened and wanted to crawl into a deep hole and die for what she'd done.

Shrugging, she decided the bed and sleep were the closest she would get.

She took off her shoes and pants, leaving her shirt, bra, underwear, and socks on. After climbing into the queen size bed, she pulled the quilt up to her neck and closed her eyes, but she didn't fall asleep.

As thoughts of Grace and Nick clouded her mind, tears slid out of her closed eyes and onto the smooth, cotton pillowcase.

Eventually, she fell asleep. She didn't hear Troy enter the room, or feel him crawl across the bed. She didn't feel him slide the blanket down her body.

Alex awoke with a start as cold hands gripped her thighs and teeth penetrated her flesh. She screamed and tried to pull away, but it was no use.

Troy's cold hands were too strong, his hunger too great, and her will to live too weak.

He feasted on her flesh, and after she died and turned, they went out into the world together, looking for food.

What was stored in the pantry wouldn't satisfy their hunger.

QUALITY SECURITY

MARIAH DEITRICK

John Marks hurried to get ready for his job interview. He didn't want to be late. Jobs didn't come around that often anymore, and he was lucky to stumble across this one. He'd been looking for work for four months–since the canning factory he worked at closed. John was thankful that he didn't have a family to support like hundreds of others that had lost their jobs along with him. He was having a hard enough time surviving with only himself. He couldn't even imagine how difficult it must be for those with families to support, but a new company was hiring one hundred new employees. That wouldn't help everyone who had lost their job, but it was a good start.

He pulled into the parking lot of Quality Security with fifteen minutes to spare. He wasn't exactly sure what they did, but at this point he didn't really care. He was two months behind on all of his bills, and his landlord had sent an eviction notice two days ago. This was his last chance before becoming a thirty-year-old living at home with his mom. He shuddered at the thought.

Inside the large, steel building was a small desk with a thin, dark haired, young woman sitting behind it and a few decorations, but nothing else, not even chairs to sit in while you waited. For a minute he thought he had come to the wrong doors.

"Can I help you?" the woman asked.

"I have an interview at ten," he told her.

"Take the elevator to level one," she instructed, pointing at a hallway hidden behind a large Ficus tree.

"Thank you," he said, and headed down the hall.

Once inside the elevator, he went to push level one, but the buttons were locked. There was a spot to put a key in each level, but no way to push it. He started getting back off when the doors slammed shut and the elevator dropped, causing his stomach to drop with it. He reached for the railing, but the ride was over before he got a hold of it.

The doors flew open to a man standing on the other side. He was a distinguished man who dressed extremely well. Obviously someone important around here, John thought.

"Welcome," the man greeted him, holding out a hand to shake John's.

"Thank you," John said, reaching his hand out in return.

"I'm Dr. Andrews," the man said, introducing himself. "I'm the head of the human resource department. You must be John Marks?"

John nodded, and Dr. Andrews led him down a long, narrow hallway to his office. They passed several other doors on the way to his office, but they were all closed, with no name plates on them.

"So, tell me about yourself," Dr. Andrews said, once he was sitting behind his desk facing John. "Do you have kids?"

That sounded like an odd question for an interview, but John answered anyway. "No," he said, and then changed the subject to his work history. "I worked at the local canning factory, before they closed down, for twelve years, and before that at the grocery store as a night stockman."

Those were the only two jobs he'd had, but he started working when he was fifteen and continued until four months ago. He hoped his impeccable work history would be enough to get him the job.

"Wow. That's quite impressive for a man your age," Dr. Andrews sounded pleased. "Most young people I've interviewed have had dozens of jobs." He opened a drawer in his desk. "Here's a quick sheet I need you fill out before you get started."

John took the sheet from the man, and a pen. It looked similar to something he had filled out when he started at the factory. It was a questionnaire about his health and lifting abilities. When he was done, he signed it and handed it back.

Dr. Andrews went on to give some history of the company, and explained the rules. None of which seemed to explain what they did here, but John didn't want to ask. It all sounded perfect to him. Not only was he getting a great job with great pay, he was getting an apartment, too–the company offered free housing to their employees.

John shook Dr. Andrews' hand again, and promised to be ready to work on Monday. Two days wasn't much time to pack and move, but with help, he got all of his belongings out of his apartment and into the new one by Sunday night.

His new place was perfect–just like the new job. A one bedroom, fully furnished apartment with a cafeteria right down the hall. What more could a single man ask for? he wondered. He had found his dream job, and he planned on keeping it.

Orientation started at six on Monday morning, and John was the first one in the meeting room. On the table in front of every chair lay a packet, notebook, and a pen. He thumbed through the packet while he waited for others to join him, but no one else came. He was the only one, until a woman walked in right at six o'clock.

"Looks like it's just you and me," John said, looking around the empty room.

"Actually," the woman said, "I'm Dr. Mason. I'll be doing your training." She chuckled and set her briefcase on the table.

"Oh," John replied, feeling foolish. "Am I the only one then?" he asked.

"There are others, but they're in another group," she went around and picked up all the packets. "They are being trained for a different job." The slender woman stopped and looked John in the eye. "Dr. Andrews must have really liked you. He has given you a very important job here."

John had a sense of pride when she said that. He had worked hard all his life, and now it was paying off.

"What exactly is the position?" he asked, feeling comfortable asking about the job now that he knew he was here to stay.

"You are going to be on quality control," she answered. "It's the best job you can start out in here, and we need to get you started right away." She pulled a new paper out of her briefcase. "I need you to read this and sign it before I can take you to the floor."

John looked over the paper she slid across the table to him. It was a contract.

"What's this?" he asked.

"Just precaution," she shrugged. "It pretty much says you aren't allowed to talk about anything you see here, or your job. It's classified information and you *will* be terminated on the spot if you break these rules."

"Sounds good to me," he said, not bothering to read the entire contract before signing.

"Thank you," Dr. Mason said, slipping the contract back into her briefcase. "Now, I need you to change into your uniform."

"I didn't get a uniform," he said.

"There are extra ones in the dressing room." She pointed to the door at the back of the room.

John jumped to his feet and hurried to get changed. The uniform consisted of all white scrubs, with a white lab coat. Dr. Mason also gave him a badge with his name on it, a spray bottle with some sort of liquid in it to keep in his pocket, and a set of keys. "Believe me. You're going to need that," she warned, pointing at the bottle. "If you need more at anytime let me know. Don't ever let it run out," she said firmly. "You'll find out its going to be your life support."

"What is it?" he asked, looking at the strange bottle.

"You'll find out soon enough, but for now you need to follow me."

John shoved the bottle in his pocket and followed her to the elevators at the end of the hall. She pulled out her keys and stuck one in the lower level button. That must be what his keys were for, he thought and smiled. He must be getting a good job if they were giving him keys already.

When the elevator doors opened, Dr. Mason headed down the hall toward the double doors at the end. "This floor is where all the research is done," she explained.

John looked in the windows as they passed. Each room had a locked door, and several employees dressed in protective suites, gloves, and face masks. They were all being extremely careful with whatever the liquid was they were holding.

Dr. Mason stopped at the last door. "This is where you can exchange your bottle for refills if you can't find me, but you must have permission first. And you need to sign out all new bottles. Each bottle has a number. You have to put that on the sheet, too." She tapped a clip board hanging on the outside of the door.

John looked through the window. There were hundreds of bottles, like the one she had given him, on shelves all around the room. She wasn't lying about needing it, he thought. They wouldn't fill that many bottles if it wasn't necessary.

"Let's keep moving," she said, unlocking the double doors.

He nodded in agreement, eager to see his new job.

Beyond the double doors was another elevator. It seemed strange to him that it was the only thing behind them. The elevators also took a key to get where you wanted to go. He couldn't understand why they needed extra security at this elevator, too.

Once again, Dr. Mason put her key in, but this time it was for a level that wasn't an option in the other elevator—Containment. He had never seen that on an elevator before. In all the elevators he had ever ridden in, they'd had numbers or letters, not full words.

"When we get down there, I want you to hurry off," she instructed, and he did while she quickly placed her key in the lower level key hole, and sent the elevator back up. "You can never leave the elevator on this floor," she warned with stern eyes.

John felt like a child getting scolded by his mother when he looked at her. "Okay," he said, not knowing how else to respond.

"We need to go in there for de-scenting," she explained, nodding toward a glass door behind him. It looked almost like a fish tank with a door on the side to him.

"What's that for?" He had only heard of people de-scenting if they were going hunting or working with animals of some kind. He didn't understand why they would need to do that here. He thought from the name that it was a security factory, and the woman had told him he would be on quality control. He assumed that was inspecting security items like cameras and alarms.

"Your job is beyond this point. Anyone crossing over has to be de-scented," she said, not really answering his question.

She pushed a button on the wall, and a man's voice came through a speaker next to it. "Good morning, Dr. Mason."

"Good morning, Chuck. We need to pass," she raised her badge to a camera and nudged John to do the same.

"Allowed," the man said.

"Thank you," she replied. "Let's go."

The glass door slid open in seconds. John peeked in before going all the way through. Large sprayers lined the walls, and another door was on the opposite side, but it was steel.

"It's okay. Just hold your breath," she said, as the chamber started filling with smoke. "It can make you cough if you breathe it in."

He took a deep breath and held it like she had instructed. Smoke filled the chamber, making it impossible to see for a moment, but then a large vacuum turned on over head and the smoke was pulled up, and out, of the chamber in seconds.

"See, not bad, eh?" she smiled. "You get used to it."

"I guess it will take some getting used to," John agreed.

"Are you ready to see what we do here?" she asked, before pushing the button again.

"I think so," John answered honestly. He wanted to see his new job, but he was anxious about what was coming next. Bears or lions? he wondered. It had to be something big.

"Ready," she spoke into the speaker again, and the door unlocked with a loud click.

The heavy door moved quickly, to John's surprise. It looked to be about three feet thick, and made of solid steel. But it still moved effortlessly across the tracks in the floor and ceiling.

"Keep your spray close," she whispered, "and keep quiet until we get past Section A."

He looked at her with wide eyes. What the hell did they have down here? he wondered. He wasn't so sure he wanted to find out anymore, but he followed her instructions and gripped the bottle in his pocket tightly, not saying a word.

She walked up to the first window—it stretched from floor to ceiling—and stopped for John to peer in.

What he saw standing on the other side was horrifying, and he gasped. That only made things worse. The creature on the other side lunged at the glass, causing an up roar all the way down the hall. Growls echoed throughout the corridor, and every creature in the section banged on the glass, trying to break free.

Dr. Mason grabbed John by the arm and dragged him out of Section A.

"What was that?" she asked furiously. "What part of, 'keep quiet', did you not understand?" she reached over and pushed a red button setting of an alarm.

"What the hell was that?" he demanded. He had never seen anything like it, and he wasn't sure exactly what *it* was. It almost looked human, but not quite–covered in blood and sores. It was repulsive.

"Zombies," she said. "Now, listen, we need to get to Section D. I'll explain everything there," she urged him forward.

He reluctantly followed her, keeping his eyes in front of him. He would surly cause a scene again if he even glanced toward the monsters, and that was obviously not something he wanted to do.

When they finally reached Section D, Dr. Mason led him into an office. "This is your office," she said, as if that was going to make everything he had just seen go away.

"What? You really expect me to stay after what I've just witnessed?" He was confused by all of this, but he wasn't stupid.

"Let me explain," she said firmly. "You signed a contract with us. You must perform the duties of your job. You are not allowed to talk to anyone outside of here about this, and I must warn you, the consequences are not pleasant."

"You can't keep me here," he argued. There was no contract in the world that was going to keep him here now.

"Listen, Dr. Andrews obviously saw something in you that he liked," she said, more gently now. "I'm going to do you a favor and show you what happens to those that do not follow the contract. There is no law suit." She explained and pulled him out of the office.

"Where are you taking me?" he asked, pulling his arm from her grasp. She didn't answer. She reached back and grabbed him again, dragging him to a staircase.

The staircase led to a grated, metal bridge across all the cells he had walked past. He was now looking down on the creatures. It was not a comfortable position to be in for John. If the bridge broke, he would be down in there with one of them. He shuddered at the thought of being trapped with one of those things.

At the end of the bridge, there was a door. Again, it was locked. She pulled her keys out and unlocked it. The room was full of empty chairs.

"It will be feeding time soon," she said. "But we'll see if we can get it started a little early for you." She pushed a black button on the wall, and a man in a bloody uniform opened the door.

"Ah, Dr. Mason. I see you have a new one." The man smirked at John. "What can I do for you?"

"We need to show him how things work around here," she said, hinting at something other than the feeding process.

"Well, I think Dr. Bronze will work nicely for this demonstration." He rubbed his chin as though enjoying the thought. "He put his notice in this morning, you know? You're getting his job." He turned to John and laughed.

"Which cell will you start with?" Dr. Mason asked.

"I think I'll start with Rocky first. Your newbie here, got him all worked up," the man smiled.

"Thanks, Frank. We'll be waiting." She nudged John back out the door. "This is why we don't break contract. Dr. Bronze tried to break his this morning. Now you get to see exactly what happens to those that try to leave." She led John back out onto the bridge, and through a door directly above one of the cells. "We'll go down here to get a closer look. Don't worry about being quiet now. They don't even notice us when their feeding." She talked about the creatures like they were her pets, and it disgusted John.

Once in the room, they were not alone. Dr. Andrews was sitting in one of the chairs in the front row. "I thought I might find you two here," he said.

"Just giving a full tour," Dr. Mason replied. "Can't let our new employee miss the fun."

The two laughed together, but then Dr. Andrews became serious again. "You're not thinking about leaving us, are you?" He raised an eyebrow as though he expected that to happen.

John shook his head. "No, sir. I only came to watch the feeding," he lied.

"That's good to hear," Dr. Andrews said, sounding pleased for picking John for the job. "Have a seat." He patted the seat next to him, and John took it. "So, what do you think so far?"

John wanted to tell him he thought they were all out of their minds, but instead he said, "It's interesting." The comment made both Dr. Andrews and Dr. Mason laugh.

"Oh, it's very interesting. Did you show him the process yet?" He leaned around John to talk to Dr. Mason.

"No, we're heading there after this," she explained.

"I think you'll rather enjoy watching that," Dr. Andrews said, nudging John to watch the glass.

John watched the creature advance into the cell in front of him. It moved almost like an old person with bad arthritis. There were clear marks of decaying flesh on its skin. John wondered how they stopped that process for a second, then reminded himself he didn't really want to know.

"It's starting," Dr. Mason said, pointing at the top of the cell.

John leaned forward in his seat to see what she was pointing at. A man in a uniform, just like John's, was teetering on the edge of an opening at the top of the cell. There seemed to be someone pushing him from behind. Frank, he thought, he must be the one pushing. He looked at the creature. It had noticed the man dangling, too. It was reaching for him and growling. John closed his eyes just as the man tipped forward.

He could still hear the man pleading for his life, but no one spoke a word. He reopened his eyes, feeling sorry for the man. He guessed the man had seen this before. He had probably sat in the very room John was sitting in now watching some other poor person became a meal to the zombie, and now he was the one dangling from the top. Somehow he had managed to catch the edge and was trying to climb back up.

In a flash, the monster jumped and caught Dr. Bronze's foot. He was now hanging from him. John's eyes widened. If the zombie decided to climb up him, he could escape. They would all be in danger if that happened. John couldn't take his eyes off the scene now. He had to make sure the zombie was locked back in its cell before he could feel safe again—well, as safe as anyone could feel this close to the madness.

Frank yelled something down to the creature, and it instantly dropped back to the ground and paced under the dangling man.

John had no idea what Frank had said, but whatever it was seemed to please Dr. Andrews.

"He sure does have a way with them, doesn't he?" Dr. Andrews said.

"Yes, he works hard with them," Dr. Mason replied. "I think they believe Frank is their leader."

The two doctors went on talking about Frank, but John didn't listen. He was too concerned with what was happening right in front of him. His eyes were glued to the man clinging for his life. How long would he be able to hold on? he wondered.

Would Frank knock him down? It was only a matter of seconds before he got his answers. Dr. Bronze came tumbling down when the door shut on his fingers, cutting them off. The creature let out a loud snarl and lunged for his prey. Dr. Bronze didn't even have a chance to get up before the monster bit a large chunk of flesh out of his throat. Blood spattered the window, and John winced.

He could hear the ripping every time the creature took a bite, but it was the hardest to watch when it bit into the heart. It was still pumping when the monster shoved it in, and blood shot out of the monster's mouth like vomit.

"I've had enough," John said, jumping to his feet. "I don't need to watch this."

Dr. Andrews snapped his head up. "Are you quitting?" he asked. It was almost like he wanted John to say yes so he could push him in with the monster himself.

"No," John said, looking him straight in the eyes. "I just don't think this is relevant to my job." He wasn't going to quit. He knew that. There was no way he was ever going to make it out alive if he did. His only choice now was to do the job he was hired for. His dream job had just turned into a nightmare. It was odd how only a couple of days ago he wished he had a job and didn't have to worry about paying his bills. Now he wished he was home and not here worrying about his life.

"I'll take you to watch the process," Dr. Mason said, and then turned to Dr. Andrews. "Would you like to come along?"

"No, thank you. I think I'd like to talk to Frank," Dr. Andrews said. "But you two have a good time. John, you'll have to let me know what you think."

There was a hidden threat behind his words that even John understood. He wanted John to let him know if he wanted to quit so they could take care of him.

"I will. Thank you," John said as politely as he could.

Dr. Andrews nodded dismissively, and the two were on their way to the process room. It was another place John was sure he didn't want to see. He wished they would tell him what his job was already. He wanted to get back to his apartment and away from the monsters they were making.

"This is the process room," Dr. Mason pointed at the door down the hall from his office. "In here is where the zombies are created, or started I should say, we start the process in this room. It gets finished in their cell."

Dr. Mason showed him the entire area, and there happened to be a transformation going on while they were in there. A young woman in her mid-twenties was unconscious on a table, with an IV in her arm. A brown liquid flowed through it, and a second bag hung from the IV pole with a clear liquid.

Dr. Mason explained the brown liquid was the poison used for the first half of the transformation, which took about two days to run its course through the body, and the clear liquid was a steroid to insure they got the strongest zombies possible.

The second half, which also took two days, was administered in the cell—that's what the different sections were for—each section was a different stage of transformation.

By the time she was done explaining the process it was after six o'clock. John was tired. He really doubted he would sleep though, knowing there were monsters in the same place he slept was not very comforting.

"So, tomorrow I'll show you your job." Dr. Mason said, walking him back to the meeting room where he had begun his day. "Oh, and the cafeteria is open all night. Feel free to grab a bite to eat. You can use your badge to charge your food."

John didn't say a word. He nodded in response to what she said, but there just weren't any words for what he had been through today.

He had a hundred questions going through his mind, like why they were even doing this, but he was sure he didn't want to know the answer.

Dr. Mason left the meeting room, and John hurried to his apartment. There was no way he was going to eat now. All he wanted to do was take a hot shower and climb into bed, and that's exactly what he did.

* * *

The next day, Dr. Mason met him in the meeting room again, and they went through the same process as the day before, to get to his office. She pulled files out of a filing cabinet and told him there was one for each zombie, and it was his job to assess them. Each file had a check list. If he couldn't put a check by everything on the sheet, the zombie was destroyed.

"If you tag a file, send it to Frank right away. He'll take care of the rest," Dr. Mason explained.

John's curiosity got the best of him and he had to ask, "Why are you creating them anyway?" He regretted asking as soon as the question came out of his mouth.

"This is the US's new army, or it will be anyway," she said. "No more sending loved ones into battle."

"No, instead send them to become a zombie. That's much better," John said sarcastically. He couldn't help himself. That was the stupidest thing he had ever heard.

"We're working on a different method." Dr. Mason defended the idea. "Using donated bodies," she chuckled.

"How the hell are you going to bring back the dead?" he asked, mad now. These people had really lost their minds.

"We've already done it once, but it didn't work out." She said it like she was talking about an employee they had hired, instead of a monster they had created. "It's all still a work in progress, but we have some of the best scientists in the world to help."

John shook his head in disgust. He couldn't believe the way they were messing with nature. Something horrible was going to come from all of this—he could feel it. "Just show me what I have to do." He wanted to get it done and over with.

"You need to do tests on them. I'll show you today how to do a complete test." She grabbed a file from the top. "This one hasn't been done in a while. Let's see how he's doing," she said.

Dr. Mason took him through the entire testing process before leaving him to do it on his own. However, she told Frank to keep an eye on him, in case he needed help. "Those things are quick sometimes," she warned. "Be sure to ask for help, and use the spray each time before you open a new cell." With those words of advice, she left.

John stood over the cell of the monster named, Bongo. He was what they called, 'a Grade A zombie'. He was fast and smart, and could tell the difference between a human and a zombie in a matter of seconds, and that was all the time John had for each test.

Then he had to shut the cell, and wait for a couple of minutes before starting the new test. If he tried to do them all, Bongo could leap up, and out, in a flash, and the opening was a good thirty feet high.

"He's spring loaded," Frank said, laughing. "You really have to watch that guy." But John didn't think there was anything funny about a zombie that could jump thirty feet in the air. He thought it should be destroyed.

Each zombie was tested for speed, agility, sense of smell, hearing, sight, and strength. The zombies that didn't make the cut, Frank shot with a dart filled with the antidote. It killed the poison in their bodies leaving only a corpse behind. He took care of the bodies, too, and within days the empty cell was filled with a new zombie for John to test.

John started to get the hang of his new job after a short time. Not that he liked what he was doing, but he felt more comfortable. He even got to take time off to visit his mom. It wasn't pleasant. She kept telling him about people who wanted to apply at Quality Security, and he tried to talk her out of recommending the place to her friends.

It was not a place he wanted anyone to come to. He had been the lucky one, and had actually gotten a job. The rest of the applicants were used as meals. That was not something he wanted hanging over his head.

* * *

By the end of his first month, John knew his job well. He even recognized the creatures and knew them by name, like everyone else that worked there. He knew their weaknesses and their strengths—which scared him most of the time, but he was doing better. He had finally come to terms with the fact that he had to do the job and keep his mouth shut about it.

He was sitting in his office entering data when Dr. Mason came in for a visit. She popped in every now and again to check on him and make sure he didn't need anything. It was her job to do the training, and supply whatever he needed, because it wasn't always easy for them to leave their posts.

"I'm on my way to the lab with my order," she said. "Do you need anything?"

"No, I think I'm good," John said. He was beginning to like her. She wasn't quite as callused as she led on. He could tell what they were doing here bothered her, too, even if she wouldn't admit it.

"Okay. I'll be making rounds again in about an hour." It was normal for her to check every hour. John went through a lot of de-scenting spray when he was testing, but today he only needed to enter data.

"Sounds good," he said, and just then the alarm went off.

"Oh, what now," Dr. Mason groaned.

There where only two things that made the alarms go off—someone had disturbed Section A, or there was a breach in the feeding room. Some people tried to escape when they figured out what was going on. John didn't blame them. He would have, too.

"I guess you'd better wait until it's over," John suggested. There was no reason for her to try and get through the chaos now. If Section A was disturbed, it was never good for anyone to enter until they were calm again.

"I guess it . . ." Dr. Mason's sentence broke off when the office door slammed shut and the lock snapped into place. "Oh my god," she said, with a horrified expression.

"What?"

This had never happened while he had been working here. The alarm was normal, but getting locked into his office was not.

"There's been a breach," she said, her eyes widening.

"You mean . . . No, it can't be," John said. He had once been waiting for something like this, but he had come to trust the security.

"A zombie," she said, confirming what he feared.

"So, now what?"

"We wait," she answered, and pulled some spray out of her pocket. "We'll have to be extra quiet and spray ourselves. We don't know what section had the breach."

John followed her instructions and sprayed himself, then picked up the phone to call Frank. He would know which one was out, and John could help by telling them how to capture it. Frank didn't answer.

"No answer," John told Dr. Mason. "He must be hunting."

Dr. Mason took a seat on the other side of the desk next to John. She didn't want to sit with her back to the door. Both she and John knew the door and the lock wouldn't be enough to stop one of them if they wanted to get in. Being on the other side of the desk seemed like a better position to them both.

The two stayed quiet for a long time, before John finally whispered, "Will someone come get us when it's over?"

Dr. Mason nodded. "The door will unlock and reopen."

He looked at the clock. It had been an hour since the doors locked. They surely should have caught it by now, he thought. He picked up the phone to try Frank again. This time he answered.

"Hey, Frank," John whispered. "What's going on out there?"

"Man, it's horrible. Someone hit the cell switch." He sounded scared to John. "Get out of the building," Frank screamed, and the phone went dead.

John stared at Dr. Mason for a long time before he could tell her anything. He was trying to think of a plan. They were in the heart of a war, and there was no escape. How the hell were they supposed to get out? he wondered.

"What?" she asked impatiently.

"We have to get out of here," he muttered. "I knew something like this would happen." He was talking to himself now. "Why did I stick around?"

"Hello!" Dr. Mason interrupted. "We have to get out now! If Frank says it's bad . . . it's bad. There's an emergency exit." She pointed at the ceiling.

John looked up, but didn't see anything but the ceiling tiles. "Where?"

"We have to get those tiles down quietly. There's a steel door above them," she said, beginning to climb on the desk.

He stood up and helped set the tiles down gently, as she handed them to him. Every time they heard a noise, they both paused and watched the door, anticipating a monster.

"Keep spraying yourself," she instructed, and he sprayed them both down in between setting tiles on the floor.

Once all the tiles blocking their escape route were down, he handed her his keys to unlock it. Dr. Mason opened the hatch as quietly as she could, but it still let out a loud, protesting screech. The door had never been used, and the hinges were beginning to rust. The two froze instantly.

"Hurry," John told her, giving her a boost. There was no way he wanted to be trapped in the office if one of those monsters came in.

Dr. Mason climbed in quickly, with John right behind. The door to the office clicked just as they got in the crawl space, and they looked at each other, wondering if they had overreacted. Frank was known for pulling pranks. Was this just another one? John wondered. The doors didn't unlock unless someone from upstairs in the lab pushed the button. There were two buttons for the doors—at the front desk in the main entrance, and in the research lab.

He poked his head out through the opening and watched. When the door opened, he half-expected Frank to jump in and yell, "Gotcha," but no one came in. There was no sound flowing in from the hallway either. All was quiet as it should be.

Dr. Mason chuckled to herself, "I guess we fell for it," she said, starting to climb back down.

"I guess we did," John said, and joined in the laughter. They both felt silly for overreacting.

When Dr. Mason put one foot back down on the desk, John froze. They were both wrong. It wasn't a joke. It was worse—the zombies were upstairs.

"Hurry back up," he told her in a whisper.

"What?" she said, but there was no time for him to explain. He grabbed her and started pulling her up just as the zombie lunged at her and grabbed her leg.

John pulled with everything he had, but he still was nowhere near strong enough. They would end up pulling her apart if he didn't do something, but he didn't know what else to do.

Dr. Mason took her foot and kicked the zombie right in the face. It didn't hurt it, but it did stun it long enough for her break free and climb back up.

"Close the door!" he yelled, trying to get his key ready to lock it.

"I'm trying," she shouted back.

The zombie was pushing the door and her up, squashing her into the ceiling. It was much stronger than she was. John hurried and put his weight on the door with hers, and locked it once it shut.

"This is bad," he said. "We need to go now. Which way is the way out?" He still had a hard enough time finding his way around the building. There was no way he was going to find his way around a dark crawl space.

"We have to follow this tunnel to the end. That will take us to the second floor," Dr. Mason said in a hushed tone.

John suddenly had an idea. He knew the zombies had already taken over the lower level. They were moving their way up fast. They needed a tranquilizer gun and some antidote. "Where is the antidote kept?"

"In Dr. Andrews' office on the first floor," she answered. "Why?"

"We need some if were going to get out of here," he said. There was no way they would make it without a weapon. He knew what the zombies were capable of, and it just wasn't possible.

They continued on their path to Dr. Andrews' office, turning every now and again to listen behind them. There was no way of knowing if one had gotten in with them. Someone else could have had the same idea, but got caught, leaving the door wide open. He knew the zombies well enough to know that at least two of them would try and climb in—Rocky and Bongo. They were the two deadliest creatures he had ever seen.

When they reached Dr. Andrews' office, John opened the door slowly. He told Dr. Mason to stay on the back side of it in case something went wrong and the door needed closed right away.

He moved the ceiling tile slowly, passing it to Dr. Mason so she could set it behind her, out of their path.

"Be careful," she mouthed, not wanting to speak out loud, and he nodded in agreement.

He pushed the door all the way open when he didn't see anything directly below. He needed to spot the gun and darts before he climbed down, so he wouldn't be stumbling around the room. He wanted to get in and out as quickly as possible. He poked his head all the way out of the opening to scan the room. When he did, he saw Dr. Andrews lying on the floor with his gun in hand.

"Dr. Andrews," John whispered, but instead of a response from him, Rocky poked his head up from around the desk.

John quickly withdrew back into the hole and put his finger over his lips so Dr. Mason would know there was danger below. If Rocky heard either of them, he would be in the hole before they could get it shut.

John took a deep breath, and held up a finger, this time signaling for her to wait right where she was. He was going after the gun.

"No," she protested, and he shushed her as quietly as he could.

He knew this was the best time. Rocky was alone and feeding. She had said it herself—they didn't notice anything when they were feeding. He had to hurry before others were drawn to the scent of his kill. That was a battle he didn't want to be in the middle of.

John sprayed himself, and slowly climbed down onto the desk top. It was not going to be easy, he knew, but he had to get that gun.

When both feet were on the desk, he stood still for a second watching Rocky. He had to make sure he hadn't been noticed. After a moment of Rocky not giving John any sign he knew he was there, he stepped slowly off the desk and ducked down behind it. He thought keeping to the floor was the best way to go. If another zombie walked past, they wouldn't see him, and he would still have Rocky in his sight.

Rocky growled—making John flinch with fear—before tearing half of Dr. Andrews' face off. John looked away for a second, trying to compose himself again. He didn't like watching them eat, no matter how many times he had seen it. It wasn't something anyone could get used to—other than Frank—but he had to keep his eyes on the prize. There wasn't time for a breakdown now.

John inched his way to the gun, never taking his eyes of Rocky as he reached his hand out, closer to the zombie's face. Rocky sniffed for a second, and John froze. His hand was trembling mere inches away from the gun. He just needed one more good stretch and he would have it in his hand.

John waited for Rocky to go in for another bite of Dr. Andrews' face, and then he grabbed it. He stopped breathing for the entire time it took him to pull the gun to his body, and then he took a slow, deep breath of relief.

He stood and passed the gun to Dr. Mason. He still needed the darts, but he didn't see them and he had a feeling Dr. Andrews kept them in his desk for easy access. There was no way he was going to be able to open a desk drawer without Rocky hearing.

Dr. Mason shut the door and locked it behind John, taking a deep breath, too. "I was freaking out the whole time," she admitted.

"Me, too," he agreed. "I didn't get the darts yet."

"You mean you have to go back down there?" her voice was shaky.

He nodded, not wanting to talk anymore. He took the gun from her to see if there were any darts in it. There were two. He pressed his head against the wall. He was hoping there would be more, and most of all, that he wouldn't have to go back down there. They didn't have much spray left, and who knew when Rocky would be done, or if he would even leave right away. He really didn't want to open the hatch if he was there and not feeding. That would not end well. Shooting him would only draw attention, and that would bring more. Then he would be down one dart and have no chance of getting anymore.

The two sat listening to Rocky growl at the body as he ripped more meat off. Even behind the door they could hear the tearing of flesh and splattering of blood, but that was good right now. They wanted to hear everything he was doing. That would help them know when he was gone, but it was stupid, too, for them to sit and wait. That was only giving the zombies a chance to make their way farther up the building, and there was no way of knowing how far they had already gotten.

Once everything was quiet, John put his key in the lock as quietly as possible. He was getting ready to check if it was safe to get the darts he needed, but just as he stuck the key in, there was a sniffing sound coming from the other side of the door. He reached for the spray bottle to cover their scent, but the bottle was empty. All they could do now was not make a sound, and move slowly away from the door.

John backed up, with Dr. Mason crawling toward him over the door. He watched her closely. If it was still Rocky down there, he could push that door up and squash her against the ceiling in seconds. There would be no time to react, but she made it across safely despite his worry. The sniffing sound turned into a growl. He was angry. John knew that Rocky could smell them.

"We have to move," he whispered, and they both sped up. There was no chance they were getting back into that room.

The two crawled away just as Rocky started banging on the door. This was exactly what John had feared. They should have left sooner, while he was still feeding, he thought. Their scent would have been long gone by now if they had.

A loud snarl ripped through the tunnel. John pushed Dr. Mason in front of him, putting himself between her and the monster that he was sure was coming. The two crawled as fast as they could. They needed to get out of the building before the zombies did. That would be the only way to save themselves and the town that the army of hybrid zombies was about to invade.

The growling faded as they got farther away. John stopped for a second to listen. Rocky must not have been growling at them. Another zombie must have entered the room. The only way he would have reacted like that is if he had a kill to protect. John didn't want to think about who might have wandered in.

When the two reached the last escape hatch, John dug in his pocket for his keys. "Damn it," he said. "I left my keys at Dr. Andrews' office." He couldn't believe this. They were trapped. They couldn't go back—it had been too close before. If Rocky was still there, he would come after them this time for sure. The only reason he hadn't before was because another zombie had interrupted, making him forget all about them, and their scent was gone by the time he was done protecting his kill.

"You know, you're lucky I'm here," she said, pulling her keys out of her pocket.

John sighed with relief. "I am," he said. "Okay, we need a plan before we open this door." He wanted to be prepared for anything, and make sure the two of them were on the same page with the plan. They needed each other to get out. With only two darts, they needed to find another weapon. "We need a weapon. We can look from up here, but it's really not going to matter. We don't want to be trapped," he said. Logically, this was not any place to be stuck. The only other way to get out would be to go back to the containment sections. That was not an option. They would never live if they went back there.

"I think we can make it from here," Dr. Mason said. "The elevator is right around the corner. We can lock it when we get in. The problem will be getting the doors to shut soon enough."

"Are you ready?" he asked, preparing to pull the door open.

"As I'm ever going to be," she answered.

John slowly opened the door like he had at Dr. Andrews' office. This time if there was a monster in there, they would both have to sneak past it with no de-scenting spray. Depending on what zombie it was, it could be difficult. The only other one that he was really worried about was Bongo. He knew where Rocky was, but they hadn't seen Bongo yet. All he could do was hope that Bongo was still on the containment floor. The two of them peeked out. The coast was clear, and they were casing the office for any blunt object they could use for a weapon.

"There," Dr. Mason whispered, pointing at golf clubs in the corner of the office.

John shut the door again to talk to her. "I'll go over and get those. I want you to wait here with the dart gun. Once I come back this way, you hand me the dart gun and climb down. We can watch each other's backs that way."

"Okay," she said. His plan made sense to her.

They pulled the door back open and had another look around before John climbed out. He wasted no time. He darted across the room and flew back to her in seconds. They were so close to the exit now, he didn't want to wait. "Lock the door," he told her, when she was out. If any of the zombies found the escape, at least the locked door would slow them down.

John went first, but he looked to her for direction. She pointed left. He looked both ways before stepping out of the office. So far there was nothing to worry about up here. Maybe they hadn't made it this far yet, he thought, but he never let his guard down. They had to be on the look out at all times.

They reached the elevator with no problems, but when Dr. Mason put her key in to get the door open, it wouldn't. The power to the elevators was out. Apparently that was part of the alarm system.

"Are there stairs?" John asked.

"All the way at the other end of the hall," she said with fear in her eyes.

He nodded, and led the way. He moved slowly down the hall, stopping before any open office doors. The first office was empty. He waved her forward with him. He wanted her to keep close behind him and keep an eye on their backs while he worried about their front and sides.

They were halfway to the stairs when John began to think they were alone on this floor. There were no signs of zombies, and they had passed several offices and closets. If there was one, it was hiding well, he thought, and started moving more quickly. He could smell the scent of freedom. They only had one flight of stairs to go and they were out of this horrid place.

Dr. Mason grabbed his free hand and squeezed it. She was feeling the freedom, too. Despite the odds, they were going to make it out alive. They both knew they would probably have a complete breakdown when they got outside and they were safe again, but for now, they had to maintain control.

John slowly stuck his head around the corner of an office door, but this time someone jumped out at him, and Dr. Mason let out a scream. John put the gun up ready to shoot when the person standing in front of him put his hands up.

"Wait, wait," he begged. "I'm not one of them."

"Shit," John sighed, trying to get his heart beating again.

"What are you doing jumping out at people, Sam?" Dr. Mason asked.

"I heard you guys coming," he said, still waving his hands in the air.

"Any sign they've made it up here?" John asked in a hushed voice, looking around the hall. If there was something on this floor, there was no way it didn't hear all the commotion and was probably moving toward them right now.

"Down there," Sam said, and pointed to an office by the staircase.

Sam was one of the lab techs, and he was alone. That told John the others had become meals, so the majority of the monsters were still on that floor, or at least he had hoped they were still contained there, but he couldn't know for sure. How any had made it this far was beyond him. He had tested the zombies every day and none showed any signs of intelligence to this magnitude. They would have had to find keys and unlock doors to move from floor to floor. Somehow one had made it, that they knew of.

John put a finger over his lips, and moved slowly toward the office with the other two flanking on either side. The gun was held in a ready position, and Dr. Mason handed a golf club to Sam. Both had them held like clubs, ready for anything.

"John," Dr. Mason whispered, pointing in an office across the hall from them.

John looked over and there he was . . . the one zombie he was hoping didn't make it past containment—Bongo stood watching them. John knew he was getting ready to attack, and acted quickly to put himself in between him and the other two.

The zombie let out a menacing growl and lunged for them. Dr. Mason screamed in response. John took a deep breath and pulled the trigger on the gun. He hoped his shaking hands wouldn't throw off his aim enough to make a difference.

The monster growled again, and a second chimed in. John looked down that hall toward the stairs. The second zombie was now in the hallway facing them. He didn't have time to watch Bongo, to see if he was hit, before he turned the gun toward the second one. Both zombies paused for a second.

The three scared workers backed away slowly, keeping their backs toward the wall. But they moved faster once the two zombies started in their direction. John was beginning to second guess his aim. When he had seen Frank do it, they dropped right away. He expected Bongo to fight, but not the other one. John recognized her. Her name was Hilary, and she wasn't very strong. He had tested her, and he and Frank were debating on when to destroy her. They knew it was only a matter of time before she wouldn't pass the tests. In an odd way, John was relieved it was her. She was the least deadly of the zombies. If he had to face one, he was glad it was her. If it had been Rocky and Bongo, John knew they wouldn't have had a chance. They were only alive now because Bongo hesitated for a moment, assessing them.

The growls continued, as if the two zombies were communicating. Their behavior was unreal. John, nor any of the other staff, knew they were capable of this kind of action. He was frightened, knowing what they could do, but now he was more afraid of what he didn't know they were capable of. Could they organize? he wondered. If they could, they were surely calling for help, especially if they had been hit.

"We need to get out of here," John urged. They had no time to waste. If they *were* calling for help, it was only a matter of minutes before they would be out numbered. "We'll have to fight."

"What?" Dr. Mason couldn't believe what he had said. This was a battle she didn't think they could win.

"There's no other choice," he said. He didn't like it any more than she did, but there was no other way.

Sam, the newest member of their group, had never worked with the zombies and decided it was better to run. He darted in the opposite direction—starting the battle.

"No!" John yelled, but it was too late. Bongo darted after him in a flash. There was no hesitation this time, and he was on Sam's back in an instant.

John hit Bongo on the head with the gun, trying to get him off Sam, but the monster was in a feeding frenzy. He ripped Sam's head almost clean off in one swift movement. Blood splattered John's face, causing him to flinch for a second, giving Bongo room to move.

Bongo stood facing him now. John was shaking. Behind him, he could hear Dr. Mason fighting with Hilary, but he couldn't risk a glance in her direction to see who was winning. He was facing the most deadly creature, standing only a couple of feet away from him. Bongo could have jumped that distance with little effort.

"Grrr!" Bongo growled, showing his decaying teeth.

"Back up!" John said sternly. He remembered Frank yelling at Rocky and it had worked, so he tried now, but Bongo held his ground. "Now!" he said, deepening his voice.

Bongo took a step back, but then came back in John's direction. His step forward put him a foot closer to John.

"John!" Dr. Mason yelled, "Come on!" She had taken care of Hilary and the path was clear to the door, but John knew he couldn't take his eyes off Bongo.

John stepped back slowly, and Bongo countered his movement. He was following. There is no way out of this without killing Bongo first, John thought. "You go," he told her. "I'll have to kill him first."

"I'm not leaving you," she insisted.

"Go!" John shouted, taking another step backwards.

Dr. Mason didn't answer this time, but John heard the door to the stairs slam shut. She had listened to him and now she was safe.

"Let's do this," John said, swinging his gun at Bongo.

Bongo dodged it, and took a quick step forward. He was fast. John had tested his speed and he was able to move at sixty miles per hour. He wasn't giving all his effort with this fight, but John watched him. He was struggling between feeding, and fighting. Bongo looked down at the decapitated body lying on the floor and growled.

He's protecting his kill, John thought and took a step back. If he could get far enough away, he was sure Bongo would feed and forget all about him, but he had to show Bongo he wasn't a threat first.

He thought of wild animals and how they protect their prey, and what the other animals did to get away. Most of them ran, but that wasn't an option for him. He needed something better. He raced through a dozen animals in his mind before settling on an answer he didn't really like, but it was all he had.

John bowed down, never taking his eyes completely off Bongo. He was trying to show him that he was giving up. He didn't want his kill. He backed away, and this time Bongo didn't make a move.

It was working.

But he froze when he saw another zombie come around the corner behind Bongo. It just kept getting worse, and he was still a good ten feet from the staircase.

Bongo let out a growl, and snapped around. The other zombie backed away, but then trained his eyes on John. If he couldn't have Bongo's kill, he was going to get his own. The zombie darted full speed in John's direction.

Bongo was no longer paying attention to the two. He was busy ripping his food apart, splattering the walls with blood. The other one was distracted by the scent of blood and turned again toward Bongo's kill bleeding on the floor, but Bongo let out a warning growl.

John heard the door open behind him.

"Run," Dr. Mason called out.

He couldn't believe she was still there. He thought she would be halfway to Mexico by now, but he did move faster toward the door now that he knew it was held open for him.

Just as he reached the door, Dr. Mason leaped out smacking the zombie in the head, allowing John to take cover in the staircase. Once she was inside with him, they both held the door shut tight.

More zombies were coming around the corner. It was turning into a hunt, and Dr. Mason and John were their prey. They must have been the only ones left alive in the building, and they were leading them out.

Dr. Mason locked the door, and the two took off up the stairs to the main lobby. John took a moment to push the desk in front of the door. He needed to stall them until he could come up with a plan to destroy the building altogether before these monsters got free. He didn't want the zombies out in the open. Nobody would be safe.

Dr. Mason headed for the door. She was ready to get out of this horrible place, but John hesitated in the hallway.

"What?" she asked.

"We can't just leave," he said. "They'll get out."

Dr. Mason shot him a confused look. "Well, what are we supposed to do?" she asked.

"We have to blow up the building," he said, but he knew it was easier said than done. They only had minutes to come up with a plan and execute it before the monsters were free and terrorizing the town.

He wished he had thought of that before. They could have stopped in the lab and grabbed flammable materials, or at least started a fire there. In the lobby there was nothing but a desk, and very little decorations. It definitely wasn't enough to start a good fire, let alone blow the building up.

He grabbed her hand and ran out of the building. Finally, she thought he had come to his senses, but he told her to get as far away as possible while he began tearing his shirt into a long strip.

"Do you have a car?" he asked.

"Yes, over there. Why?"

"Bring it around," he said, and ran toward his own car, but because he didn't have his keys anymore, he would have to hot wire it, and he really wasn't sure how to do it, but he had to try.

Dr. Mason was waiting by her car when he finally pulled up in his. The zombies were in the lobby.

John got out and shoved part of his shirt into the gas tank as far as it would go, lighting it on fire before hopping in. Dr. Mason looked at him like he was crazy, but he didn't care.

He held one foot on the brake and weighed the gas pedal down with a book he had in the back seat. He slammed it into reverse and hopped out, removing his foot from the brake, sending the car crashing right through the front doors of the building.

Dr. Mason followed his lead, and tore her shirt around the bottom, shoving it into her gas tank. John ran to help, knowing they needed to get far, far away before the car blew. They were too close to the blast.

It took them two seconds to send her car flying into the building as well, and then they ran to find a getaway car. They both wanted to watch the building explode before they drove off, so they moved to the back of the lot.

"It's taking too long," John said. He wasn't an expert on these things, but in movies it always exploded before they had a chance to take cover. "Something's wrong."

"You don't know that," she said, knowing that he would go back in and check it out if there wasn't an explosion soon.

"Look." John pointed at one of the zombies making its way out of the rubble. "I'm going back in."

"John, you can't," she protested. "It's not our prob . . ." her sentence was cut off by a loud boom.

Both of them ducked in their seats, and the car rocked from the force. Debris hit the windshield, shattering it. John covered his head with his hands, and when the blast was over, they both looked up at the flaming building.

An arm twitched on the hood of the car, and there were other monsters lying on the ground in flames. Their job was done. They had made it out and destroyed the building. They both cheered with joy, and instantly started crying.

"Is it really over?" Dr. Mason asked sobbing.

"Yes," John answered, putting the car in drive. "Let's get out of here." He didn't want to spend another minute looking at the place that had been his nightmare for weeks.

On their way into town, they passed fire trucks and police cars. John and Dr. Mason both agreed it was their problem now, and they didn't look back.

ABOUT THE WRITERS

Rebecca Besser lives in Ohio. Her writing has appeared in the Coshocton Tribune, Irish Story Playhouse, Spaceports & Spidersilk, joyful!, Soft Whispers, Illuminata, Common Threads, Golden Visions Magazine, and Stories That Lift. She also has short stories in multiple anthologies by Living Dead Press, where she is currently an editor, and a story in The Undead That Saved Christmas, a charity anthology. Visit her site to learn more about her and her publications: www.rebeccabesser.com

Julian Boote is an actor, author, screenwriter and filmmaker with a BA Honors in Film & Art from Reading University in the UK, with four feature film credits to his name in the roles of producer, co-screenwriter, and second unit director. Julian has recently returned to his first love; acting, and is thriving now in front of the camera. Creating stories has been a pleasure for him since childhood, and he hasn't stopped; his current project being a novelization of one of his feature scripts. He also writes short stories in his (copious) free time, including tales for children.

Mariah Deitrick currently lives in Iowa with her husband and four children. She is a graduate from the Institute of Children's literature, and enjoys writing fiction for all ages.

David H. Donaghe lives and works in the high desert of southern California. In his spare time, David writes short stories and novels. He has had several short stories published in the past, four of which appear in other, Living Dead Press anthologies. David is currently enjoying life and working on his next novel. He invites you to follow him to Face Book and My Space, to join his reader network at www.authornation.com/MCRIDER and to check out his author web page at http://dhdonaghe.weebly.com/index.html

John Foster was born in Sleepy Hollow, NY, and has been afraid of the dark for as long as he can remember. A writer of horror and strange fiction, Foster spent many years in the ersatz glow of Los Angeles before relocating to the relative sanity of New York City where he lives with his lady, Linda, and their cat, Lucy. He can be reached at jfosterpro@yahoo.com.

David French is a history buff and enjoys vintage horror films. Recently he started writing horror stories and finds it relaxing. He hopes others find his stories fun and enjoyable.

Anthony Giangregorio is the author and editor of more than 45 novels and anthologies, almost all of them about zombies.

His work has appeared in Dead Science by Coscomentertainment, Dead Worlds: Undead Stories Volumes 1-7, and Wolves of War by Library of the Living Dead Press. He also has stories in End of Days: An Apocalyptic Anthology Vol. 1-4, the Book of the Dead series Vol. 1-5 by LDP, Zombie Zoology by Severed Press, and two anthologies with Pill Hill Press.

He is also the creator of the popular action/zombie series titled Deadwater and his action/ horror novel Dead Rage is being optioned for a movie.

Check out his website at www.undeadpress.com.

Domenic Giangregorio is 13 years old. When he's not just being a kid, he writes for the fun of it. His other stories are in "Family of the Dead" with his father and brother and Dead Worlds: Undead Stories Volume 4.

Dane T. Hatchell grew up in Baton Rouge Louisiana and has lived there all his life. In his youth he was a fan of old school horror movies, and a collector of magazines such as Creepy and Eerie. Now in his early fifty's, he is devoting his free time to writing to satisfy a lifelong passion. You can contact Dane at Enadious@gmail.com. Special thanks to Sarah Graves for her contributions as my copy editor.

Mark M. Johnson is a horror and sci/fi fanatic, known on-line as, The Black Empty. Amongst other things he'd rather leave to your imagination, he enjoys writing as a hobby. By the grace of good and extremely patient editors, his short fiction has appeared in many fine anthologies found on his Amazon.com author's page.
http://www.amazon.com/MarkJohnson/e/B001KMO6M0/ref=sr_tc_2_0?q id=1276365531&sr=1-2-ent

Sean T. Page, based in London, manages the influential anti-ghoul website, www.ministryofzombies.com. His publishing credits include the Official Zombie Handbook UK through Severed Press & numerous short stories. The undead trouble him greatly so follow the madness on his website & blog.

Rich Restucci lives in Pembroke, Massachusetts with his wife Donna, their three children, and a living-dead cat. When not writing about zombies, Rich works as a marine chemist.

Alan Spencer has published two novels, entitled, "The Body Cartel" (Damnation Books) and "Inside the Perimeter: Scavengers of the Dead" (Living Dead Press). Look for his work in many of the Living Dead Press anthologies, including "Love is Dead," "The Book of Cannibals," and "Book of the Dead 2," to a name a few. This fall, his story "Mother's Solace" will appear in the anthology "Toe Tags 2."

PLAYING GOD: A ZOMBIE NOVEL
by Jeffery Dye

It was supposed to be a regeneration virus to help soldiers on the battle-field—regrowing limbs and healing wounds— but a simple act of carelessness unleashed it on an unsuspecting world.

For the virus was not perfected, and once exposed, the host quickly dies, only to rise again as one of the undead.

As countries are quickly overrun, scientists and military teams battle to contain the outbreak.

There is no other option.

If the infection continues to spread, soon the entire globe will be consumed. And perhaps that will be a just punishment for a mankind that dared to try to play God.

DEAD HOUSE: A ZOMBIE GHOST STORY
by Keith Adam Luethke

The old mansion on the edge of town, aptly named Dead House, has a history of blood, pain, and death, but what Victor Leeds knows of this past only scratches the surface of the true horrors within.

But when his girlfriend is attacked by a shadowy figure one rainy night, he soon finds himself caught up in a world where the dead walk and ghostly wraiths abound. And to make matters worse, a pair of serial killers are fulfilling carefully made plans, and when they are done, the small town of Stormville, New York will run red. The last ingredient to open the gates of Hell, and plunge this small upstate town into madness, is rain.

And in Stormville, it pours by the gallons.

The Lazarus Culture
by Pasquale J. Morrone

Secret Service Agent Christopher Kearns had no idea what he was up against. Assigned on a temporary basis to the Center for Disease Control, he only knew that somehow it was connected to the lives of those the agency pro-tected...namely, the President of the United States. If there were possible terrorist activities in the making, he could only guess it was at a red alert basis.

When Kearns meets and befriends Doctor Marlene Peterson of the Breezy Point Medical Center in Maryland, he soon finds that science fiction can indeed become a reality. In a solitary room walked a man with no vital signs: dead. The explanation he received came from Doctor Lee Fret, a man assigned to the case from the CDC. Something was attached to the brain stem. Something alive that was quickly spreading rapidly through Maryland and other states.

Kearns and his ragtag army of agents and medical personnel soon find them-selves in a world of meaningless slaughter and mayhem. The armies of the walking dead were far more than mere zombies. Some began to change into whatever it was they ate. The government had found a way to reanimate the dead by implanting a parasite found on the tongue of the Red Snapper to the human brain. It looked good on paper, but it was a project straight from Hell. The dead now walked, but it wasn't a mystery. It was The Lazarus Culture.

DEAD RAGE

by Anthony Giangregorio
Book 2 in the Rage virus series!

An unknown virus spreads across the globe, turning ordinary people into bloodthirsty, ravenous killers.

Only a small percentage of the population is immune and soon become prey to the infected.

Amongst the infected comes a man, stricken by the virus, yet still retaining his grasp on reality. His need to destroy the *normals* becomes an obsession and he raises an army of killers to seek out and kill all who aren't *changed* like himself. A few survivors gather together on the outskirts of Chicago and find themselves running for their lives as the specter of death looms over all.

The Dead Rage virus will find you, no matter where you hide.

CHRISTMAS IS DEAD: A ZOMBIE ANTHOLOGY

Edited by Anthony Giangregorio

Twas the night before Christmas and all through the house, not a creature was stirring, not even a. . . zombie?

That's right; this anthology explores what would happen at Christmas time if there was a full blown zombie outbreak. Reanimated turkeys, zombie Santas, and demon reindeers that turn people into flesh-eating ghouls are just some of the tales you will find in this merry undead book. So curl up under the Christmas tree with a cup of hot chocolate, and as the fireplace crackles with warmth, get ready to have your heart filled with holiday cheer. But of course, then it will be ripped from your heaving chest and fed upon by blood-thirsty elves with a craving for human flesh! For you see, Christmas is Dead!

And you will never look at the holiday season the same way again.

BLOOD RAGE

(The Prequel to DEAD RAGE)

by Anthony Giangregorio

The madness descended before anyone knew what was happening. Perfectly normal people suddenly became rage-fueled killers, tearing and slicing their way across the city. Within hours, Chicago was a battlefield, the dead strewn in the streets like trash.

Stacy, Chad and a few others are just a few of the immune, unaffected by the virus but not to the violence surrounding them. The *changed* are ravenous, sweeping across Chicago and perhaps the world, destroying any *normals* they come across. Fire, slaughter, and blood rule the land, and the few survivors are now an endangered species.

This is the story of the first days of the Dead Rage virus and the brave souls who struggle to live just one more day.

When the smoke clears, and the *changed* have maimed and killed all who stand in their way, only the strong will remain.

The rest will be left to rot in the sun.

THE BOOK OF CANNIBALS

Edited by Anthony Giangregorio

Human meat . . . the ultimate taboo.

Deep down, in the dark recesses of your mind, can you honestly say you never wondered how it might taste?

Honestly, never wondered if a chunk of thigh tasted like chicken or pork?

Or if a hunk of an arm was similar to steak? And what kind of wine would be served with it, red or white?

Would a human liver be no different than one from a cow, or a pig?

For all we know, human flesh is as tender as veal, better than the finest tenderloin. And that is what the stories in this book are about, eating each other. But be warned, after reading these tales of mastication, you may just become a vegetarian, or at the very least, think twice before taking your first bite of that juicy steak at your local restaurant.

THE TURNING: A STORY OF THE LIVING DEAD

by Kelly M. Hudson

The Dead Walk!

And no place on earth is safe from their ravening hunger. Civilization falls, leaving groups of struggling survivors to navigate a world that has descended into Hell.

Jeff Richards is one such survivor. He and his lover Jenny flee their home in the Bay Area and take a perilous journey through Northern California into Oregon, seeking shelter in rural areas to avoid both the living dead and that most treacherous animal of all: their fellow humans.

But can a man who has lost everything, including his humanity, ever be reborn? When the dead walk, will any of us survive?

Or will we all join the ranks of the undead to forever walk the earth.

VISIONS OF THE DEAD: A ZOMBIE STORY

by Anthony & Joseph Giangregorio

Jake Roberts felt like he was the luckiest man alive.

He had a great family, a beautiful girlfriend, who was soon to be his wife, and a job, that might not have been the best, but it paid the bills.

At least until the dead began to walk.

Now Jake is fighting to survive in a dead world while searching for his lost love, Melissa, knowing she's out there somewhere.

But the past isn't dead, and as he struggles for an uncertain future, the past threatens to consume him. With the present a constant battle between the living and the dead, Jake finds himself slipping in and out of the past, the visions of how it all happened haunting him. But Jake knows Melissa is out there somewhere and he'll find her or die trying.

In a world of the living dead, you can never escape your past.

DEAD MOURNING: A ZOMBIE HORROR STORY
by Anthony Giangregorio

Carl Jenkins was having a run of bad luck. Fresh out of jail, his probation tenuous, he'd lost every job he'd taken since being released. So now was his last chance, only one more job to prevent him from going back to prison. Assigned to work in a funeral home, he accidentally loses a shipment of embalming fluid. With nothing to lose, he substitutes it with a batch of chemicals from a nearby factory.

The results don't go as planned, though. While his screw-up goes unnoticed, his machinations revive the cadavers in the funeral home, unleashing an evil on the world that it has not seen before. Not wanting to become a snack for the rampaging dead, he flees the city, joining up with other survivors. An old, dilapidated zoo becomes their haven, while the dead wait outside the walls, hungry and patient.

But Carl is optimistic, after all, he's still alive, right? Perhaps his luck has changed and help will arrive to save them all?

Unfortunately, unknown to him and the other survivors, a serial killer has fallen into their group, trapped inside the zoo with them.

With the undead army clamoring outside the walls and a murderer within, it'll be a miracle if any of them live to see the next sunrise.

On second thought, maybe Carl would've been better off if he'd just gone back to jail.

ROAD KILL: A ZOMBIE TALE
by Anthony Giangregorio

In the summer of 2008, a rogue comet entered earth's orbit for 72 hours. During this time, a strange amber glow suffused the sky.

But something else happened; something in the comet's tail had an adverse affect on dead tissue and the result was the reanimation of every dead animal carcass on the planet.

A handful of survivors hole up in a diner in the backwoods of New Hampshire while the undead creatures of the night hunt for human prey.

There's a new blue plate special at DJ's Diner and Truck Stop, and it's you!

DEAD THINGS
by Anthony Giangregorio

Beneath the veil of reality we all know as truth, there is another world, one where creatures only seen in nightmares exist.

But what if these creatures do actually exist, and it is us that are only fleeting images, mere visions conjured up by some unknown being.

Werewolves, zombies, vampires, and other lost things that go bump in the night, inhabit the world of imagination and myth, but all will be found in this collection of tales. But in this world, fiction becomes fact, and what lurks in the shadows is real. Beware the next time you sense you are being watched or catch movement in the corner of your eye, for though it may be nothing, it might just be your doom.

THE DARK

by Anthony Giangregorio
DARKNESS FALLS

The darkness came without warning.

First New York, then the rest of United States, and then the world became enveloped in a perpetual night without end.

With no sunlight, eventually the planet will wither and die, bringing on a new Ice Age. But that isn't problem for the human race, for humanity will be dead long before that happens.

There is something in the dark, creatures only seen in nightmares, and they are on the prowl. Evolution has changed and man is no longer the dominant species. When we are children, we're told not to fear the dark, that what we believe to exist in the shadows is false.

Unfortunately, that is no longer true.

SOULEATER

by Anthony Giangregorio

Twenty years ago, Jason Lawson witnessed the brutal death of his father by something only seen in nightmares, something so horrible he'd blocked it from his mind.

Now twenty years later the creature is back, this time for his son.

Jason won't let that happen.

He'll travel to the demon's world, struggling every second to rescue his son from its clutches.

But what he doesn't know is that the portal will only be open for a finite time and if he doesn't return with his son before it closes, then he'll be trapped in the demon's dimension forever.

SEE HOW IT ALL BEGAN IN THE NEW DOUBLE-SIZED 460 PAGE SPECIAL EDITION!

DEADWATER: EXPANDED EDITION

by Anthony Giangregorio

Through a series of tragic mishaps, a small town's water supply is contaminated with a deadly bacterium that transforms the town's population into flesh eating ghouls.

Without warning, Henry Watson finds himself thrown into a living hell where the living dead walk and want nothing more than to feed on the living.

Now Henry's trying to escape the undead town before he becomes the next victim.

With the military on one side, shooting civilians on sight, and a horde of bloodthirsty zombies on the other, Henry must try to battle his way to freedom.

With a small group of survivors, including a beautiful secretary and a wise-cracking janitor to aid him, the ragtag group will do their best to stay alive and escape the city codenamed: **Deadwater**.

DEAD END: A ZOMBIE NOVEL
by Anthony Giangregorio
THE DEAD WALK!

Newspapers everywhere proclaim the dead have returned to feast on the living!

A small group of survivors hole up in a cellar, afraid to brave the masses of animated corpses, but when food runs out, they have no choice but to venture out into a world gone mad.

What they will discover, however, is that the fall of civilization has brought out the worst in their fellow man. Cannibals, psychotic preachers and rapists are just some of the atrocities they must face.

In a world turned upside down, it is life that has hit a Dead End.

ZOMBIES IN OUR HOMETOWN
by Gary Wedlund

All Joe Jefferson wants to do is go fishing.

But little does he know, three days later he'll be leading a ragtag group of survivors through a zombie-infested town. A mortician's skin treatment has done its job a little too well. Aunt Millie makes a miraculous recovery and goes on a murderous rampage, to the amazement of the mourners.

Friends, relatives, the mortician, and even the televangelist, Reverend Purswell, are left to sort out the leftovers. Nobody knows what the mess is all about until confronted with the exponentially born again. As more of the recently deceased munch on the town, the police have one idea about how to confront the zombies, and the Reverend Purswell another.

While everyone is engaged with tom-foolery, Officer Sandra Anderson and Joe get to the bottom of the horror, one grave encounter at a time.

Not much of a first date. Will they ever get to a simple dinner and movie?

ANOTHER EXCITING ADVENTURE IN THE DEADWATER SERIES!
DEAD SALVATION
BOOK 9
by Anthony Giangregorio
THE HANGMAN'S NOOSE!

After one of the group is hurt, the need for transportation is solved by a roving cannie convoy. Attacking the camp, the companions save a man who invites them back to his home.

Cement City it's called and at first the group is welcomed with thanks for saving one of their own. But when a bar fight goes wrong, the companions find themselves awaiting the hangman's noose.

Their only salvation is a suicide mission into a raider camp to save captured townspeople.

Though the odds are long, it's a chance, and Henry knows in the land of the walking dead, sometimes a chance is all you can hope for.

In the world of the dead, life is a struggle, where the only victor is death.

INSIDE THE PERIMETER: SCAVENGERS OF THE DEAD
by Alan Spencer

In the middle of nowhere, the vestiges of an abandoned town are surrounded by inescapably high concrete barriers, permitting no trespass or escape. The town is dormant of human life, but rampant with the living dead, who choose not to eat flesh, but to instead continue their survival by cruder means.

Boyd Broman, a detective arrested and falsely imprisoned, has been transferred into the secret town. He is given an ultimatum: recapture Hayden Grubaugh, the cannibal serial killer, who has been banished to the town, in exchange for his freedom.

During Boyd's search, he discovers why the psychotic cannibal must really be captured and the sinister secrets the dead town holds.

With no chance of escape, Broman finds himself trapped among the ravenous, violent dead. With the cannibal feeding on the animated cadavers and the undead searching for Boyd, he must fulfill his end of the deal before the rotting corpses turn him into an unwilling organ donor. But Boyd wasn't told that no one gets out alive, that the town is a death sentence. For there is no escape from *Inside the Perimeter*.

DEADFALL
by Anthony Giangregorio

It's Halloween in the small suburban town of Wakefield, Mass.

While parents take their children trick or treating and others throw costume parties, a swarm of meteorites enter the earth's atmosphere and crash to earth.

Inside are small parasitic worms, no larger than maggots.

The worms quickly infect the corpses at a local cemetery and so begins the rise of the undead. The walking dead soon get the upper hand, with no one believing the truth.

That the dead now walk. Will a small group of survivors live through the zombie apocalypse? Or will they, too, succumb to the Deadfall.

THE DEAD OF SPACE: BRAVE NEW WORLD
by Jeremiah Coe

Welcome to the future of the walking dead! The Earth is freezing over. After a deep space probe returns with information of another habitable planet at the end of our galaxy, a desperate attempt to save mankind is implemented. The Intrepid, a massive starship with a crew of 500, is sent to investigate the world designated E-eleven-two for possible habitation of the human race. The world looks perfect, clear springs, tall mountains, open fields, even the remnants of the planet's native inhabitants still exist, right down to the structures they one lived in. And there are no native species to threaten the newly arrived human population. It's perfect...it's paradise. A mystery arrives in the form of the planet's previous inhabitant's corpses, found frozen under the polar ice caps, thousands of them, all perfectly preserved.

The scientists, in their excitement, hastily bring back fifty of the bodies to base camp, each one perfectly preserved and ready to be dissected and studied. As the bodies thaw out and await dissection, first one, then another begins to move, and soon, they start to walk; despite being dead for hundreds if not thousands of years The crew of the Intrepid are about to find out what happened to the natives of E-eleven-two, and are going to discover to their horror that they didn't die out naturally.

In fact, there was nothing natural about their demise.

The future isn't full of hope...the future is dead.

UNITED STATES OF ARMAGEDDON
by Jeffrey Thomas Crooms
THE END OF A COUNTRY!

America's enemies plot a sadistic plan to destroy the population and armed forces so they can swoop in and rule the country.

Terrorists called the Horsemen smuggle in a deadly biological weapon straight to the heart of the United States and release it.

The result is a land covered with corpses, bloated bodies strewn from sea to sea.

A few desperate survivors battle through the blighted landscape on a last ditch mission to save the country from total domination.

But the biological weapon has a side effect, one no one would have ever foreseen, one too unimaginable to even contemplate.

Welcome to the future. Welcome to the Unite States of *Armageddon*

BOOK OF THE DEAD
A ZOMBIE ANTHOLOGY VOL 1
ISBN 978-1-935458-25-8
Edited by Anthony Giangregorio

This is the most faithful, truest zombie anthology ever written, and we invite you along for the ride. Every single story in this book is filled with slack-jawed, eyes glazed, slow moving, shambling zombies set in a world where the dead have risen and only want to eat the flesh of the living. In these pages, the rules are sacrosanct. There is no deviation from what a zombie should be or how they came about. The Dead Walk.

There is no reason, though rumors and suppositions fill the radio and television stations. But the only thing that is fact is that the walking dead are here and they will not go away. So prepare yourself for the ultimate homage to the master of zombie legend. And remember... Aim for the head!

REVOLUTION OF THE DEAD
by Anthony Giangregorio
THE DEAD SHALL RISE AGAIN!

Five years ago, a deadly plague wiped out 97% of the world's population, America suffering tragically. Bodies were everywhere, far too many to bury or burn. But then, through a miracle of medical science, a way is found to reanimate the dead.

With the manpower of the United States depleted, and the remaining survivors not wanting to give up their internet and fast food restaurants, the undead are conscripted as slave labor.

Now they cut the grass, pick up the trash, and walk the dogs of the surviving humans. But whether alive or dead, no race wants to be controlled, and sooner or later the dead will fight back, wanting the freedom they enjoyed in life. The revolution has begun!

And when it's over, the dead will rule the land, and the remaining humans will become the slaves...or worse.

KINGDOM OF THE DEAD
by Anthony Giangregorio
THE DEAD HAVE RISEN!

In the dead city of Pittsburgh, two small enclaves struggle to survive, eking out an existence of hand to mouth.

But instead of working together, both groups battle for the last remaining fuel and supplies of a city filled with the living dead.

Six months after the initial outbreak, a lone helicopter arrives bearing two more survivors and a newborn baby. One enclave welcomes them, while the other schemes to steal their helicopter and escape the decaying city.

With no police, fire, or social services existing, the two will battle for dominance in the steel city of the walking dead. But when the dust settles, the question is: will the remaining humans be the winners, or the losers?

When the dead walk, the line between Heaven and Hell is so twisted and bent there is no line at all.

RISE OF THE DEAD
by Anthony Giangregorio
DEATH IS ONLY THE BEGINNING!

In less than forty-eight hours, more than half the globe was infected.
In another forty-eight, the rest would be enveloped.
The reason?
A science experiment gone horribly wrong which enabled the dead to walk, their flesh rotting on their bones even as they seek human prey.
Jeremy was an ordinary nineteen year old slacker. He partied too much and had done poorly in high school. After a night of drinking and drugs, he awoke to find the world a very different place from the one he'd left the night before.
The dead were walking and feeding on the living, and as Jeremy stepped out into a world gone mad, the dead spotting him alone and unarmed in the middle of the street, he had to wonder if he would live long enough to see his twentieth birthday.

THE CHRONICLES OF JACK PRIMUS
BOOK ONE
by Michael D. Griffiths

Beneath the world of normalcy we all live in lies another world, one where supernatural beings exist.

These creatures of the night hunt us; want to feed on our very souls, though only a few know of their existence.

One such man is Jack Primus, who accidentally pierces the veil between this world and the next. With no other choice if he wants to live, he finds himself on the run, hunted by beings called the Xemmoni, an ancient race that sees humans as nothing but cattle. They want his soul, to feed on his very essence, and they will kill all who stand in their way. But if they thought Jack would just lie down and accept his fate, they were sorely mistaken. He didn't ask for this battle, but he knew he would fight them with everything at his disposal, for to lose is a fate worse than death.

He would win this war, and he would take down anyone who got in his way.

THE WAR AGAINST THEM: A ZOMBIE NOVEL
by Jose Alfredo Vazquez

Mankind wasn't prepared for the onslaught.

An ancient organism is reanimating the dead bodies of its victims, creating worldwide chaos and panic as the disease spreads to every corner of the globe. As governments struggle to contain the disease, courageous individuals across the planet learn what it truly means to make choices as they struggle to survive.

Geopolitics meet technology in a race to save mankind from the worst threat it has ever faced. Doctors, military and soldiers from all walks of life battle to find a cure. For the dead walk, and if not stopped, they will wipe out all life on Earth. Humanity is fighting a war they cannot win, for who can overcome Death itself? Man versus the walking dead with the winner ruling the planet. Welcome to *The War Against Them*.

DEADTOWN: A DEADWATER STORY
B OOK 8
by Anthony Giangregorio

The world is a very different place now. The dead walk the land and humans hide in small towns with walls of stone and debris for protection, constantly keeping the living dead at bay.

Social law is gone and right and wrong is defined by the size of your gun.

UNWELCOME VISITORS

Henry Watson and his band of warrior survivalists become guests in a fortified town in Michigan. But when the kidnapping of one of the companions goes bad and men die, the group finds themselves on the wrong side of the law, and a town out for blood.

Trapped in a hotel, surrounded on all sides, it will be up to Henry to save the day with a gamble that may not only take his life, but that of his friends as well. In a dead world, when justice is not enough, there is always vengeance.

END OF DAYS: AN APOCALYPTIC ANTHOLOGY
VOLUMES 1-4
Edited by Anthony Giangregorio

Our world is a fragile place.

Meteors, famine, floods, nuclear war, solar flares, and hundreds of other calamities can plunge our small blue planet into turmoil in an instant.

What would you do if tomorrow the sun went super nova or the world was swallowed by water, submerging the world into the cold darkness of the ocean? This anthology explores some of those scenarios and plunges you into total annihilation.

But remember, it's only a book, and tomorrow will come as it always does. Or will it?

Blood of the Dead
A.P. Fuchs

Bits of the Dead
edited by
Keith Gouveia

Axiom-man
The Dead Land
A.P. Fuchs

$15.99
(Trade Paperback)
ISBN: 9780984261017

$15.99
(Trade Paperback)
ISBN: 9780984261024

$15.99
(Trade Paperback)
ISBN: 9780984261055
(Also Available in Hardcover)

Visit www.pillhillpress.com
For the best in speculative fiction!